Praise for Kim Moritsugu's Previous Books

The Oakdale Dinner Club

"Under the author's deft pen, her small community comes to life;
her plot weaves back and forth through time with skill."
— *Publishers Weekly*

"*The Oakdale Dinner Club* is light and entertaining and goes
down as smoothly as the free-flowing dinner-party wine."
— *Quill and Quire*

"Toronto writer Kim Moritsugu's clever sixth novel is sheer
entertainment from beginning to end."
— *The Waterloo Record*

The Restoration of Emily

"A very funny, sometimes suspenseful novel for grown-ups …
Moritsugu writes with dash and irony."
— *Quill and Quire*

"A fun, light, and adept piece of writing."
— *Globe and Mail*

"Funny, wise and sharp, this is a character all of us can see a little
bit of ourselves in."
— *Chatelaine*

The Glenwood Treasure
(shortlisted for the Arthur Ellis Best Crime Novel)

"*The Glenwood Treasure* has suggestions of the late Timothy
Findley and more than a hint of the old Nancy Drew mysteries.
But, given the strength of this book, it seems more fitting to
drop the comparisons and allow Moritsugu her own place on the
literary landscape."
— *Globe and Mail*

"Kim Moritsugu is a witty social observer and the book deftly
blends a comedy of manners into the mystery."
— *Toronto Star*

"A cozy read … Moritsugu is a good writer with an appealing
central character that will awaken the inner girl in all of us."
— *National Post*

THE
SHOWRUNNER

THE
SHOWRUNNER

KIM MORITSUGU

DUNDURN
TORONTO

Cover design: Laura Boyle
Cover image: istock.com/LPETTET
Printer: Webcom

Library and Archives Canada Cataloguing in Publication

Moritsugu, Kim, author
    The showrunner / Kim Moritsugu.

Issued in print and electronic formats.
ISBN 978-1-4597-4097-6 (softcover).--ISBN 978-1-4597-4098-3 (PDF).--
ISBN 978-1-4597-4099-0 (EPUB)

    I. Title.

PS8576.O72S56 2018   C813'.54   C2017-906242-5
                                      C2017-906243-3

1 2 3 4 5   22 21 20 19 18

We acknowledge the support of the **Canada Council for the Arts**, which last year invested $153 million to bring the arts to Canadians throughout the country, and the **Ontario Arts Council** for our pub-lishing program. We also acknowledge the financial support of the **Government of Ontario**, through the **Ontario Book Publishing Tax Credit** and the **Ontario Media Development Corporation**, and the **Government of Canada**.

Nous remercions le **Conseil des arts du Canada** de son soutien. L'an dernier, le Conseil a investi 153 millions de dollars pour mettre de l'art dans la vie des Canadiennes et des Canadiens de tout le pays.

Care has been taken to trace the ownership of copyright material used in this book. The author and the publisher welcome any information enabling them to rectify any references or credits in subsequent editions.

— *J. Kirk Howard, President*

The publisher is not responsible for websites or their content unless they are owned by the publisher.

Printed and bound in Canada.

VISIT US AT

dundurn.com | @dundurnpress | dundurnpress | dundurnpress

Dundurn
3 Church Street, Suite 500
Toronto, Ontario, Canada
M5E 1M2

AUGUST

1

Stacey was in her office with the door closed, reading a script, when she heard her producing partner, Ann, bray her name from outside her door. "Stacey! You in there?"

She marked the spot that she'd read to and pictured Ann steamrolling down the hallway. Three, two, one: Ann flung the door open and stepped inside. "There you are. I want you to meet someone."

Stacey did not grimace at the interruption. She made her eyes go bright and friendly and held up the script. "Hold on, I'm halfway through the latest draft of episode 5."

"I'll be quick. And that script is fine; I already approved it."

If Stacey were keeping track of Ann's little put-downs, that would be the first of the day, the fifth this week. On a Tuesday morning.

Ann pulled in from the hallway a slim, pretty actress whose credits included the lead in a low-budget horror movie, a four-episode guest arc on *Gossip Girl*, and featured roles in the ensemble casts of two short-lived cable shows. She had also done a TV spot in the previous year for The Olive Garden, as a perky waitress, if Stacey was not mistaken. But what was she doing in the office?

Ann said, "Jenna, I'd like you to meet Stacey McCreedy, the second woman in *Two Women Walking*, and co-creator of *The Benjamins*. Stacey, this is —"

The second woman? Make that slight number six. Stacey said, "Jenna Kuyt, isn't it?," stood, shook hands, and hoped Ann had not gone behind her back and cast this Jenna without Stacey's consent. She had nothing against the girl, but there were protocols in place for who did what when and consulted with whom. Protocols Ann was inclined to forget.

"It's such a treat to meet you!" Jenna said. "I was just telling Ann how much I loved *Mothers and Daughters*, and you worked on it, too, right?"

"I did, yeah. And hey, I liked your work in *East Side, West Side*."

"You mean you were one of the ten people who saw an episode before it was cancelled?"

Jenna was enough of an actress that Stacey couldn't tell if the modesty shtick was false or true. What she could see was that Jenna's face was a study in the golden ratio that defines physical beauty. Up close, she was breathtaking, in a pan-ethnic, olive-skinned, green-eyed, auburn-haired kind of way. Like a citizen of the future, an ambassador of the planet. Next to Ann, she looked like Baby New Year alongside Mother Time.

"But thanks," Jenna said. "It's good to know someone watched the show other than my parents and my boyfriend."

Okay. What was Jenna doing there? And why were Stacey's calf muscles tensed, and her heart rate elevated?

Ann said, "Jenna's going to be my assistant while Candace is on maternity leave." And to Jenna: "Stacey is number one on my contact list. We call each other eight times a day, minimum. And text or message countless more times. Right, Stacey?"

"Sometimes," Stacey said, "we even speak to face-to-face, like we're doing now."

Jenna smiled politely, Ann rambled on about the nature of their partnership, and Stacey wondered what Ann was up to with this hire. Maybe Jenna's acting career had slumped (The Olive Garden, for Christ's sake) from C-list to off-list in the last year, and she was reduced to doing temp work, so why not become an assistant to an industry heavyweight like Ann? And it would be just like Ann to take pleasure in bossing around — she would call it mentoring — a pretty, semi-known actress. That was probably what was happening: the two of them were engaged in mutual exploitation, and Stacey's fight-or-flight response was an overreaction. "I should get back to this script," she said. "Welcome aboard, Jenna. I hope you like it here."

"I'm sure I will. It'll be fun to learn how the business works from the other side of the camera."

Yeah, non-stop fun was what they had, all right. Stacey said, "Ann, a quick question — what happened to the pool house sex scene? I didn't see it in this draft."

"I moved it to ep 6. And like I said, don't worry about that script."

"Me, not worry? Is that even possible?"

Ann ignored that, and on her way out, said to Jenna, "Stacey started in the business as my assistant a few years back. I took her on straight from college, and now her office is almost as big as mine."

Ann's version of the how-they'd-met story positioned her as a wise old bitch and Stacey as a young, eager-to-please pup plucked from a litter of interns and trained until she became Ann's top dog. It was true enough that Stacey didn't need to hear it again. She got up to close the door and heard Jenna ask, "So, which one of you is the showrunner?"

Good question. Stacey waited, doorknob in hand, to hear Ann's reply.

"I am. On the creative side, anyway. I'm the *éminence grise* around here."

"The what?"

"The head honcho."

Stacey shook her head. Ann would take full credit until forever for their combined work, and for the work of the three hundred people that their production company employed to produce *The Benjamins*, a primetime dramedy (the inevitable tagline: "It's All About Them") centred on the hopes, dreams, and weaknesses of an interracial L.A. showbiz family.

Glory-taking was Ann's way, and there was no denying that her track record of thirty-one years in television — take this in: she'd started in TV the year Stacey was *born* — had helped sell the show to the network. But the *Benjamins* concept had been all Stacey's to begin with. She'd dreamt up the concept during her non-existent spare time while producing Ann's last show. She built and devised the storylines, characters, and arcs for the entire first season and put together a complete show bible before she even brought the idea to Ann. Before Ann had tweaked it and assumed ownership of it.

Ann said, "Stacey's a rock, but her role is to look after the logistical side of things. She's got an accountant's mind — she's all about dotting *i*'s and crossing *t*'s."

Stacey eased her office door shut. The secret to survival when working with Ann was to pick out the occasional tiny gold nugget of approval from the dross she blurted out daily. So Stacey would take being called accountant-ish and rock-like as a compliment, and she would get back to work.

As of that August morning, two episodes, post-pilot, of the eight-episode first-season order of *The Benjamins* were in the can, the fourth was in production, the premiere was slated to air in a month, and Stacey was so busy she had to compartmentalize. She picked up the script and tried to focus in on it, but she couldn't concentrate — her mind skittered and bounced over the words on the page. She lifted her head, dropped her jaw, and placed two fingers on the pressure point beneath her collarbone. She breathed in and out and ordered her brain to calm itself, to de-tense. That was better.

When she'd finished reading the script, she made some notes on it and gave it to her assistant, Topher, to distribute, though without employing any of the techniques Ann had used in Stacey's assistant days. There were no imperial summons or hollered orders, and no throwing of papers across the room. Instead, Stacey got up from her desk, opened her office door, and waited until Topher finished his phone call before *asking* him to please pass the script on.

"On it," he said. "And sorry about Ann barging in on you before. I told her you wanted some alone time, but she pretended she didn't hear me."

"Thanks for trying. Did you meet the new assistant?"

"The actress? Yes, I did." He gave Stacey a knowing look from behind his hipster glasses. "You want in on the office pool for how long she lasts?"

"Now, now. Let's be nice to her for at least a week or two."

Topher arched one eyebrow, a trick he was good at. "So I'll put you down for two weeks? My bet is on ten days."

"Topher."

"I should deal with this script," he said, and hustled off.

Back inside her office, Stacey picked up her phone and read a text from Ann:

Did u talk to Ryan yet?

Ryan was the actor who played *The Benjamins'* resident heart-throb, one of the adult grandsons of the Benjamin patriarch. Thanks to a panty-melting grin, a well-proportioned and ripped physique, and a willingness to remove his shirt at the drop of a clapperboard, he had built up a vocal online fan base of gay men and straight women on his last show, and Stacey was counting on Ryan's pecs and abs to pull in some early eyes to *The Benjamins*. So far, he'd kept his body in shape, shown up on time for his calls, and dutifully attended the second-rate red carpet events the studio publicists had arranged to have him invited to and photographed at. His acting was one-note — his role as a charming slacker was made for him. So he'd caused no concerns until word had reached Stacey from an on-set spy that he'd become extra-friendly with Vanessa, the seventeen-year-old nymphet actress who played the role of his seventeen-year-old nymphet *sister*.

Ann and Stacey had discussed the issue the day before on their mid-morning walk — a leisurely stroll from the studio to a nearby coffee shop and back — during which they covered the usual seven or eight items of business, Ann did not mention that she'd hired a new assistant, and Stacey was elected to have a chat with Ryan to warn him off the jailbait.

"He'll take it better coming from you than me," Ann had said. "From someone closer to him in age. If I talked to him, I'd probably come off parental, and that would be so not cool. For him and for me."

Stacey agreed that she should handle Ryan, but not because they were of the same generation. More because she was immune to Ryan's charms, and Ann wasn't. Stacey knew better than to pursue or lust after any guy that handsome. She'd learned that lesson in high school, after a good-looking alpha male she'd yearned for all senior year had rewarded her devotion by letting her give him a blowjob at a grad party. Whereas Ann, despite her eminent greyness, had a way of dropping her boss woman persona in Ryan's presence and turning girlish and giggly. And a little pathetic.

Stacey had practised both parts of the upcoming conversation the night before, at home, where she'd adopted a jocular, between-us-guys tone, and had Ryan match her in kind. So, she was rehearsed when a flustered-looking Topher — Christ, not him, too — showed Ryan into her office.

She began with a compliment on Ryan's read of a line in the last scene she'd seen in dailies, a scene he played with Vanessa. As if his read had been in any way remarkable.

He said, "Yeah? You liked it? I was trying to show that my character has a vulnerable side."

"Smart thinking. The fans love that in hot guys like you. And way to make the feelings between you and Vanessa look strictly fraternal during that big hug on the couch. No one would guess what's going on in real life."

Ryan was a rare thing among young actors, a graduate of a halfway-demanding college program in economics, and the many hours he'd spent on tanning beds had not completely fried his brain, so he was fairly quick with a response. "Who said there's something going on?"

"Is there?"

He did his signature jaw-clenching move. "Nothing that would make this meeting necessary."

"Good. I figured as much, but you know how people talk. And how the gossip hounds are ready to jump on any little indiscretion. Especially an indiscretion like statutory rape."

He blue-steeled her a ray of such active dislike that she would have been devastated if she were crushing on him like everyone else in the building. When she didn't falter, he said, "You don't think Vanessa's a virgin, do you?"

"I think we'll all have something to celebrate when she turns eighteen in January. I know *I'll* be sending her flowers."

"January's a long way off. Who knows where we'll be by then? The show could be cancelled."

She'd underestimated him, hadn't realized he'd be up for a fight. She tried to look amused, as if she enjoyed their sparring, but her pulse sped up to an anxiety-making rate, and for the second time that morning. "We won't be cancelled. With talent like you and Vanessa on board and the wicked storylines the writers are fleshing out, we'll get a full-season pickup and an early renewal. Take it from me: good things come to those who wait." They'd better, or her whole life plan would be shot to hell.

Ryan stood and stretched — he lifted his sculpted arms in the air, and his T-shirt rode up, exposed his eight-pack. "Okay. Message received. I'll hold Vanessa off. No matter how much she begs." The douchebag grinned. "Is there anything else you wanted to see me about?"

"No, that's it." It was time to throw him, douche or not, a carrot. "I'm glad we had this chat. I'm going to think about that vulnerability idea. There might be some interesting paths we can take your character down that we haven't thought of yet. So thanks."

He turned the charm back on. "Any time."

Ann came by as Ryan was leaving — so she could experience the thrill of brushing past him in the doorway, Stacey suspected — and said, "Hey Ryan, how's it hanging?"

He said, "Low," treated her to his sexy grin, and sauntered off.

Ann stood in the doorway, awash in his Eau de Stud scent, and watched him walk away. While Stacey opened her desk drawer, found and swallowed some Advil, and avoided the sight of Ann flushing an embarrassing shade of menopause.

When he was out of earshot, Ann said, "How'd that go?"

"It looks like he'll steer clear of Vanessa until she's eighteen, or until he gets tired of her, whichever comes first."

"Glad to hear it."

"And they say gallantry is dead."

Ann said, "He's a good guy. He won't let us down."

Stacey wasn't so sure, but she knew better than to disagree. "About your new assistant: are we hiring actresses to do clerical work now?"

The besotted glow faded from Ann's face and was replaced by something harder and colder. "You disapprove?"

"Hiring her just seems a little like mixing church and state."

"I can't believe we're wasting time talking about who answers my phone. Why exactly is this a problem?"

The Advil had better kick in soon. "It's not a problem. In fact, what were we talking about just now? I forget."

"Good. You ready to walk? I want to discuss the cast retreat."

2

Ann's Journal

This is me keeping a journal. Which I'm doing because, one, I'd rather type stream-of-consciousness banalities on my laptop than engage in conversation with my new driver, name of Miguel. He seems tolerable — quiet and not too much of a talker. But no bonding with the help for me, thanks.

Two, now that I have a driver, I have eighty more free minutes a day than I did when I drove myself to and from, AND I don't have to worry about enabling another raccoon to commit car suicide by hurling itself into my path like one did on Mulholland a few months ago. No one gives a shit if raccoons die, but some people do apparently care about domesticated animals, so it would be in my best interests NOT to kill someone's pet, which I might have done if I'd kept driving at night on the unlit hill roads.

And three, in a production meeting the other day a question came up about one of the locations for that episode and no one could remember for a minute what we'd decided, and Stacey made a big deal out of looking up the specs on her laptop in something she called her work journal.

When I said, "You keep a work journal?" she smugly announced that she keeps detailed daily notes of every meeting she attends, because she thinks it's important that our company in general and The Benjamins in particular develop some "institutional memory." To which I was like, you don't actually think anyone is impressed by that passé business jargon you're slinging, do you?

Also: OCD much?

Anyone can play this journal game, and I'm the writer here, so what the hell, I'll give it a whirl for a day or two. Not least because I had the impression, during that meeting, that she was trying to show me up, and expose me as the not-really-computer-literate, past-her-prime oldster who isn't as sharp anymore as young, bright-eyed, bushy-tailed, super-efficient Stacey.

Seeing Jenna looking all shiny and happy and worshipful today because I'm her boss and a TV icon made me want to say to Stacey: remember when you looked up to me and hung on to my every word because you thought I had something valuable to teach you? I'd like to see more of that respectful attitude nowadays, more gratitude for how far I've pulled you up the ladder, and fewer comments like, "So, what — we're hiring actresses to do clerical work now?"

Producing partner or not, when she said that, I thought, We who, honey? We fucking who?

3

After her first day on the job, Jenna's boyfriend Andrew wanted to take her out to Nobu for dinner. Jenna didn't think that doing temp work because she couldn't book an acting gig to save her life was worth celebrating, but he was trying to be supportive, and it never hurt to be seen out and about, so she put on a dress and heels and went along. She wasn't hungry, though. Not even when the server recognized her before taking the food order. "I loved *East Side, West Side*," he said. "Such a shame it was cancelled."

Jenna thanked him, ordered some sushi she had no intention of eating, and took a sip of a margarita. And another sip.

Andrew said, "Tell the truth: do you regret taking the job?"

She stopped checking the room for boldface names, or anyone she knew, and focused on him. "No. Not at all!" Or not yet, anyway, not as long as she thought that being Ann Dalloni's assistant would lead her somewhere she wanted to go.

She'd heard about the job from her actress friend Kerry, who knew someone who knew Ann's pregnant assistant. Jenna aced the interview — she was bubbly and energetic, and told Ann she was a big fan of her last series, which she raved about like she hadn't just read recaps of its final season's back half and watched a couple of clips online the night before. She'd also claimed that while she might go out for an audition now and then, her stalled acting career would not get in the way of being an assistant. When in reality, she intended to be gone the minute she got a good part. If she ever got a good part again.

She said, "Ann seems nice. She asked me to sit in on some meetings today to get an understanding of what she does and who she works with. And you know what? She goes for a walk every day with her partner, Stacey, to a coffee shop down the road; it's their little ritual. That's why they called their company Two Women Walking. Isn't that cool?"

"I should have known you'd be positive. Good for you."

Andrew was eighteen years older than Jenna, forty-six to her twenty-eight, and sometimes acted fatherly, but Jenna didn't mind the age difference. For a suit, he was fit and handsome, he wasn't out-of-it old, and he was smart and good at his job — he was an entertainment attorney. He was her attorney, that's how they'd met seven months before. She said, "Who knows? This might lead to a whole new career for me. Ann told me that Stacey worked her way up to executive producer from nothing. Or from less than I'm starting with, anyway."

"As long as you're not uncomfortable about working on a show that could have cast you as a lead — that *should* have cast you. In your shoes, I couldn't do it."

The relaxing effect of the alcohol as it seeped into Jenna's bloodstream was worth every calorie. She said, "The way I see it, I wasn't meant to be on *The Benjamins*, and I'm okay with that.

What's the expression? When one door closes, another one opens. Maybe that'll happen for me."

"I think it's a window that opens when a door closes, but sure. And that's one of the things I love about you: your optimism."

Jenna smiled modestly, eyes downcast, a bit she'd perfected when she played an Amish girl in a Lifetime movie.

Andrew said, "I like that you value your independence, too, but working at this job might be pushing the independent woman act a bit far."

"Not if I want to pay my rent."

"Speaking of that, what would you say" — he shifted in his seat, and for a terrible second, Jenna was afraid he might go down on one knee — "if I asked you to move in with me?"

Boy, did she *not* want to move in with Andrew. He made good money, and was okay to hang with when her career was in limbo, but she could do better. She was still young, and hot, and she didn't want to get serious and play house unless her housemate had more top-end potential. But until she found that special someone, she didn't want Andrew to go away either, not while he could fulfill the function of a presentable, well-connected date who bought her drinks and dinner in fancy restaurants and liked being seen with her.

So, she said, "Oh, my!" Still doing the Amish girl.

"Speaking selfishly, I like the thought of waking up every morning and seeing you in my bed. I like it a lot."

She squeezed his hand, pushed her voice up half an octave, and made her eyes twinkle. "And I think you're so sweet to suggest it!"

The twinkle worked: he smiled. "But?"

"No buts. It's a tempting offer. So tempting! It's just that moving in together — giving up my apartment, fitting my stuff in with yours, living together for real — would be such a huge change. Huge! So I'd like to think about it. Can I think about it?"

"You may, but don't keep me waiting too long with your answer. You know how impatient I am."

She knew how prematurely he ejaculated, too.

"Where's our food, anyway?" he said.

Had the room gotten colder? To warm it up, Jenna considered kissing her fingertips then reaching over and touching them to his lips, but the gesture was too cutesy. She searched for a new subject instead. "Have you ever met Stacey McCreedy?"

"No, I only know of her. Why?"

"She's younger and prettier than I expected."

"No competition for you in the looks department, though."

Uh, no. "She's not gorgeous or anything, but she's thin, and pale, and has great hair. It's long and wavy and reddish blonde. It's almost as good as Connie Britton's hair."

Andrew looked around for the server. "You're impressed with her hair? There's more to her than that — I hear she's very sharp. She'll be running her own shows before long, and leaving Ann in the dust."

What made Andrew think this, Jenna didn't ask. He was a know-it-all about the entertainment business. About sports, too. He could go on for hours about pro basketball, analyzing the game and the players and the coaching — hours.

She said, "Ann's a legend. She's not going anywhere."

"I just hope the legend doesn't try to push you around."

"Don't worry about me. I can take care of myself."

She steered the conversation to his work after that, and half-listened to him talk about his day and a contract he was negotiating; then a studio executive Andrew knew came by to say hello, and when she saw an actor she'd worked with once who'd landed a series regular spot on a hit sitcom, she congratulated him as if his success did not make her feel sick.

After dinner, on the way out of the restaurant, a couple of the paparazzi stationed outside took Jenna's picture, though she heard another guy, who lowered his camera at the sight of her, tell them not to bother, she was no one.

She'd have to see about that.

4

At 8:00 p.m., Stacey texted her friend Zach, asked him to come over later, and left the office. During the drive from Manhattan Beach to her condo in Santa Monica, she listened to a CD the show's music supervisor had burned — suggestions for songs to be used in the next episode. Once home, she ran 5K on her treadmill while watching audition clips on her tablet for guest spots that the casting director had sent over. A hot shower and dinner of a pear, a chunk of cheese, and five almonds took some of the day's edge off. Sex with Zach would sand down the last bit.

Stacey had met Zach at USC, a college she chose to attend because she was offered a partial track scholarship by the athletic department, and also because it was twenty-five hundred miles away from home, her parents, and anyone she knew.

She did *not* go to USC intending to enter the School of Cinematic Arts — she barely knew it existed when she began her freshman year in sciences and met Zach, her smart but lazy sometime lab partner. Stacey had made herself over during the summer between high school and college. She had undergone a painful transformation from a skinny, red-haired, freckled, way-late-to-develop virgin into a generically pretty (and no more) college student. She started colouring her hair the strawberry blonde shade she'd worn ever since, and learned how to style it. She coerced her parents into giving her, as a graduation present, money to pay for the services of a dermatologist, who burned off most of the freckles from her face. She learned how to apply makeup, she bought some flattering, California-girl clothes. And she developed a confident air, which fooled Zach into thinking she was the kind of popular shiksa he'd pined for since puberty.

She rewarded him for buying her act by making him her casual sex partner for a year or two. During that time, she studied hard, made A's, and ran track (her event was middle distance), while he smoked weed, played video games, and maintained a C average. He also displayed a willingness to try anything sexual she suggested, and she briefly experienced the pleasant sensation of being sought after.

In her junior year, Stacey took a few film and television electives, met some ambitious, head case-ish, creative students who saw the benefit of allying themselves with an organized, disciplined person who could be relied upon pick up the pieces on group projects, and started down the career path that led her to become a show creator. Zach, meanwhile, did his junior year abroad, then transferred to a college in the northeast. They'd lost touch until he'd messaged Stacey on Facebook five months ago to say he was back in California, teaching high-school biology at a progressive private school in L.A., and how about they go for a drink sometime? They'd been hooking up semi-regularly ever since.

When Stacey let Zach in at 10:00 p.m., she had on a tank top and shorts, her hair was piled up on her head with a banana clip, and she was wearing no makeup, but Zach said, "Hey, beautiful." And, "There's a small dog with a big head out here."

Stacey looked where Zach pointed. Buddy, a white terrier that belonged to her elderly neighbour, was lying in the hallway at the halfway point between the two apartments, his back against the wall. Stacey came out and squatted next to him. "Hey, Buddy." He lifted his head and looked at her, wagged his tail. "What are you doing out here?"

Zach said, "Friend of yours?"

"He lives next door. Go on in, I'll take him down there."

Outside her neighbour's door, Stacey listened for signs of life, heard the telltale sounds of Fox News, and knocked. "Pauline? Are you there? It's Stacey, from down the hall. I've got Buddy with me."

A middle-aged black woman Stacey had never seen before, dressed in a nurse's getup — a floral print top and purple pants — opened the door. "Did the dog get out when I wasn't looking?" she said. "Come on in, Buddy, there's a good boy. Thanks for bringing him back."

"You're welcome. Is Pauline okay?" She'd seemed okay, or mobile, at least, the last time Stacey had seen her, about a month back.

"She's on oxygen full-time now, and she's stable," the woman said. "She's sleeping at the moment, but if you want to see her, you could come by in the daytime."

Stacey wasn't close enough to Pauline to visit her if she was sick, or to ask any more questions about her condition — their relationship consisted of lobby and elevator small talk. But she said, "Could she use some help with Buddy? I work late, but I could maybe take him out for an evening walk sometimes."

"That's nice of you, hon. I'll tell Pauline and the day nurse you offered. You're from next door, you said?"

"Yes, from number 405. My name is Stacey."

Back in her apartment, Zach sat on the living room sofa, feet up, an open beer bottle in his hand, a baseball game playing on TV.

"Dog get home okay?" he said.

"Yeah, but my neighbour seems to be sick. A nurse answered the door."

"That's too bad." He took a swig of beer. "And how's my shawty?"

"Let's pretend you didn't just call me that."

"My girl?"

"Your Thursday-night hookup is a little tired."

"Tough day at the office?"

Jenna's face and freakishly large eyes — like an anime character's — popped up on Stacey's mind screen. "Long day. What about you? How was school?"

"So-so. The kids were restless, I had to sit through a staff meeting about green initiatives at lunchtime, and when I got out of the meeting, I had twelve emails to answer from over-involved parents questioning me about their over-privileged kids."

"Sounds like you love your job."

"I'd like it more if it required less politicking and ass-kissing."

Oh, Zach. "Every job involves that shit. The trick is to get yourself into a position where yours is the ass that's being kissed."

"Like you've done?"

"Like I'm working on doing. Do you know how many people my show employs?"

"You didn't let me finish about my day. This afternoon, we did a lockdown drill. That's always a laugh riot."

"I can imagine." And a high school lockdown drill might make a good scene choice for the teenage characters on *The Benjamins*.

Zach said, "And this shitty thing happened during it."

Stacey was already mentally laying out a lockdown scene for the show, but she put it away for later and listened.

"I was in my classroom with a bunch of ninth graders, everyone sitting on the floor under the desks. We're crouched down, silent, listening to the clock tick and waiting for the all-clear, when this one girl, Courtney, who is chubby, and doesn't seem too smart — her pants split. Down the back, down her ass. Because of the way she was sitting, I guess. And everyone heard the ripping sound and turned and looked at her."

He had Stacey's full attention now. "Instant humiliation," she said.

"I'd put the kids under strict orders to be silent in the drill, and the freshmen don't know any better yet than to obey the rules, but a few started to whisper and laugh at her, and I'm telling them to quit it when the bell rings and the announcement comes over the PA system that the drill is over."

"And?"

"We all got up, and Courtney grabbed her backpack and ran out of the classroom. I think she was crying, and she didn't come back."

In the baseball game on TV, a batter popped out. Stacey said, "Is that the end of the story?"

Zach said, "I felt bad for her."

So did Stacey, in theory — for all the good it would do the girl (none). She said, "You're too soft-hearted to be a teacher." He was too soft and weak to work in any field that would bring him into contact with regular human cruelty.

"It was such a small incident, maybe she's already forgotten about it."

"Maybe." Though Stacey remembered every single embarrassing or shameful thing that had ever happened to her, starting with the time she cried when she was made It during a game of hide-and-seek at school in first grade and couldn't find anyone, through to the day in middle school when she didn't discover until she got home that she'd had a large menstrual blood stain on the back of her pale-blue shorts, and finishing with the mistake she'd made that morning, when she'd questioned Jenna's hiring and Ann had shot her down.

It was like she had a logbook hardwired into her mind that listed, with supporting video and audio, every blush she'd blushed, every foolish word she'd spoken, every misstep she'd taken. And she was compelled to read and reread that logbook often, and remember why she was breaking her back at work: so she could become known as a maker of quality television, and rub her success in the face of every person who had ever rejected, ignored, shamed, or failed to appreciate her.

Zach said, "Let's face it, adolescence sucks."

"Mine sure did."

"No, it didn't. There's no way a girl who looks like you came close to feeling real angst. Did you even have acne?"

"No, not really, but —"

"I'll bet you had some popular-guy boyfriend by your sophomore year of high school, and the male teachers flirted with you, and you were oblivious to the fact that when you strolled through the halls every day, that hair floating around you, your tight little ass bouncing up and down with every step, you fuelled the fantasies of every pimply, horny-as-hell, violin-playing loser like me who lusted after you from afar and jerked off nightly to the thought of seeing you naked."

It was true that Stacey never suffered from acne, but otherwise, Zach had it wrong. She'd been a geeky kid who played French horn, ran cross country and track, did well in math and science, and was, by her estimate, unknown to 80 percent of the 500 kids in her year. By devoting herself to schoolwork, the music stand, and the running trails in Toronto, where she grew up, she had managed to graduate without experiencing sex, drinking, or drugs, and with a 91 percent grade average, to go with an honours diploma in invisibility.

Her high-school life had been nothing like the standard hot-girl, coming-of-age-movie existence Zach imagined she'd had, but what was the point of shattering his illusions? If what got him over to her place once a week to service her sexual needs was the idea that she represented every girl he'd wanted but couldn't have, she saw no reason to set him straight.

They fucked, they came, he left.

At eleven o'clock, Stacey ran through her nightly beauty routines, went to bed, and fell asleep. At 4:00 a.m. on the dot, she opened her eyes, turned on the bedside lamp, and reached for her laptop. A stray image lingered in her mind from a transparently symbolic bad dream she sometimes had, about climbing stairs in a tall tower, stairs without end. She shook it off and opened her work files.

Part of her 4:00 a.m. routine was to annotate the work journal she kept on her computer. She recorded the outcomes of meetings, made note of significant decisions and discussions, brought forward items that required follow-up. She found it soothing to keep close track of everything.

She was halfway through her notes about the previous day when a chill ran through her, an echo of the apprehension she'd felt in her office when Ann introduced her to Jenna.

Ann had been bossy and dismissive, but what else was new? Sure, she was more arrogant and impatient now than when Stacey had started working for her seven years before. Back then, Ann had tempered her megalomania with some roguish charm and a wicked wit. But power was supposed to corrupt, and age wither. So it hadn't bugged or surprised Stacey too much the week before, for instance, when Ann had shown up at the office in a chauffeur-driven town car and announced that it was her new ride. A ride she intended to charge to the production budget, not to her own expense account.

Stacey wouldn't let Ann get away with that kind of creative bookkeeping — there were some advantages to being overseer for the company's administrative functions — but she was used to Ann's grasping ways. Ann was who she was, and of all the adjectives Stacey could use to describe her, dangerous wasn't one.

Still. If she hadn't been distracted that morning by the script she had to approve, and by the inadequacy she felt whenever faced with the Jennas of the world — people who were born beautiful and had been blessed with good fortune all their lives — she might have suspected Ann of amping up the aggression level the minute she walked in. And when she'd told the story about how Stacey and Ann had met.

Shit, what if the day's minor manoeuvres were a continuation of a campaign Ann had been secretly waging since *The Benjamins* had been picked up?

Looked at through that filter, the slings and arrows of the past few months started to add up — like the creative decisions Ann had made without consulting Stacey, and the I'm-the-boss tone she'd begun to use more often lately to freeze out Stacey's input in meetings.

What if the tensions Stacey had attributed to Ann feeling her age, seeing herself slow down, and trying to fight her inevitable decline, were actually — how could Stacey have missed this? — reactions to the threat to her dominance that Stacey embodied? Ann must have seen that Stacey was brighter, and more in touch, and had fresher story ideas, and could spin the same old family-drama tropes — a teen pregnancy scare, a cheating husband, the reappearance of a child given up for adoption, the physical and mental decline of a grandparent — into something new. When Ann couldn't, not any longer. She must have realized that Stacey couldn't and wouldn't be confined forever to dealing with budgets and contracts and production details. And that Stacey had as much right — more — to run the show as Ann did.

Hell, if Stacey were in Ann's shoes and had figured all that out, she might launch a counter-attack too.

She squared her shoulders, slapped her own face, hard, and felt the sting on her cheek. She was too smart, too good at seeing through people, at seeing past their polite public faces to spot the ugly, grasping ambition within — she always had been — not to have figured out before now that Ann must have regretted going into partnership with Stacey from the moment they'd signed their company into being.

Unless.

Maybe Stacey had succumbed to 4:00 a.m. paranoia and was reading too much into that morning's encounter. Maybe Jenna's arrival wasn't a salvo, and Ann wasn't out to get Stacey, not this week. Maybe Ann's arthritis had acted up and made her cranky.

Maybe this, maybe that — what was certain was that Stacey would be extra vigilant from now on, around Jenna and Ann both.

5

Two weeks into the job, Jenna took a morning off to audition for a part on a medical show as a business executive, the sister of one of the doctor characters. Her agent, Tasha, had talked her up to the casting director and recommended Jenna because she slightly resembled the actress in question. "The only problem is that you're prettier than she is," Tasha said. "So wear something office-y to the audition, and don't look too stunning. Act humble, but fun. Make them like you!"

Yeah, yeah.

Jenna had asked Ann for the morning off work, and the night before, she rehearsed the sides alone in her apartment. Her character's key lines in the scene were:

```
I'm not sorry that my job involves
making money. We can't all be life-
saving saints like you.
```

She read the lines cold and calculating, she read them with a bitch face and a finger snap, she read them depressed and defeated. Then she tried to imagine how Stacey would deliver them. Stacey was a real-life businesswoman, sort of, and the right age, thirtyish, and for meetings outside of the office she wore expensive little jackets over her expensive little floaty dresses or five-hundred-dollar jeans. She had a way of being friendly when she spoke to Jenna, but distant at the same time. Like you could never say she wasn't nice, but you couldn't really know her either.

Jenna gave Stacey's warm/cool approach a try with the lines but it didn't work for her. It wasn't that attention-getting or memorable on Stacey — she was not the most charismatic person. As producers went, Ann had way more star quality.

In the end, Jenna decided on the bitch-face version of the lines, without the finger snap. Maybe she could start a new phase of her career and play bad girls.

She arrived on time for the audition, and did not let herself be shaken by the presence of eight other actresses of her age range and physical type sitting in the hall, some with better resumés than hers, including a former child star who had headlined a popular sitcom fifteen years before. She silently chanted her confidence mantras, and when she was called into the audition room, she went in and killed the scene. Killed it.

The casting people thanked her for coming in. They had a few others to see, they'd let her know. She said she'd love the opportunity to work on the show, then left. If she let a tear of self-pity drop down her cheek on the drive to the studio, no one would have known it by the time she walked in and sat at her desk. But when Ann came out of a meeting an hour later, picked up her messages, asked Jenna where she'd been, and said, "Oh yeah. How'd it go?" Jenna told her, in detail.

"I wouldn't be too discouraged," Ann said. "It doesn't sound like much of a part."

"What will be will be, I figure. And on one level, I'm already over it."

Ann flipped through her messages. "You can't take that kind of rejection personally. There are so many factors that go into a casting decision that have nothing to do with the actor. Right, Stacey?"

Stacey had come down the corridor. "What are we talking about?"

"Jenna went to an audition this morning. I was telling her that if she didn't get the part, it's probably not her fault."

Stacey made such direct eye contact that Jenna wondered if she'd imagined her being distant before. "For all you know," Stacey said, "you reminded the casting director of a girl who was mean to her in high school, or of some slut her boyfriend hooked up with last week."

Was that supposed to make Jenna feel better? Before she could decide, Stacey said, "And if you won over the casting director, something arbitrary about you — like your nose, or your hair colour, or your name — could rub one of the producers or the director the wrong way. Casting is such a crapshoot."

Jenna had always thought her nose was crooked, though when she'd asked Andrew for his honest opinion about it, he'd said he didn't see it. She said, "Maybe I'm not meant to act anymore. Maybe I'm meant to become a producer instead. Like you two."

Stacey said, "I've always thought looks like yours belonged in front of the camera, not behind it with us drudges. But stranger things have happened."

Ann eyed Stacey over the top of her reading glasses. "We should ask Jenna what she thinks about the retreat idea. From her dual perspective as talent and management."

Stacey: "If you want."

"Go ahead. Ask her."

Jenna didn't know what they were talking about, but she was already used to Stacey and Ann speaking to each other as if no one else were around.

Stacey said, "Ann thinks we should organize a team-building weekend away. For the cast, writers, and producers."

Ann: "Here's something to know if you want to be a producer, Jenna. It's important to encourage a sense of family in the early stages of a show."

Jenna had never done any team- or family-building activities on her previous shows, but okay.

Stacey said, "We'd pick an inn or small resort away from the studio, ship everyone out there, organize some low-key activities like yoga classes, or maybe pedicures — wasn't that what you said, Ann?"

"I never mentioned pedicures, but that's a good idea. And Jenna, so you understand: the idea is to give people a chance to bond, away from the set, out of the office, before we get too far into the shooting schedule."

"Yeah, I get it. What did you want to ask me about it?"

Stacey and Ann exchanged a glance and Jenna started to sweat, like she was being tested at school. She'd never been good at tests.

Stacey said, "To begin with, what do you think about that idea from a cast member's point of view? If you were a cast member, I mean, would you want to do something like this, or would you consider it an ordeal?"

Maybe Jenna wasn't cut out for management work after all. Maybe she could only sound decisive and smart when reading lines. She tried to think. She didn't mind hanging out with actors, except for the divas who thought they were better than everyone else — the older, established actresses with movie backgrounds who were reduced to playing grandmas late in their careers were often like that. And you had to avoid the show creep. There was always one — a guy who was too free with his hands, and who made raunchy comments that he called flirting and Jenna called disgusting. But aside from those types, other actors could be okay to hang with, and party with. And if the idea was Ann's, she should support it, right? "A weekend like that could be fun, sure."

Stacey said, "What about from a staff point of view? If you came along, would you feel awkward socializing with actors, not to mention with your bosses and superiors?"

If they thought they could consult Jenna about a retreat, then not invite her to it, they were wrong. A weekend of networking with the cast and producers could pay off no matter which career path she chose. "Speaking for myself," she said, "I'm a real people person, so I'd love it."

Ann said to Stacey, "Sounds like we should do this."

Stacey picked up a pen from the desk, flipped it in the air, and caught it. "I'll get Topher to look into some possible venues."

They'd forgotten about Jenna again. She said, "I know just the place! Because of my friend Cooper? He's a real sweet guy. I've known him since high school. I used to think I'd marry him someday. He has a long-term girlfriend now, though, she's a pro beach volleyball player?" Shit, she was babbling, and uptalking, and losing them. Stacey had stood up like she was about to leave, and Ann's face had gone slack like it did when she tuned out of a conversation. "Anyway, Cooper has a bike shop and he runs biking and hiking tours out of an inn called Haven in the mountains near Malibu. Do you know it?"

Ann said, "Is it one of those crunchy ashram-type places, all spartan and vegan?"

"No, I've been there with my boyfriend, and it's pretty fancy. It's a Cali-style mountain lodge, with a spa and a gourmet restaurant with a good wine list."

Stacey said, "You're being so helpful today, Jenna. Haven, you say? I'll have Topher check it out, put it on our list of places to consider. Thanks for that."

"I'd be happy to call Cooper and ask him to arrange a group discount and a special bike or hike outing, if you like."

"We'll see," Stacey said, and walked off like the conversation was over. She was fifteen feet away when Ann yelled, "Stacey! What about our walk?"

Ann's bossy tone would have stopped Jenna in her tracks, but not Stacey. She looked back over her shoulder, said, "I'll meet you at the front door in five. I'm going to change my shoes," and kept on.

"What's up her ass?" Ann muttered. As if Stacey had been difficult, when Jenna didn't think she had been. Aside from the part when she'd walked away while being yelled at.

Jenna said, "Did I talk too much there? You know actors — sometimes we overshare."

"You did fine. Maybe you went on one sentence too many. Or two. But enthusiasm is good. I like enthusiasm." Ann lowered her voice. "Stacey's uptight, that's all. She likes to 'run shit,' as the young people say. Don't worry about her. You answer to me, and I think you're doing a swell job."

And that was what mattered, as far as Jenna could see.

6

Stacey wasn't keen on the cast retreat idea. Call her cynical, but did no one else see the irony in trying to form a fake happy family out of people who worked on a show about a treacherous, double-dealing one?

She hadn't liked it when Ann first proposed it, and she liked it less after Jenna said she'd love to go for a free high-end weekend getaway with the cast members because she was a "people person." Jenna was big on world peace too, Stacey was sure. And for the talent portion of the beauty contest, Miss San Fernando Valley will now perform a monologue from *Legally Blonde*.

One reason Stacey was against the retreat idea was that Ann had done it before. For their last show, she'd dragged everyone out to an exclusive resort near Newport Beach. The producers and writers welcomed the perk of a few days of luxury living on the company tab, and the cast came out to please Ann. For two days, they played the roles of actors who got along, except when they were sneaking out for smoke breaks and bitching to each other, or calling their significant others to complain on their cellphones behind the resort. Which Stacey knew about because her room overlooked a courtyard where the complainers thought they could speak without being overheard.

Afterward, Ann had pronounced the event a big success, and Stacey hadn't disputed that assessment because there was no upside to disagreement, to puncturing Ann's high self-regard, not with *The Benjamins* coming down the chute, and Stacey's new role as co-creator in development. No point in saying the retreat was a bad idea this time either.

And what was with Ann asking for Jenna's opinion on the subject? Why should a C-list actress who'd worked with Ann for two weeks have input on a management decision or be invited to come along? If she did, Stacey would have to look at those doe eyes and listen to her Thought-of-the-Day insights into human nature all weekend and please, no.

Stacey stopped at Topher's desk and asked him to research possible retreat venues according to a clear, concise set of parameters. She made no mention of Haven. Inside her office, she sat down and tried to find her centre. She also slipped out of her shoes and into her sneakers so she could walk with Ann.

She tied up one sneaker, reached for the second, and — hold on. It might actually be a crafty idea to ship the crowd out to Haven, with Jenna along. If the venue didn't work out, Jenna's judgment would be criticized. If it proved satisfactory, the probability was still high that Jenna would make social gaffes, either by being too familiar with the actors she considered her peers, or with Ann, who, Stacey knew from experience, liked to decide how and when to bestow favours like intimacy on her protégés.

The presence of the Cooper guy — from the sound of her description, Jenna's Man That Got Away — manfully leading hikes might cause trouble for Jenna, too. Stacey could sic one of the nubile actresses on him, to piss Jenna off and make her jealous. Or, if he was a tall, rugged type, he could rub the male actors the wrong way, bring out their competitive natures — it wasn't easy managing actor egos, and it would be harder still when they were collected in one place. If the men got ticked off, again Jenna would be blamed, yip-yip.

Stacey woke up her computer and looked up Haven. She clicked off the drippy New Age music that played on its website, and saw that it was a mid-size, high-end inn "nestled" in the Santa Monica mountains, with elegantly appointed suites, a full menu of spa services, and all the amenities, including optional hiking and mountain biking tours organized by an adjunct company with the hippie name of Hike, Bike, Love.

On the way out to meet Ann, she asked Topher to add Haven to the list of venues under consideration. "It's out Malibu way. And it comes with a personal recommendation from Jenna Kuyt."

"Is that a good thing?" he said.

"Yet to be determined. Could you please check it out anyway, as soon as you can?"

"Will do."

Ann was waiting for Stacey at the front door. Uh oh. Ann hated to wait, wished always to be the one waited for, but she was talking on her phone, so she was preoccupied. Or not. She indicated with an irritated flick of her hand that they should head out, waited for Stacey to open the door for her, and walked through it.

Into the phone, she said, "No, not the Malbec, the Burgundy. How many times do I have to tell you?" Then, "I should be home by eight. Or nine." A sigh. "Goodbye." She ended the call. "Why'd it take you so long to change your shoes? And why are you walking so fast? Slow down. My knee's bothering me."

Stacey was not walking fast, but she slowed her pace, and carefully chose a response from among the several that occurred to her. "Was that John on the phone? How's he doing?"

John, Ann's older-than-her husband, was a history professor at Pepperdine who had a reputation — Stacey had looked him up — as a magnetic lecturer and sleazy skirt-chaser. He also, according to Ann, pouted and whined if she wasn't around to keep him company on the evenings he chose to stay home. Why Ann wanted to remain married to him Stacey had never understood — in every show Ann had worked on, she'd created husband/patriarch characters who were kinder, nobler, and less selfish than John appeared to be. Her fantasy husbands, no doubt. As opposed to the fantasy lover character she'd created for Ryan to play.

The saddest part of the story was that Ann wanted to grow old with John. She'd admitted as much to Stacey a few months before, under the influence of three mojitos, at an upfronts party. She'd leaned in too close, exhaled a poisonous combination of alcohol fumes laced with garlic from the potsticker hors d'oeuvres that had been passed around, and said, "Here's the thing about John: I'd rather be with him than be alone."

Now, Ann said, "He's fine. Aside from bothering me about which wine we should drink with dinner."

"Is this his last year of teaching? How old is he now?"

On the mojitos night, Ann had confided that John wanted her to retire when he did, despite the huge gap in their salaries, because he intended to travel the world, with her. And on her millions, presumably. Ann said, "He's only sixty-four."

Stacey did not say a word, or words, like, "what do you mean, *only?*" but Ann gave her a side eye anyway, and said, "You know, Stacey — one day, you, too, will be old."

That was not quite true. On Stacey's thirtieth birthday, she'd made a suicide pact with herself, to be executed (yeah, she'd be here all week) the day she turned fifty. But it wasn't something she'd told anyone about, or that she couldn't decide to opt out of. "And I won't be good at being old, I can tell."

"Fuck!" Ann stopped walking, and grimaced in pain. "My knee is in spasm."

Stacey stood by while Ann started in on the kind of heavy breathing that pregnant women do in movies when they're in labour. In Stacey's opinion, Ann should consider retirement regardless of John's wishes. Had there been any day recently when she hadn't suffered from some ailment or ache — her knee, her foot, her shoulder, a cough? Stacey waited till Ann's face cleared and she stopped panting. "Do you want to turn back?" she said.

Ann said no, the pain had mostly passed. "I'm okay as long as we walk slowly and stick to the agenda." She pulled from her pocket a strip of paper on which she'd written the topics she wanted to discuss. She brought out a list like this every day during their walk. "What were we talking about before my knee went out?"

"Retirement. But we're done with that. What's the first item on your list?"

She peered at it. "Damn. I forgot my reading glasses."

"They're around your neck."

Ann felt for the glasses on the lanyard, put them on. "I still can't read this. What's that first word?"

Scrawled in comically large print was a word that started with a capital C. "Does it say Candace?"

"Yes. You heard Candace had her baby last night? A girl. And she's named her Camisole. No joke. After the article of clothing — that is, the article of lingerie. Maybe she can call her next child Girdle."

"Or Corset. Then she could say, 'Have you met my daughters, Camisole and Corset? We call them Cami and Corsy for short.'"

"And their little brother is named Body Shaper."

Stacey heh-hehed. Ann could still make her laugh. "Should we send her something?"

"I'll have Jenna send a gift basket from me and flowers on behalf of the company."

She would expense both gifts to the company, then take personal credit for them — what else would Stacey expect? "Okay."

Ann said, "I don't think Candace will come back from maternity leave, by the way. She's probably still tripping from the drugs and hormones, but when she called me, she said that mothering — and that's the term she used — is her true calling. Could have fooled me. Before she got pregnant, it seemed like club-going and star-fucking were her twin vocations. Did she ever tell you about her one-nighter with Chris Evans? Or was it Chris Pine?"

"No, she didn't. But then, Candace and I were never within confiding distance."

Ann stopped walking, and rubbed her knee. "I like that: 'within confiding distance.' Did you just make that up?"

"I don't know. Maybe."

"Let's use it, give it as a line to Arielle. Remind me tomorrow when we're in the writers' room."

Stacey would remind Ann, but it was such a power play, that remind-me line. The same as saying, "I'm too busy and important to remember this thing we're talking about, so hey you, lesser person? Remember it for me."

Ann said, "I'm going to encourage Candace to embrace her new-found maternal instincts and not come back. I like Jenna better. She's more personable and presentable, and she has more potential."

"Potential for what?"

"To move up the ranks. Like you did."

Stacey could have pointed out the ways that she was intellectually superior to Jenna, including that she'd had an M.F.A. in Film and Television Production when she started working for Ann, but what use had Stacey's college education been, really? Except to introduce her to the professor who admired her obsessive work ethic and recommended her for an internship with the prof's old pal Ann.

Stacey said, "You think Jenna is ready to give up her acting career? She wasn't half-bad in her last show."

Ann stopped again — at the rate they were going, they'd be lucky to reach the coffee shop by nightfall — and sniffed the air in a manner intended to make fun, but that made her look like a large-nostrilled rabbit. "Hey — do I smell jealousy?" She chuckled. "Come now, Stacey, you can't honestly feel threatened by Jenna." She performed a vintage style double take, complete with popped eyes and head reared back so far that her chin tripled. "*Can* you?"

If this were a scene in *The Benjamins*, the person on the receiving end of an assholeish put-down like that would respond by walking away, without a further word. Possibly while flipping the bird. But people rarely walked away mid-conversation in real life, Stacey had noticed. And the way to manage Ann was not to engage, but to diffuse. Calmly, she said, "No, I don't feel threatened by Jenna."

"You're sure? Because I thought maybe she reminded you of some girl who was mean to you in high school."

Stacey squeezed out a credible-sounding laugh, like she could enjoy a joke made at her own expense. "Good one, Ann. That's funny. And clever, how you linked back to our conversation in the office. I'm glad to see your knee problems haven't affected your mind."

The flattery worked: Ann relaxed.

"What's next on your agenda?" Stacey said.

7

Ann's Journal

So many people to hate this week.

Like the network goons whose notes on the episode 6 script suggested that we reduce the number of sex scenes featuring Ryan from 2 to 1 in favour of beefing up the political corruption story line (their snoozy idea to begin with).

They of all people should know that if anyone understands what the target demographic of straight, frumpy, TV-watching women aged 18–49 are looking for in a nighttime soap, it's me, and what those sad sacks want is pretty-faced, hunky-bodied guys who can be their TV boyfriends.

The same goes for boomer women of my advanced age and spending power: united we multigenerational women stand in mooning over the blue-eyed, cheekbone-blessed, hard-abbed guy who's probably gay in real life but who cares, because this is our dream world.

The goons don't know nothin'. To the point where I might have to stop taking their notes and reading their emails. How great would that be, if I just ignored them from here on out? Pretty fucking great.

Then there was the optometrist Miguel drove me to for what was supposed to be a quick eye exam so I could get a new glasses prescription. "I don't like the look of your retina, and I strongly recommend you see a specialist," said Mr. Bottom of his Class in pre-med who yearns to be more than a dispenser of eyewear. More than a fucking eyewear retailer.

He came on heavy enough that fine, I'll set up an appointment with a real eye doctor. But this had better not be a waste of my time, like with my knee — all those tests and ineffective physical therapy treatments and no cure offered aside from a prescription for a paltry amount of painkillers. Doctors are so useless unless they're on TV shows or save the lives of children who are stricken with terrible diseases. Though in the case of children, sometimes you have to wonder what made the parents think having a child was such a good idea in the first place. Seriously.

I crack myself up. But I'd better make sure this document is password-protected. I don't want my anti-child or anti-pet or anti-everyone sentiments ending up online in a public forum somewhere when I get hacked.

Okay, did that. And now the one place where I can express my misanthropy without any filters is cloaked in secrecy, as it should be. Three cheers for private media. As opposed to social media. Hell, if I kept it real on Twitter, every tweet would be a variation on "you suck," "fuck off," and "Am I the only person in this room/town/country who knows anything?" Imagine how the fans would go for that.

Also a piss-off: when Stacey voiced her disapproval that she thinks she hid, but did she ever not, of the cast retreat idea.

It's like whenever Stacey and I talk about work lately, which is all the time, there's a power struggle subtext going on. A storm-the-Bastille undercurrent to what she says.

Could she be trying to usurp me?

She's intelligent and thorough and competent, no question. And I'll give her that the concept for The Benjamins was golden, especially after I improved it. And the timing was right for the whole biracial, cross-cultural thing being in vogue with Obama being in power and all. But granting her a co-creator credit was one thing — she can't possibly think that a skinny-ass pisher like her could be smarter than me, and know better than me, about how to run a show, could she? I mean, come on.

Let's hope she's just champing at the bit right now, and not contemplating gnawing through the reins (or whatever they call those strappy restraints horses wear on their heads — the tack?) and trampling me to death.

Because I'll sink her like a stone if she keeps on challenging my authority. Sink her like a stone, then dynamite that stone and blow it all to hell.

Hahaha.

There's nothing like a little unbridled — that's the word, bridle — metaphor mixing and threat uttering to make me feel better.

Way to go, journal. Talk soon.

SEPTEMBER

8

After a long day's work, Stacey came home, took Buddy for an evening stroll, and had Zach over for a pre-coital drink (Stacey drank flavoured water, Zach had a beer) in front of another baseball game on TV.

They made idle conversation — What percentage of people in North America normally wear white on any given day, do you think? she asked, when the camera panned over the fans in the stands. Twenty-eight point three was Zach's typical, not funny, meant-to-be-a-joke response that she overlooked in order to still entertain pleasurable anticipatory thoughts about him going down on her later. Thoughts that were interrupted by the rarely heard ring of her landline.

She checked the call display. It was her parents, to whom she hadn't spoken in over a month, so she said sorry to Zach, and hello into the phone.

Her mother, Deb, said, "Grant, Stacey answered the phone. Pick up."

When Stacey's dad had come on the line, with much noisy

handling of the extension receiver, Deb said, "We're calling to discuss our trip to L.A. in October for my conference."

Grant said, "You haven't forgotten we're coming, have you?"

Stacey picked up her cell and opened her calendar app. "No, I haven't. You're here on the sixteenth, right?"

"We land on the Wednesday, yes."

Whizzes at math and science, the two of them, and they couldn't retain the number of their arrival date. To needle them, Stacey said, "Wednesday the sixteenth?"

Deb: "Yes, the Wednesday of that week."

Grant: "We'd like to see you Thursday evening for dinner and Sunday for lunch. And your sister will be there; she's attending the conference as well."

"You call that a strike?" Zach said, louder than he should.

Deb said, "Do you have someone over? Should we call you back tomorrow night?"

Grant said, "We can't, Deb. I'm giving that speech tomorrow night."

"We can talk now. There's no one here. That was the TV. I'll turn down the volume."

Deb said, "I'd ask if you're dating anyone, but I know how much you like that topic."

"I like that topic so much that if I *were* seeing someone, which I'm not, I wouldn't tell you about him."

Zach pouted at Stacey. Or was it a mock pout? She turned her back on him, and cursed herself for regressing into the twin states of insolence and petulance at the sound of her parents' voices. "About the dinner, I won't know till that day if I can meet you. But I should be able to make lunch on the Sunday. Is Ellen bringing Hugo along on this junket?"

Grant said, "No. He's staying behind with the kids. It's too bad you can't commit. We'd like to see you. Let's hope you can make it. Now, let me give you our hotel info."

She convinced them to email her the details instead of dictating them, started to wrap up the call, and saw in her peripheral vision that Zach was miming exaggerated reactions to the ball game — he jumped up and down, and pumped his fists, and mouthed words he would be yelling if Stacey hadn't denied his presence. She might have found this physical comedy routine mildly amusing if Grant and Deb weren't being so annoyingly Grant-and-Deb-ish. Might have.

Deb said, "Grant, what was the other thing I wanted to talk to Stacey about?"

"What your secretary said about Stacey's show."

"Oh yeah. The new secretary at the clinic is a big TV fan. She watches three or four hours a night, can you believe it? And she was very interested to hear you work in TV."

The secretary was bound to be more interested than Deb, Grant, or Ellen were. "Uh-huh."

"She said your boss is a very well-known showrunner."

"Ann's not my boss anymore, she's my producing partner."

"Right. But my secretary said she'd never heard of you. She said Ann is on Tweeter —"

"It's called Twitter," Grant said.

"— and she has hundreds of thousands of followers, and gets interviewed on TV internet sites all the time."

"All of those things are true."

"Why is Ann the spokesperson if you're partners? Why aren't you doing that?"

Stacey had not developed a higher media profile because Ann wouldn't dream of sharing the spotlight. She'd been the public face and voice of every show she'd produced, and she wasn't about to let that change because *The Benjamins* had been Stacey's idea.

"That's just the way it is," Stacey said. "Ann and I share some responsibilities and split others." That is, Ann did the prestigious, for-credit tasks, and Stacey did everything else.

She still had her back turned to Zach, but when she looked over her shoulder, she saw that his eyes were closed and he was making soft snoring noises, pretending to be asleep. He had better be pretending.

"I have another call coming in," Stacey said, "Gotta run. Email me those details, bye." She hung up. "Fuck me."

Zach opened his eyes. "At the end of the inning, I promise."

Again with the not funny. She said, "You'll have gathered that was my parents."

"I also gathered that I won't be meeting them when they come to town. On Wednesday the sixteenth, was it?"

What the hell? Did Zach think theirs was the kind of relationship that called for meeting parents? She had no time or energy for that kind of thing. She took a couple of calming breaths. She could use an orgasmic release of the non-self-induced variety, and Zach couldn't make that happen if she booted him out the door, now could he? "Believe me," she said. "You don't want to meet my parents. Unless you have a throat disorder or diseased eyes."

"I don't. So, you're right. I don't want to meet them." He came over, kneeled at her feet, and slid his hands under her skirt, up her thighs. "I'd rather be the secret lover no one knows about; mild-mannered teacher by day, sex god by night."

Sex god? Try sex minion. He was not without skills, so she'd let him stay, but she already knew, when she closed her eyes and spread her legs, that it was time to cut him loose.

9

Jenna had been friends with Kerry Langdon since they'd worked together on a sitcom that was cancelled after one season. At age twenty-one, Jenna played a teenage alt girl with an eyebrow piercing and a wig of spiky hair coloured in blue, green, and purple chunks. Then twenty-four, Kerry was the blonde cheerleader best friend and next-door neighbour of Jenna's character on the show, because cheerleaders and alternative girls with punk hair are often friends in real life. Not.

Since then, Kerry had carved herself out a niche as a vixen on a long-running daytime soap that taped in L.A., and she'd met and married a business guy who was in real estate, or land development, Jenna wasn't sure which. All she knew was that Eric was wealthy — their house in Hancock Park was a borderline mansion. And now here Kerry and Jenna were, getting their highlights done side by side in a Melrose hair salon, like they did every eight weeks, and it was Jenna's turn, for once, to be sympathetic about Kerry's career, because her soap had been cancelled, after forty-five years on the air.

Kerry said, "Talk about the end of an era. You should have seen the old-timers in the cast when they heard the news. Imagine all those plastic surgery faces crumpling up in tears. Or trying to crumple up."

"That's so sad." Jenna didn't know whether to feel sorry for Kerry or nervous that they might start competing for parts. "How bummed are you about this? On a scale of one to ten."

"I don't know. Seven? I mean, I hate losing a stable, full-time gig, but maybe this is a sign."

"Of what?"

"That I should do something else. What are the odds of me getting hired to do primetime or movies? Look at you. You're younger, and you've got that exotic, biracial look going. If you can't make it after all these years of trying, how can I?"

Jenna felt the Jell-O-ish mass that was her confidence quivering inside her chest. "I can still make it big. So can you. All it takes is one good part, one hit show."

"The thought of going out on auditions for guest spots on police procedurals makes me want to puke. I'm thinking that when my show wraps, I'll go into interior design. Remember that little house I flipped in Echo Park? I liked doing that, and I made some money on it. I'll get Eric to bankroll me on the first couple of properties, and I'll take it from there. What do you think? You in?"

"What? Me? No. I'm not handy. Or design-y. And I don't have a rich husband to back me."

"That reminds me: how's it going with Andrew? Have you given him an answer on moving in?"

"No, not yet." Jenna hadn't told Kerry the real reason she was hesitant to commit to Andrew. She'd said she didn't want to be tied down, rather than admit she was aiming higher. "Anyway," Jenna said, "I still want to act. And maybe produce."

"Yeah? How's the job going? And how weird is it to work for Ann Dalloni? On a scale of one to ten."

"It's weird hearing people talk about the talent like I'm not there. Which I'm not. As talent. But it's interesting to see how a show runs from the production perspective."

"From the dark side, you mean?"

"Aren't the networks officially the dark side?"

"You're right. Networks are the most evil, then the studios, then the production companies. But spill with some gossip. Are Ann and that Stacey McCreedy lesbian lovers, or what?"

"No. Ann's married to a college professor, a man. She has been for years."

"What about Stacey? What's her story?"

"She's low-key compared to Ann. I'm not sure if she's single, or has a boyfriend, or what."

"Some source of dirt you are."

Jenna tried to think of something scandalous to tell Kerry. "They're not that tight, Ann and Stacey. There's tension between them sometimes, for sure."

"That doesn't surprise me. I auditioned for Ann once, a few years ago, and she came across as a stone-cold bitch. Is she still like that?"

"I'd call her a warm bitch, actually," Jenna said, and they laughed, like when they'd hung out together in the sitcom makeup trailer, bonding over their love for old movies, sure they'd gotten their big break and stardom was coming their way.

Kerry clutched Jenna's arm. "I just realized what you're doing — you're working your way onto the show through the back door. What a stealth move! How soon do you think till they cast you?"

"That's not why I'm there. I want to learn about production." Though a few days before, Jenna had overheard a couple of the writers talking about a new recurring character she'd be perfect for — an attractive college student doing an internship at the music company one of the second-generation Benjamins ran. She could play that role with her eyes closed. She *wanted* to play the role. Way more than she wanted to help organize the retreat, which was scheduled for the following weekend. Six days away.

Jenna was nervous about the retreat, stage fright–type nervous, when she had no reason to be. It wasn't like she would be performing. "Maybe you're nervous about performing your job," Andrew said, a few days before the retreat was to begin, when they were getting ready for bed at his place. "You'll be fine. And it's just a temp job anyway, so who cares?"

She turned on her electric toothbrush. There was no point in telling him that the job hadn't felt like a temp job lately, what with Ann assigning her important tasks to do with the retreat weekend. She'd made and distributed copies of the schedules, and asked everyone whether they smoked or not and which of the optional activities they wanted to participate in. She'd done a first run-through of the room allocation chart, though Stacey had ended up taking over that task and doing it her way, which was fine — she had strong opinions about who should sleep where, just like Ann, who had insisted on doing the seating arrangements for the Friday night dinner and consulting with the chef on the food and the wines for the meals.

Jenna was just an assistant, but she added value to the company. And anyway, Andrew should have known that not everyone went to a big-name law school and became a partner in a law firm with junior staff reporting to them. Some people were the junior staff. Temporarily. When they weren't wondering if a casting director would ever book them again.

"Are you coming to bed?" Andrew said.

Jenna stopped the toothbrush and spat. "I'll be right out."

Another reason Jenna didn't want to talk about why her job mattered was because if she did, Andrew might ask if she'd decided about moving in with him, and she didn't want to discuss that topic, not with her birthday coming up. She was hoping his gift to her would be a new car. One of the smaller Mercedes models would be good, to match his Mercedes SUV. Though if he bought her a car, she'd probably have to move in with him.

She closed the bathroom door and started to floss. What if no one liked Haven and it was her fault? What if the food didn't meet Ann's high standards, or the spa staff took pictures of the actors naked and sold them to TMZ? No, everything would work out. The writers, producers, and actors on the show weren't assholes; they'd be polite. And the inn staff would be used to celebrities, and be discreet.

One aspect of the weekend Jenna wasn't worried about: the optional hikes she had arranged with Cooper and his business partner, Riley: an easy pre-dinner sunset hike on the Friday night, and a morning hike the next day for the early risers. She didn't know Riley, but she was sure Cooper would be a hit: he was a guy's guy who also got along with women. He wasn't good-looking — his hair had no flow, and his eyes were small and a muddy shade of brown. But he was tall, and lean, and mellow.

Jenna and Cooper had dated for most of their junior year of high school, in the Valley, and he'd had those same qualities then, but she'd dumped him a couple of months after she was discovered by a modelling scout at the mall. Her mom signed her up with a talent agent and a manager, she started acting in commercials and on teen shows, and she quickly outgrew all her high-school friends, including Cooper.

She rinsed her mouth and checked her reflection. No makeup, and she still looked amazing. She dabbed some perfume on her pulse points, turned off the bathroom light, and went out to join Andrew in bed. As soon as she sat on the bed, he laid his hand on her thigh. "Hey, baby. Give me two minutes to see the sports highlights, then I'll tap that fine ass of yours."

Jenna slipped between the Frette sheets and settled into the big goose-down pillows Andrew had piled up on his bed. Cooper wouldn't have high-end linens like these. He still lived in the Valley. Not with his parents anymore, but Jenna could picture him in a shitty apartment, furnished with down-market furniture from Ikea to go with his down-market life. Though when she'd called him to set up the hikes, he hadn't sounded miserable. He'd sounded friendly.

They'd reconnected at a ten-year high-school class reunion the previous winter and become Facebook friends, exchanged a few messages and birthday greetings. That's how Jenna knew Cooper led biking tours, and had a tall girlfriend who played professional beach volleyball.

When they'd spoken on the phone about the retreat, Cooper had said he'd love to take the group for some hikes at Haven. "But do you think the actors will be up for it? You know that hikes involve walking outdoors, in nature, right? Do you think *you'll* be up for it now that you're a movie star?"

"I'm hardly a star," she said, but she liked that he thought of her as one. Maybe she was his celebrity crush. She'd tried to keep the flirt out of her voice, seeing as neither of them was single, but she might have let a few notes slip through. "And I'd be up for a hike. I'm into fitness and fresh air."

"I'll look forward to seeing you out on the trail then," he said, and she'd gone and bought a pair of short, sexy hiking shorts and some shoes she could hike in. Not because she was planning to try anything with Cooper, but just so she would look her best, like her mother had always told her she should.

Andrew clicked off the TV with one remote, dimmed the lights with another, and turned onto his side to face her. "You're so beautiful," he said. Jenna lifted the men's undershirt she wore to bed, rolled it up over her tits, and let him fondle them with both hands in his standard sequence: cup, squeeze, push together, release, tweak nipples three times. The same sequence he performed every time they had sex.

On cue, she arched her back, moaned seductively, and reached for his dick.

"And you're so fucking hot," he said.

She preferred he not speak during sex, but at least he had his facts straight.

10

According to the fifth and final version of the itinerary Stacey had received from Jenna, twenty-three people were confirmed for the retreat: Stacey and Ann and their assistants, four executive producers, five writers, and ten principal cast members. Only twelve of these turned up for the Friday evening pre-dinner hike. Everyone else was around, on-site — the group had driven out to Haven from the studio in a fleet of Escalades (not Stacey's idea), as if they were politicians in a motorcade, or gangster drug dealers — but as soon as they arrived, Ann had wanted to go check in with the chef about the dinner menu. Not that she would have hiked anyway.

There would be no athletic activity all weekend for Topher and the two youngest writers, either. They didn't do outdoor exercise. The male producers were having pre-drinks in their rooms, if Stacey knew them. That left Bonnie the senior writer, Stacey, and some assorted cast members on the hike, including Ryan and the older actors who played his parents, uncles, and aunts. A twenty-two-year-old party girl named Carly, who played Ryan's onscreen cousin, had also shown up, probably because she hadn't read as far as the word *optional* on the itinerary.

Jenna was there in her role as event organizer, and when Stacey approached the group standing outside the lodge's main building, at a calculated three minutes before the appointed meeting time, Jenna was chatting up a surfer dude with shaggy blond hair, blue eyes, and an over-tanned, wiry build — the old flame, no doubt.

She said to him, "You really saw *Go Ahead and Scream*? The whole thing?"

"I sure did. That scene when the killer had you chained to the wall, spread-eagled, and your shirt was ripped off, and he was cracking his whip? You acted the shit out of that! And you looked crazy sexy, too!" He had an affected drawl, but Jenna seemed to be into him.

Another guy, carrying a clipboard and dressed in the same Hike, Bike, Love T-shirt and cargo shorts uniform as the surfer dude, came over and, in a normally inflected voice, said, "Hi there. Would you be Stacey McCreedy?"

"I would."

He ticked her name off his list and offered her his hand to shake. "I'm Cooper. Nice to meet you."

This guy was Jenna's Cooper?

He called to the blond dude, "Yo, Riley. The gang's all here. Let's get started."

Riley broke off his conversation with Jenna, jumped up on a rock, and started giving a speech-slash-stand-up routine in his tiresome drawl about the hike to come, how long it would be, their route, what they'd see, and what safety rules should be followed. He talked and joked, and Stacey moved to a vantage point where she could watch people watch him, and check out the group chemistry.

Down in front, Peter, one of the middle-aged actors who played a second-generation Benjamin, looked interested and engaged — he was a well-mannered guy. Next to him, Kate, who played his wife, was engrossed in her phone (not so polite.) At the side, Jenna leaned over and whispered something to Cooper, who shook his head, gently, and put a finger to his lips. Yay Cooper.

While Ryan did a hamstring stretch, Carly — clad in Uggs, the idiot — fiddled with the flap of a mini-backpack so small it probably only fit her lipstick, her phone, and her recreational drugs. She snapped and unsnapped the flap, snapped and unsnapped it, until Stacey was tempted to snatch it away from her. Instead, she walked over and offered Carly a piece of gum, which she took and popped into her mouth.

From his rocky perch, Riley said, "So Cooper will bring up the rear, and I'll lead. Are we ready to go?"

"Ready!" Peter sang out — he had a Broadway theatre past. Ryan threw in a woot-woot noise, and people chuckled, some of them merrily. Like they were having fun.

Riley said, "Then let's go! And can we have a round of hell yeah's for Jenna, cause she had the bright idea to hire Hike, Bike, Love to take you all out on this hike today? Jenna, why don't you come up here, take a bow, and help me lead these wonderful people?"

Jenna hesitated, looked back at Cooper, then jumped up on the rock with Riley anyway, like a good sport, and took her bow. And Stacey had to hand it to her: she looked fetching in her hiking outfit, with her long, toned legs.

The time was 5:05 p.m. The hike would only take an hour, and it would cover gentle slopes. If Stacey were on her own, she would run the route, or at least walk faster than the leisurely pace Riley and Jenna set. But this walk wasn't about fitness or mind-clearing, it was supposed to be about team building. So, Stacey made herself go slow and hang back, the better to observe the people ahead.

Near the front of the single-file line the group fell into, Peter chatted with Bonnie, and warmed her and anyone else in earshot with his natural bonhomie, while Ryan jogged back and forth, up and down the line, like a brain-damaged prizefighter in training.

Carly was positioned behind Stacey and in front of Cooper, but she brushed off Stacey's matchmaking conversational gambits, pulled out an iPod, and said, "The music will help me connect with the landscape." Stacey wouldn't have believed that even if she hadn't heard the opening riff from one of Carly's own music tracks — she was trying to launch a music career — leak from the earphones.

The group walked on, following Riley and Jenna's lead, and spaced itself out along the trail. About ten minutes in, when Stacey knelt down to retie her shoelace, Carly moved past her, and Cooper stopped to wait by Stacey's side. She apologized for holding him up, and had just risen to standing when he said, "Look! Up to the right. A kestrel."

A hawk-like bird, with bright-orange tail feathers and dappled black and white wings, soared above them.

"Cool," Stacey said. The bird's bright colours and graceful shape, set against the clear blue-sky backdrop, looked like prime nature-channel footage. They watched it dive-bomb toward the ground and disappear from view over a ridge, and Cooper said, "It must have sighted some prey. A rodent maybe, or a lizard."

They resumed walking, but they'd fallen behind and were about twenty feet back from an oblivious Carly. Cooper said, "We should pick up the pace a little, not leave too big a gap."

Stacey walked faster. "How's this?"

"Good. Beautiful day, isn't it?"

The day *was* fine — sunny and not too hot. The late afternoon air carried a hint of fall, of crispness. She tried to take in the mountain views, the clear air, and the silence, and appreciate them, and she succeeded for a few minutes, until up ahead, Riley turned and said something to the people near him. She didn't catch what he said, only the lazy tone, and the sound of laughter in response.

She said, "Your boy Riley — is he an actor, or a comedian?"

"He's a wannabe actor. He's done a couple of small parts on TV, but he's still waiting for his big break. How'd you guess? Takes one to know one?"

Shrieking bird noises — the kestrel again, closing in on more prey? — had cut through his words. "Sorry. What'd you say?"

"You act too, right? On the TV show everyone here works on? What's it called?"

"*The Benjamins.* And I don't act. I'm one of the executive producers."

"Sorry. I thought everybody here was an actor. Executive producer, huh? Does that mean you're the boss?"

"I'm a co-boss, with another woman who's back at the lodge. Our production company is called Two Women Walking. Two Dubs, for short."

"So you've walked before."

When she turned back to see if he was kidding, he was smiling and showing his dimple. One, on the left side of his face. "Yeah," she said, "once or twice."

They'd caught up to Carly, who was now three feet in front of them on the path. Her narrow ribcage and tiny waist were centred in Stacey's sightline, and three feet beyond Carly — what was that reddish, sandy-coloured lump on the trail? A rock? Or, holy shit, a rattlesnake, slithering out of its coil and into an upright position?

Stacey sprang forward, stepped in front of Carly, and backed up, blocked her from moving. "Stop!"

Carly bumped into Stacey, said, "What the fuck?," and removed an earbud.

"Snake," Stacey said, and Carly said, "Oh, my God," but like she was more angry than scared. Frozen in place, they watched the snake rise, its rattle sounding, into striking position. Close behind them, Cooper murmured, "Don't panic, and don't scream. We're going to step back slowly, all three of us together. Right leg first. Ready?"

"Set," Stacey said.

Carly held onto Stacey's waist with both hands, and when Cooper said go, the legs of all three worked together, like they were a six-legged insect. They stepped back — right, left, right, left, right, left — until they were well out of striking distance, and waited for the snake to sense that the threat had gone away. They waited for it to silence its rattle, collapse onto the ground, and slither down the hillside, away from the trail.

Cooper was gripping Stacey by the shoulders from behind, tightly enough that she found faint marks on her skin later, impressions of his fingertips made through the fabric of her top. "That was exciting," she said. He released his grip and they broke their formation.

Cooper asked if they were okay; Carly said, "We shoulda got a picture of that thing. It was huge." She pulled out her phone and started texting. Stacey said, "I'm fine," though her head ached from the adrenaline rush. "How are you doing?"

"I'm good," Cooper said. "Glad no one got bitten. That was quick thinking on your part. Carly, you saw that Stacey protected you, right?"

Carly didn't look up from her phone. "Yeah, thanks."

"When in doubt, save the talent," Stacey said. And to Cooper, "You were admirably calm and collected."

"Thanks. Just doing my job." His dimple put in an appearance again. He was cute, in a country boy way. "One question: what was that move you used on Carly? It looked like you were boxing her out."

Her turn to smile. "I think I was. All the years I played house league basketball as a kid — my muscle memory must have kicked in."

From the crest of the hill ahead, Riley bellowed, "Coop! What's going on down there?" and everyone in the group stopped, turned, and looked their way.

Cooper placed his hands — gently, this time — on Stacey's shoulders, and called out, "We're coming. We had a rattlesnake encounter."

Someone up top gasped so loudly that Stacey could hear, and before Cooper let go, Stacey thought she saw a flash of consternation cross Jenna's expressive face. In the instant that Jenna had seen her being held in Cooper's arms, had annoyance registered, or jealousy? Lovely, kestrel-viewing, snake-avoiding day or not, Stacey sure hoped so.

11

When Jenna got back to the lodge, Stacey's assistant, Topher, was sitting on the veranda with his laptop open in front of him. "Ann's looking for you," he said, and he didn't wag a finger at her, but his voice did. Jenna didn't think she liked him and his retro Ray Bans very much. And did he have to so obviously give Riley the once over?

She checked her phone, which she'd turned off for the hike. Shit. There were four missed calls from Ann, plus a text commanding her to come up to Ann's suite, pronto, and another sent ten minutes later asking where the hell she was. So she couldn't stay and talk to Cooper, who had become friendly with Stacey after they'd encountered a snake on the path and Stacey had maybe sort of protected Carly from it. Everyone had heard the whole story when they stopped for a water break before heading back. And now Stacey was laughing at something Cooper had said, and he was touching her arm. A lingering kind of touch.

Jenna said thanks and see you later to Riley anyway. He'd turned out to be a funny guy, and a hit with the older cast members, so that was good; her recommendation hadn't been a disaster.

Another text came in from Ann:

WHY AREN'T YOU HERE?

She waved at Cooper, mouthed, "See ya tomorrow," and ran upstairs to Ann's room, where Ann was waiting, her makeup applied and her hair in rollers. She was dressed in black wide-leg pants, a silk shell that exposed her crepey-skin cleavage, and pointy-toe kitten heels — an outfit that didn't seem right for a dinner at a mountain inn, but Jenna wouldn't have told her that any more than she would have told her own mother what to wear.

"You look pretty," Jenna lied. Ann's style reminded her of Oprah's, with the massive bust, in a full-support bra, leading the charge. Too bad Ann lacked access to Oprah's wig collection — Jenna could tell that Ann's hair, rollers or not, would fail.

"Thank you, Jenna. That's not what you're wearing tonight, is it?"

"No, I just came from the hike. I was going to my room to change —"

"You'll have to do that later. Right now, I want you to help organize the after-dinner games."

"What games? I thought we were doing karaoke." Jenna had come prepared to sing if the opportunity arose. "Single Ladies" was her go-to karaoke song. She did it complete with dance moves, so she looked funny *and* sexy.

"No," Ann said, "the writers nixed that idea. Too performance-based and catering to the actors, they said. We're going to play a round of Family Feud instead."

Family Feud?

She said, "I had Stacey's assistant find a list of questions and answers online while you were out. He'll project them in PowerPoint on a screen for the game, and we've set up teams: Adults versus Children."

"What do you mean? What children?"

"Over-Forties versus Under-Forties — same thing. I'll ask Peter to act as host. Your job is to source props, like buzzers or bells for people to ring, a banner that says Family Feud, and some prizes. Here's a list." She handed over a piece of the lodge stationery, on which she'd made notes in her large handwriting. "And I've emailed you a script for Peter. Find a way to print it, go see Stacey's boy, and if you have to work through dinner, let me know and I'll have the kitchen send up plates for the two of you with a bottle of wine, okay?"

Jenna said okay.

"What a hassle I had, by the way, while you were out gallivanting on the trails. Trying to organize the wines with the kid this joint passes off as a sommelier was like trying to explain what vaudeville was to the boys in the writers' room. He would have served the Grigio with the burrata if I hadn't intervened, and made me look like an ignoramus in front of anyone who's already looking for ways to undercut me. I have to watch my back every minute lately, every goddamned minute."

Jenna didn't know what Ann was talking about, or who was trying to undercut her, but she said, "I have your back," because it seemed like what she should say, though what she was thinking was where the hell was she supposed to find a stopwatch and a cowbell, the top two items on the list. And she was not happy about missing dinner at the grownups' table, and what about her shower, and so much for doing her hair, but that's what happened when you were an assistant to a senior executive — you had to pay your dues and suck it up. That's what happened in workplace movies anyway, like in *The Devil Wears Prada*.

Ann said, "Before you go, do me one more favour and help me get these rollers off. I'm afraid of pulling my hair out with them." She sat down at a vanity counter outside the bathroom and waited for Jenna to come over.

Jenna was grossed out by the idea of touching Ann's hair, which was thin on the top and at the back, so thin that her pink scalp showed through. But Ann could see Jenna's reflection in the mirror, so Jenna hid her disgust and unwound the first roller.

Ann drank from a glass that didn't seem to contain water — maybe vodka and tonic. Or straight vodka. "How was the hike?" she said.

"Good! The guys who led it? Riley and my friend Cooper? They were real nice and they set an easy pace. You should come for the morning hike tomorrow." One roller down, seven to go.

"I'll see. I'm not much of a sportswoman. Not like Stacey. Was she there? She probably ran the route. She boasts about her athletic prowess all the time, about how she runs fifty miles every day, and did track in college, big whoop."

"She runs fifty miles a day?"

"Something like that. Tell me you didn't do sports in college too."

"I've been acting full-time since I was in high school. I didn't go to college."

"You didn't? And I still hired you?" Ann laughed, and not kindly.

"I may not have a college education," Jenna said, "but I make up for it by having a high EI score."

"A what score?"

"EI — Emotional Intelligence. It means I read people well. And I'm street smart."

"Did Stacey run on this hike or not?"

"She didn't run, she walked. She was at the back of the group and I was at the front." Jenna didn't mention the snake incident and how Stacey had come off as some kind of hero, when, come on — had there even been a snake on the trail? Ann would hear all about it at dinner anyway. While Jenna scrounged around for props.

"Ow! Be careful. I can't afford to lose any more hair."

"Sorry. I'll go slow."

While Jenna worked at untangling the sparse hairs, Ann stared at herself in the mirror. When she'd taken another shot from the glass, she said, "Between us: what do you think about Stacey? Honestly."

Honestly? "She seems nice. And smart. And organized. And she has good hair. Does she wear extensions?"

"I think it's all hers. Though if there's any justice in this world, one day she'll thin out on top too."

Jenna worked the problem roller free at last. "Got it!"

"You've worked for me long enough to see and hear what goes on around the office, correct?"

More pop-quiz pressure. "I guess so."

"Then use your emotional intelligence and tell me: do you think Stacey is trying to get rid of me, oust me off my own show?"

What? Whew. Jenna didn't have to lie. "After everything you two have accomplished as a team? And all the time you spend together, all those meetings, and the walks? No way is she trying to split up your partnership. You guys are like parents and the show is your baby." She unrolled the last roller, placed it on the counter, and hoped she wasn't expected to comb that mess. To head off the idea, she walked over to the sink and washed her hands, with extra soap.

Ann picked up a small hairbrush and started fluffing her hair with it. "*I* think she *is* trying to throw me over, the ungrateful little cunt."

Whoa, language. And was Ann drunk, or was there something to what she said? "Why do you think that?"

"Because I see what she's up to, with her snippy comments about my age and retirement. I see how she subtly undermines my authority every chance she gets. And if she thinks I won't rise to the challenge and take her down before she gets even close to toppling me, she's wrong."

Jenna's mind had wandered while Ann was talking, but she caught the last half of the last sentence just fine. "You're like Scarlett O'Hara," she said.

Ann stopped brushing, and the look she shot Jenna through the mirror was deadly. "What are you saying? That I'm an ancient white racist?"

"No! I mean, you're like —" Jenna put on a Southern accent. "As God is my witness, I'll never be hungry again."

Ann still looked pissed.

"You're just so strong, and so determined not to let anyone knock you down."

Ann picked up a lipstick. "Yeah. Indefatigable Ann — that's what they call me."

Jenna didn't want to ask what that word meant. She said, "I should go and round up the Family Feud supplies."

"Yes, you should. Thanks for your help."

"You're welcome. Your hair looks good. And soft."

Jenna was at the door when Ann said, "And I don't have to tell you to keep our conversation tonight confidential, do I?"

Jenna made a lip-zipping gesture. "No loose lips here."

"Good. Come tell me when everything's arranged. Let's make this game a blast."

12

The early-bird hike organized for day two of the retreat was scheduled to depart at 8:00 a.m. By the time Stacey set out for the meeting spot at ten minutes to, she'd updated her work journal, gone for a run, showered, blow-dried and styled her hair, and had coffee and a yogourt, but she was glad of an excuse to leave her room again. She could use a diversion from stewing about how well the previous night's activities had gone over with the cast and producers.

Who would have thought that a lavish, locavore-ish, multi-course dinner, each dish announced by the chef, and served with a specially selected California wine introduced by Ann — using language so overripe Stacey couldn't believe anyone could utter it with a straight face — would go over well with a crowd that, as a rule, avoided food? Not Stacey, but the company embraced the foodie/drinkie experience as if to the pretentious-dining-table born. Except for underage Vanessa, who pushed a few morsels around on her plate, chugged a glass of every wine on offer, and made frequent, lengthy bathroom trips to either ingest banned substances or purge herself of what little she had eaten. Stacey couldn't wait for her to be either legal or off the show, to make her someone else's problem.

The group had sat at the table for two long hours, during which more than a few people behaved as if Ann, the wine connoisseur, had interesting knowledge to impart. When that got old twenty minutes in, Stacey started table-hopping. She made sure that everyone was noticed and ego-stroked and included in conversations, and that the producers didn't leer too openly at the young actresses, and she counted the minutes until she could go back to her room and wipe the good-listener smile off her face.

After each person was served a glass of dessert wine (would the meal ever end?) and an oozy dark-chocolate brownie studded with pine nuts, topped with an artisanal marshmallow, and encircled by the words "Long live the Benjamins" written on the plate rim in strawberry coulis (a dessert that contained, at minimum, 700 calories, in Stacey's estimation), the gang was released from the table, only to retire to a lounge for after-dinner games.

Karaoke had been planned, which would have been painful to sit through but wouldn't have required Stacey's participation. Unlike the Olds versus Youngs version of Family Feud that Ann, helped by Jenna and by Stacey's own Topher ("Ann *made* me do it," he'd said when asked why he'd aided and abetted), sprang on the group — a game that the Olds won. Because the secret to winning, the mostly drunk Youngs realized too late, was not to come up with the truest or cleverest answers to the inane questions, but to predict the responses of the idiots who answer the telephone surveys that feed the game's content.

For example, when asked What is the first thing you do upon waking in the morning?, survey respondents had not come up with any of the answers the Under-Forty team suggested in the huddle: jerk off, smoke a joint, watch online porn, or call in sick. The Youngs also failed to rise to the challenge of naming with any degree of seriousness something that a woman puts in her hope chest.

The capper to the evening had been listening to Ann gloat about the Olds' victory, sing "We Are the Champions" off-key, and yell that Stacey and the Youngs team knew nothing about anything. So much fun.

The morning air was cool and clear when Stacey stepped outside; the earlier fog had blown off. Birds cheeped somewhere nearby, and the gravel in the path crunched under her feet. She shivered for a moment in her hoodie and running pants, but it was a pleasant shiver — coming outdoors lightened her mood. So did the sight of Cooper. When Stacey arrived at the meeting spot, he was there, leaning against a wall, his hat pulled low over his forehead, writing in a notebook. Even before he looked up, she felt her shoulders drop and the set of her jaw soften. As if his innocence from Ann's put-downs and arrogance made him the antidote to the one-upwomanship Stacey battled daily.

They exchanged good mornings. He said, "Did I drive past you earlier? Running down the hill road, around six-thirty? In a jacket with phosphorescent trim on it?"

"Yeah, I'm an early riser, and I like to run in the mornings."

"And now you're up for a hike, on top of the run? A hike without any snake sightings, I hope."

"I'm a glutton for exercise, I guess." She looked at her watch, and at the empty path. "But if no one else shows up, you don't have to take me out alone."

"I'd be happy to take you alone, but there should be a few more coming. I have ten names on the signup list."

"They might be sleeping off the effects of last night's dinner. It was like a fine wine seminar in there, with all the sampling and tasting going on, plus four courses of rich food. Some people might have gotten carried away and overindulged."

"Not you, though. You didn't get carried away." He put the smile lines around his eyes into play, a look that worked for him.

"No, I didn't."

"Because your only gluttony is for exercise?"

"I guess."

"Good morning!" Jenna called. She'd come out through the lodge doors, followed by Peter and Ryan, all of them dressed to walk, and by Ann. Ann, who normally refused to interact with other humans before 9:00 a.m., was sporting a baseball cap over bedhead hair and black activewear that clung to her several spare tires.

"Here are our hikers," Cooper said.

Stacey wanted to pull his focus for a minute longer, now that Jenna could see them together. But all she could think of to say was, "Where's Riley today?"

"We traded off. I'm leading the hike this morning, and he's doing a bike tour in Topanga Canyon this afternoon."

Jenna bounded up like an eager dog, and two more Olds emerged from the lodge. One of them, an exec producer named Rob, started talking about the night before. He said that Jenna had done a great job running the game, and much as it irked Stacey to admit it, the praise was deserved — Jenna had introduced some charm to the proceedings in a clueless but sweet way, when she called out the answers at the end of a round, punctuated by chime noises played on her phone.

Stacey added her voice to the chorus of compliments, and watched Rob lean close to Jenna and ask her if she'd ever worked on a real game show, because she was a natural. What was he playing at? Stacey also congratulated Ann on the success of the evening, because it would have been churlish not to, and because being gracious was what she did.

Ann said, "It did go well, didn't it? But after all that good food and wine, a hike is definitely in order. For those of us who ate and drank, that is."

Was that supposed to be a shot at Stacey? Misfire. She didn't feel bad about not pigging out or drinking — she felt good.

Ann said, "And wasn't it clever of Jenna to set up this hike, everyone? She's a woman of many talents." She turned to Cooper and looked him up and down. "You must be Jenna's guy. I'm Ann. The boss of this outfit."

Cooper introduced himself, welcomed her, and to Stacey's amusement, ignored the two misstatements Ann had made, though they begged to be corrected.

Jenna said, "Cooper's not 'my guy,' he's just a friend."

Ann had already moved on to Ryan, who was on the ground doing sit-ups. "Way to work those abs, Ryan," she said, and she might as well have smacked her lips, like a cartoon coyote about to devour its dinner.

The small group set out, and Stacey let Jenna — who stuck so close to Cooper that she was in danger of treading on his heels, while still stringing along a clearly smitten Rob — go ahead. Next came Ryan, followed by Ann, who struggled to keep pace with him. Stacey brought up the rear again, with Peter, an old pro who had experienced both fame and obscurity in his twenty-five-year career. He was grateful for a gig like *The Benjamins*, and knew it might not last. He and Stacey chatted amiably about the New York theatre scene after she told him that her parents, who admired live drama as much they disdained television, had seen him on Broadway a few years before, in a Eugene O'Neill play.

Twenty minutes into the hike, Cooper brought the group to a halt and delivered some commentary on the landscape. He spoke in a low-key, knowledgeable, self-deprecating manner that was the opposite of Riley's stand-up routine of the day before. What he said about the flora, fauna, and geological features of the mountains did not interest Stacey, but she liked the sound of the tenor notes in his voice, and from the back of the group, she studied him.

He had a small horizontal scar beneath his right eye. A fresh-looking scratch on his neck might have been a shaving cut. The bridge of his nose and apples of his cheeks were dusted with twelve or fifteen freckles of an adorable variety that made Stacey's head-to-toe thousands look like the marks of a disfiguring disease.

A dragonfly buzzed near Stacey's head and she dodged it, but not before it almost flew into her mouth, which was hanging open, about to let forth drool. What was happening to her? The sun, the fresh air, and the competitive presence of Ann and Jenna must have pushed her off track. Because when was the last time she'd thought of anything as adorable, without irony?

Cooper finished his talk. Peter said, "On we go," and Stacey followed him, head down. Maybe she was sick, and was hallucinating Cooper's appeal. Maybe she had sunstroke, or had been bitten by a virus-bearing insect. She asked Peter how his kids were doing, and while he listed their current statuses, she pulled herself together and cleared her head of rose-tinged, Cooper-related thoughts. From further up the line, she could hear Ann lecturing about the current state of television drama at a volume that was sure to disturb the wildlife. Left unfettered, Ann might chip away at the goodwill she'd built up the night before by being an obnoxious loudmouth this morning. That would be good.

At the end of the hike, the group was walking on a well-groomed dirt path close to the lodge's main building when Ann tripped. She cried out, lurched forward, sank onto one knee, and toppled over onto her ass. Those who were closest expressed concern and knelt down to help, so that by the time Stacey ran over, Cooper was squatting next to Ann on one side and Jenna was on the other. They each gripped one of Ann's arms, and Cooper spoke in soothing tones — had she injured any body part, could she get up? No hurry, they would wait till she was ready.

Ann barked, "I'm fine, get off me," and, "stupid fucking tree root," though there was no extruding root or rock in the path that Stacey could see.

"How's your knee?" Stacey said, and Ann said, "Who asked you to come over here and butt in? For fuck's sake, leave me alone."

Peter said, "Let's give her some breathing space," and almost everyone moved back.

After a minute, Ann allowed Cooper and Jenna to help her up, then shook them off. "You're making way too big a deal out of this," she said. "There. End scene."

Cooper said, "Hey everybody," and all eyes turned to him. "I want to thank you for coming out this morning. I've enjoyed meeting and talking with you folks this weekend. Good luck with your TV show —"

"You be sure to start watching it!" Ann yelled. "And tell your friends to watch it too!"

Cooper chuckled as if he did not find the interruption rude. "And with the rest of your retreat. That's it for me, except that if you'd like to hear more about the tours that Hike, Bike, Love runs in and around L.A., please take a brochure. And if you'd care to leave your email addresses on this signup sheet, we'd love to add you to our mailing list. Enjoy the day!"

The group applauded and said goodbye, and Jenna gave Cooper a long, close hug, complete with murmured sweet nothings in his ear, a bit of business that prompted Rob to call out, on his way inside with the others, that he would save Jenna a seat at the brunch table. Stacey would have liked to escape to her room and have a few minutes alone before sitting down to a meal, but Ann was right in front of her, and she didn't want to accompany her inside, or be anywhere near her. So she turned back to Cooper, still being embraced by Jenna, and asked for a brochure.

He freed himself from Jenna's clutches, pulled a brochure from the stack, and passed it to Stacey. His hands did not touch hers, but two seconds of direct contact with his smiling eyes gave her goosebumps, and her mouth was open again.

He said, "You should sign up for our newsletter, and come on a bike tour sometime. I think you'd like it."

She said sure, picked up his clipboard, and wrote her email address on his list.

Jenna popped back up, a mosquito to be swatted. "What about me? You don't think I'd like a bike tour?"

"You should come too," Cooper said. "The more the merrier. I asked Stacey because she seems athletic."

Jenna pouted. "Because she did track in college, you mean?"

Cooper and Stacey spoke at the same time. Stacey said to Jenna, "How'd you know that?" and Cooper said to Stacey, "What event?"

Stacey admitted to her middle-distance running career at USC, Cooper said he'd done high jump at Arizona State, and Jenna said, "But you two wouldn't have competed at the same track meets, would you? Stacey is like, ten years older than us. What are you, Stacey, thirty-seven?"

Stacey smiled. "I'm thirty-one, but if I seem older, that's cool — I'm a little tired of being known as a wunderkind." While Jenna tried to parse that sentence, Stacey pulled Cooper into a between-us-jocks handshake/hug. "Thanks again, Cooper. If I'm ever up for a bike tour, I'll be sure to think of you."

His hand was big, the skin on his fingers and palm callused, his grip firm. "Do that," he said, and Stacey turned away, flushed with what she hoped looked like exertion, but what she feared was a girlish blush, a sign that she was as taken with Cooper as Rob was with Jenna.

13

Ann's Journal

Ouch, ouch, ouch. My knee has swelled to the size of an elephant's, and is aching rhythmically, like I'm a bass drum pounded by a pimply teenager in a hell-bound marching band. And that's despite the handful of pain-killers I popped at the lodge before crawling into the car and bidding Miguel to take me home. Stupid rock or branch or whatever it was that I didn't see.

I bet Stacey saw the obstruction in my path, didn't say anything about it on purpose, and was waiting for me to trip over it. I bet she placed it there.

It drives me insane when she smiles that smile she thinks hides the contempt she feels for every-one she's so sure she's smarter, younger, and quicker than. Principally me. I caught the gloat rays she sent my way from behind her sunglasses when I fell. I'm surprised she didn't look around for a shovel to dig my grave with.

Miguel just got on the intercom to ask how I'm doing back here. Shut up and drive, Miguel.

My little spill aside, haha-the-fuck-ha on everyone (that is, Stacey), the retreat was a roaring success, thanks to me. Starting with the attentive, isn't-this-fascinating looks on their faces when I introduced the group to some fine wines at the first dinner. Their ignorance of the subject was so vast you'd think they'd been raised in trailer parks, or in Buttfuck, Idaho, which most of them probably were, but that's okay. I'm happy to be the guru who leads them out of the backwoods into the cultured light of urban sophistication. Happy to be The Wise One.

Hell, until I fell down today, the weekend was going so swimmingly that I managed to forget about the eye specialist who tortured me for an hour on Friday morning with the bright lights and eye drops and high-tech testing equipment and then had the nerve to tell me my eyesight is failing, big-time, and nothing can be done about it.

Fuck him. There are other, better doctors in the sea, other opinions to seek. I refuse to go blind. Or to go quietly into any night, good or otherwise.

And what about that Family Feud game last night? Some of the Olds were laughing so hard they cried. Because I know how to make fun, how to entertain. I'm the goddamned Queen of Fun. While Stacey is the queen of nothing. And a major pain in my ass and knee and life.

She's too smart for her own good, that's the problem, and too smart for mine.

OCTOBER

14

Jenna was on the phone, confirming some arrangements for an upcoming *Benjamins* viewing party — a big deal at a bar in Hermosa Beach, with the cast members attending and a few hundred fans invited — when Rob came by, stood in front of her desk, and waited for her to hang up.

She finished the call to the event planners Ann had hired — Jenna was supposed to double check and triple confirm that the food and drink for the VIP section would be prepared by Ann's preferred chef and caterers, not the bar's line cooks and regular bartenders — and said, "Sorry, Rob. How are you?" as if she didn't know or mind that he had a crush on her. "Ann's down the hall at an edit."

Rob was married and fiftyish and forty pounds overweight and talked way too much about his fly fishing hobby, which Jenna could not find less interesting. But he had some clout, so she acted friendly when he dropped by, which was too often since the retreat.

"I don't want Ann, I want you," he said. "Happy birthday!" He handed over the object he had hidden behind his back, which was a bottle of Cristal, tied up with a tacky multi-coloured cluster of curly ribbon. As presents go, it beat the box of Sprinkles cupcakes in Ann's favourite flavour that she had the office manager order in on every staff member's birthday, but it seemed cheap from a guy who might set Jenna up in a luxe condo with a decent wardrobe budget if she gave him the chance.

"Thank you so much! I love Cristal!" She took the bottle and stowed it away in an empty file drawer in her desk. "But you shouldn't have! Now everyone in the office will expect champagne on their birthdays."

He lowered his voice to a near-whisper. "I wish I could have gotten you a better present: a part in the show. I'm still working on that."

He'd been promising her a part — and not just a guest spot, but a recurring role — for weeks now. She'd believe that when she saw it, likely never. She grabbed her bag and got up. "I have to run, but thanks so much for the gift!"

She didn't have to turn around on her way down the corridor to know he was watching her ass as she went.

When she came back from the restroom, Ann and Stacey were standing near her desk, talking quietly. Were they arguing? Things had been a little frosty between them lately. They still spent hours together every day in meetings, but they didn't do their daily walks anymore. Supposedly because Ann had injured her knee on the retreat hike, though it looked to Jenna like Ann walked the same as she had before the fall — not very well.

From ten feet away, she heard Ann say, "Here's what *I* don't get — where do you get off making that kind of decision?"

Stacey glanced at Jenna, took a beat, and said, "But how pumped are we by the overnights?"

Ann gave Stacey a cold stare, while Jenna silently counted the seconds — one-Mississippi, two-Mississippi, three-Mississippi, four. Ann said, "Yeah, up 2.0 to 10.1 mill is pretty damn good. I'm going to celebrate with lunch. Can you order me in some Thai food, Jenna? I'm starving."

Jenna pulled out the desk drawer that contained menus from Ann's short list of acceptable restaurants, and handed her the Thai place's menu. Ann squinted at it, then tossed it back on Jenna's desk. "Get me number eight and number twenty-five. No, wait. Eight, twenty-five, and forty-seven. I'll take the leftovers home for dinner."

Jenna considered and decided against exchanging a glance with Stacey about the large quantity of food Ann wanted, and had picked up the phone to call in the order when Stacey said, "Is that a bottle of champagne in your drawer, Jenna?"

Caught. "Yes! It was a birthday gift. Today's my birthday." She smiled her widest, toothiest smile to distract them from asking who'd given her the bottle. In case Rob came through one day on that part, the less Ann and Stacey know about his feelings for her, the better.

They both said happy birthday, and Ann yelled over to Lisa, the office manager, asked if she'd ordered the birthday cupcakes. She had; they would arrive shortly.

Stacey reached into the drawer, and turned the bottle so its label faced up. "And not just champagne, but Cristal. Someone was generous."

Ann saved Jenna from saying who that someone was. "Better phone in that lunch order, Jenna. Get something for yourself, too, if you like."

Jenna said no thanks, and dialled the number. She wasn't eating lunches all week in preparation for the alcohol calories she planned to consume that weekend.

Ann said, "I don't suppose you want any food, Stacey, do you?"

"No, thanks."

"You're going to stick with your Zone salad, or the kale juice you brought in? I don't know how you can eat that crap for lunch every day."

"Each to her own," Stacey said, and headed down the hall to her office.

Ann muttered "skinny bitch" — about Stacey, Jenna hoped — and went into her office, shut the door. So much for the argument Jenna had walked into, she thought. But when Ann's food arrived, Jenna took it in to her and Ann told her to close the door and sit down, she wanted her opinion about something.

Ann fiddled around on her computer for a minute, and a song began to play through her speakers, a house music track Jenna had heard before. Ann pointed to her ear to indicate Jenna should listen, opened one of the takeout food containers, picked out a shrimp with her fingers, and popped it in her mouth.

"What am I listening for?"

"Give it a minute or two and we'll talk about it."

The song was the kind that starts out with an instrumental passage of beats and synthesizer, and you wonder is this an intro or what, then a vocal track is added, and layers of sound, one by one, and you anticipate and anticipate, and when you can't stand to wait anymore, the beat drops, and it doesn't matter what the words are or mean. Jenna nodded and bumped in her chair, and whatever this song was called, she hoped it would be played when she went out for her birthday, because she could really get into it on the dance floor. And she should make sure to get hold of some Molly for that night too, do it up right.

Ann turned off the song before it finished, and from around a mouthful of her Thai food, said, "You liked it."

"It has a good beat, yeah. What's it called?"

"Never mind. What genre of music would you say that song is?'

"EDM?"

"What the fuck is that?"

"Electronic dance music?"

"Of course it is."

Ann had all the containers open now, and the strong garlicky smell of the food was making Jenna feel queasy.

"Let me ask you, Jenna: what am I famous for doing in the shows I've created? When it comes to music."

That was a tricky question, because was Ann famous, technically? Jenna had known of her before she started working at Two Women Walking, because she looked at more of the trades than Andrew thought she did, and she heard industry gossip from people like Kerry, and followed the bigger entertainment websites. But how many of the millions of people who watched Ann's shows knew her name, let alone what, if anything, she'd done with music?

Jenna was irritating Ann by taking too long to answer, she could tell, and now she remembered reading a magazine profile, the one up on Ann's office wall, framed, that said something about emo music, so she blurted, "You were one of the first people to use contemporary emo-type songs in your scenes and then, like, plug the song afterward in the end credits?" She should have left off the question mark at the end of that sentence, but it was too late to take it back.

Ann gestured with the hand that held chopsticks, waved them in the air. "Exactly. I'm known for exposing heartland viewers to independent artists by underscoring the emotional highs and lows in my scenes with plaintive, heartfelt, gem-like folk-rock songs. And what I am *not* known for? Having anything to do with this kind of druggy dance shit."

Why were they talking about this song, or music at all, unless it had something to do with Ann being mad at Stacey? It must have. Jenna said, "Does someone want to use that EDM song in an episode of *The Benjamins*?"

"You catch on quick. Yes, someone does. And you can probably guess who that someone is: that skinny bitch Stacey."

Enough with the skinny comments. "Stacey's not that skinny. I'm as thin or thinner than she is."

"Nonsense. She has the figure of a child. You, at least, have some curves, some hips."

Fine. Jenna wouldn't eat lunch for the next month, not even salad, if that's what she had to do to shrink her hip measurement. "If you don't like that song, why don't you tell the music people to find something else?"

"An excellent question. There's a reason I don't veto it, why I don't tell the music supervisor and the editor and the writer and the director of the episode that the song doesn't fit my vision of the scene. And the reason is that our very own Stacey suggested we use it over a montage that cuts back and forth from Nate and Julie having sex, to Abe having a heart attack, to Arielle dancing, high, at some all-night raver. She claims it builds up to a climax the same way the scenes do, like the buildup to a goddamned orgasm, she said, and the writers were all 'ooh,' and 'yeah,' and 'this'll be so cool,' and my voice, the voice of experience, didn't get consulted. No one wanted to hear what I had to say, about how the mood of the scenes would be sullied by the use of that soulless song. Because I am no longer in charge around here, apparently."

While Ann spoke, Jenna had pictured a montage like she described, scored to the part of the song she'd played, and she saw exactly how it would work. "Stacey has a point about the song being like a tease. EDM tracks are all about the buildup and the drop."

Ann set her chopsticks down, and wiped her mouth with a napkin. "Did I ask for your opinion?"

"Uh, yeah?"

"I asked you what kind of music this was, not if it would fit with the scene."

"I thought you wanted me to —"

"Jenna, don't you see?"

Jenna wanted to say "that you're an asshole?" But she didn't, and Ann carried on.

"The problem is not the song, nor the montage, nor how people who've worked with me for years — people whose loyalty and good work under pressure I have rewarded with steady employment, artistic challenges, and good pay — are now turning on me and trying to climb on the bandwagon of that manipulative little upstart. The problem is who she is: a pretender to my throne."

The whole situation — being captive in Ann's office, Ann speaking in long dramatic paragraphs and eating greasy food — reminded Jenna of the speeches villains give in spy movies, when they're about to kill the main guy, only the speech is so long that James Bond or whoever manages to escape. Which made Jenna wonder where Ann was going with this rant. She said, "What are you going to do about this? About Stacey. You're not going to kill her or anything, right?"

"Kill her? Are you crazy?"

"I meant" — what the hell did she mean? — "you're not going to kill her career, are you?"

Ann's oily lips formed a wicked smile that revealed a strip of green onion caught between her teeth. "Ooh, I like that idea."

"No, but seriously. The worst you would do is fire her, right?" If only someone would knock on the door or call, and get Jenna out of there.

"I can't fire her," Ann said. "We both report to the studio. Only it or the network could fire her. Or me."

"Oh, right."

"But that doesn't mean Stacey won't be fired." She winked. "If you catch my drift."

So the feud was very much still on, and Jenna could look forward to being caught in the crossfire. Great.

Ann looked at her watch. "I have a meeting in fifteen minutes, but can you go get me a latte? And pick up some air freshener while you're at it, nothing too floral, and spray it around in here? Thanks."

Jenna was almost out, and glad to be going, when Ann said, "Close the door behind you. I'd like to finish my lunch in peace."

"I'll let you do that," Jenna said, and made her escape.

15

Stacey met her parents and sister for dinner at Pizzeria Mozza in West Hollywood, their choice of restaurant. High-end food was one of her parents' hobbies, along with travel, and they never went anywhere without researching where people of their specific discerning and particular taste preferences liked to eat.

Stacey was on time for the reservation, but her parents were twenty minutes late, since they were Busy Important Doctors, even when away from home at a conference. She used the time alone at the table to deal with some emails, and toasted herself with her glass of water for her accomplishment of the day: the insertion of an inspired song choice into episode 8. Who said she couldn't have creative input? All day, every day.

Deb and Grant walked into the restaurant inside the bubble that they inhabited when they were together, and only located Stacey because they were with her sister Ellen, who, though also a doctor — a radiation oncologist — was adept at everyday transactions like walking into restaurants. She checked in with the hostess, saw Stacey, and led their parents over.

"Sorry we're late," Ellen said. "Mom had trouble reading the directions she'd printed out, so we got lost."

The 'rents were only in their early sixties, but they didn't own a DVR or a smartphone, couldn't text, and had no knowledge of contemporary pop culture, all of which might have made Stacey suspect she was adopted, only she had her father's brown eyes and her mother's colouring with the wall-to-wall freckles and the brick-coloured hair, so there was no doubt she was theirs.

"Hi guys," she said.

They turned toward her, blinked in unison, said hi, and asked how she was. "You look well," Grant said, and Deb added, "She always does." They sat down and studied the menu.

Two minutes later, Ellen said, over the restaurant's din, "Why don't we get a couple of pizzas and some antipasti, maybe a salad, and share everything?" This reasonable suggestion started Deb and Grant off on a lengthy discussion of the menu offerings and what they wanted to eat here, what did the chowhounds recommend, and look, there's the fennel sausage pizza, right there, the third one listed, see?

While that went on, Ellen said to Stacey, "You do look good. That hair! I can only imagine how many hundreds of dollars a month you spend on its upkeep."

How classic of Ellen to perpetuate the oldest-child stereo-type, Stacey thought: to still, at age thirty-four, resent Stacey for displacing Ellen by being born. Ellen had pleased the parents by becoming a married-with-kids doctor and buying a house six blocks away from their family home in Toronto, yet she still felt a need to put down Stacey's hair. And how mean-girl was that of Ellen anyway, since her ticket in the genetic lottery had won her hair in a flattering chestnut shade, and a complexion that was more pink than deathly pale? Digs at Stacey's frivolous job, one that didn't save lives, were due any minute.

Stacey said, "How are Hugo and the kids?"

"They're well. The twins are at a lovely, lively stage. They're so bright and funny and communicative."

They would be.

"How's your work going?" Ellen said.

"It's crazy busy, but I like it."

"And you find it fulfilling?"

There was Ellen's weak shot, and within the first five minutes of the conversation. Stacey ignored it. "Yeah, when the show numbers are good. Which they have been so far."

Deb looked up. "*The Benningtons* is popular?"

Ellen: "The show is called *The Benjamins*, Mom. The family it's about is Jewish. And black. Right, Stacey?"

They would know what the show was about if they'd watched one entire episode of it, like the pilot, for example. Deb and Grant were already distracted by and talking too loudly about an egg and potato pizza at a nearby table. Of course they didn't follow her show. Why would they, when there were fascinating things like egg and potato pizzas to obsess over? During a momentary lapse in their chatter, she said, "Ellen's right. The family on the show is mixed race and mixed religion: white Jewish and black Christian. Like Peggy Lipton and Quincy Jones — Rashida Jones's parents? — they were my original inspiration couple for the show."

Grant said, "You know why Mom calls the show *The Benningtons*? Because we used to take the dog to a vet called Dr. Bennington. Remember that, Deb? For years, we went there."

"That's right," she said. "Good old Dr. Bennington."

Stacey said, "I might get a dog."

That got their attention. All three turned to her with questions: why, what kind of dog, where from?

Stacey explained that her neighbour Pauline had written her a letter to say she was dying, of lung cancer, and would Stacey consider adopting Buddy, a seven-year-old Westie, when the time came.

"Why you?" Ellen said.

"Pauline doesn't have anyone else to take him. Her husband died ten years ago, and they had no kids. And Buddy knows me: I've been taking him for evening walks since she's been sick." Pauline had also written in her letter that Buddy was good company, and would be a faithful friend for a woman living alone. As if Stacey's married-to-her-work state and Pauline's widowed one were similarly lonely. When Stacey wasn't lonely at all. She didn't have time to be lonely.

"How long has she got?" Ellen said. "Lung cancer usually moves fast."

"It seems like it's a matter of a few months."

Deb said, "I don't see how you could look after a dog with your work schedule," and Grant said, "It would be charitable of you, but I'm not sure it would be smart, or practical."

"I'm going to say yes." She hadn't responded yet to Pauline; she'd only received the letter the night before. But she didn't mind Buddy, didn't mind his bright eyes, cocked head, and funny, quick gait. And he always seemed happy to see her when she came over to take him out. Possibly because he liked the walk as much as the walker.

She'd write a note to Pauline when she got home and say she would like to adopt Buddy. "I can always hire a dog walker, and I might bring Buddy to work some days." Though she could see Ann, who was no animal lover, objecting to that.

The waitress appeared to take drink orders. Stacey stuck with her mineral water, but Ellen suggested wine, which prompted Deb and Grant to debate the wine choices for five minutes. Once that decision had been made, food orders were placed. Deb and Grant changed their minds, twice, about ordering the deep-fried squash blossoms, because Grant was supposed to be watching his cholesterol, as Deb told the waitress and anyone else within earshot. They settled at last on twice as much food as Stacey would have ordered for a party of four.

For her next conversational foray, Stacey asked how the conference was going, and heard that Ellen's paper, presented that day, had been well-received; that Deb looked forward to a session the next day on a new technique used for laryngoscopies; and that Grant hoped to get in a round of golf with a doctor friend from Texas. The conference talk lasted through the arrival of the wine, but the first food item — bruschetta made with chicken livers — silenced the table for the time it took Deb and Grant to fall upon it, chew, and swallow a few bites. Adjective-laden comments about its flavour and texture followed — Stacey heard the pâté described as silky, rustic, smoky, and earthy. She was surprised they didn't make tasting notes in a dedicated notebook. Or take photos.

Ellen said, "You don't want any, Stacey?"

"No, thanks. I'm not that hungry. I had a big lunch." Or Ann had.

"So listen," Ellen said. "I should have asked you before I came down, but I'd love to do something active and outdoorsy while I'm here. Are you free tomorrow or Sunday to go for a hike or something?"

At the mention of the word "hike," an image popped into Stacey's mind of Cooper standing on a canyon cliff, on a blue-sky, sunny day — a picture featured on the home page of the Hike, Bike, Love website. Cooper looked tanned and fit in the picture, and his biceps and dimple were both on display. That is, the bottom half of his left bicep was visible, below the short sleeve of his T-shirt, and because he was smiling in profile, his dimple could be seen. Which Stacey knew because she'd looked at the pic once or twice or three times a day in the two weeks since the retreat.

She'd had no contact with Cooper. He'd sent her a promotional email, a group message to everyone on the company's mailing list that was in no way personal or personalized, but he had not communicated with her otherwise, nor she with him. Yet she felt a kind of comfort when she looked at the photo, as if she were a soldier away at war, and he was her small-town sweetheart waiting at home, the person she fought the good fight for.

"I don't know, Ellen," she said. "I may have to work." This was halfway true — Stacey could work fifteen hours a day, every day of the week, if she wanted to. But now that it had come up, the thought of spending time with Cooper, in the fresh air, with Ellen's visit as her excuse for seeing him, was more appealing than anything else she had planned. She reached for her phone. Was Cooper doing any bike tours that weekend?

"Please?" Ellen said. "Take a few hours off, show me around." She leaned closer and spoke into Stacey's ear. "If I don't go somewhere with you, I'll have to spend more time with *them*."

The notion that she and Ellen were conspirators was ludicrous, though the one opinion they shared might be their annoyance with the parents' foibles. Stacey brought up the Hike, Bike, Love website on her phone, swiped past the picture of Cooper, and found a calendar that listed canyon bike tours on both Saturday and Sunday. "Maybe I could blow off work for a morning," she said. "Would you be up for some biking?"

16

J enna drove over to Andrew's house with her overnight bag at nine, with the idea that they'd smoke a little weed, watch some TV, have sex, and go to sleep at eleven, all very mature and adult.

The plan was to celebrate her birthday the next night, a Friday, with Andrew and some friends: a couple of his, more of hers, eight in total. They'd go to the Marmont for dinner and drinks, then somewhere else for dancing and more drinks. Andrew wasn't much of a club-goer, but Jenna insisted they do more than dinner, because what was a birthday without a VIP booth, bottle service, and dancing?

She didn't expect any gifts from him, not yet, but as soon as she walked in, Andrew presented her with a piece of antique Art Deco furniture — a polished wooden dresser with a big round mirror attached to it, a vanity that you were supposed to sit at to brush your hair while wearing a peignoir set, like actresses did in movies set in the 1930s. Though this piece might have been even older than that.

She guessed the gift was supposed to be major, *though it wasn't a car*, because when she walked into Andrew's bedroom, it was set against the wall with a wide satin ribbon tied around the mirror, and an expensive-looking satin nightgown and robe were folded in a La Perla box on the matching stool, and Andrew said happy birthday like the gift was nothing, when clearly it was something special that he'd chosen for her — except to his taste, for the bedroom that he thought would soon be theirs.

Jenna was disappointed, but she said, "You bought this just for me? It's beautiful!" and examined it like she loved it.

She had a great-aunt who was the all-time champion of gift receiving, a title she earned (and re-earned every year) at family Christmas celebrations. No matter what anyone gave her — a piece of kindergarten macaroni art, bath beads, tea towels, drugstore chocolates — Aunt Miranda always reacted like she'd received the best gift ever, and she was very convincing. She was the first good actress Jenna had seen perform live.

Jenna drew on Aunt Miranda's techniques now. She said how gorgeous the dresser was, how luxurious it would be to sit when she put on her makeup instead of standing up over a bathroom sink, and how glamorous she would feel doing it in the silky nightgown.

He hugged her and kissed her on the forehead. "I knew you'd love it. It's for when you move in."

Jenna still hadn't committed to that. She probably should, if only because Andrew's house, an impressive three-thousand-square-foot mid-century modern in the Oaks of Loz Feliz, was a big step up from Jenna's cute but in no way impressive apartment in Silver Lake.

She definitely should. She could always move out if she got bored with Andrew, or found someone better to couple up with. And it wasn't as if the auditions she'd gone to in the last few months — all five of them — had worked out for her, or like she had any faith in Rob's promises. It wasn't as if her confidence was high. Shit, after the conversation with Ann earlier that day about the dance music song, her off-camera job prospects weren't looking too good either.

"I'd love to move in," she said. "I'll give notice to my landlord tomorrow. Now how about some birthday champagne?" But not her Cristal. She'd save that for the day when she had something big to celebrate.

If that day ever came.

17

In the car on the way to Topanga Canyon, Ellen asked if Stacey was dating anyone, and Stacey said no.

"No? Mom said you had a guy over when she called you a few weeks ago."

There was no reason for Ellen to know about Stacey's fuck-buddy arrangement with Zach. Make that her former arrangement. She'd told Zach that after *The Benjamins* premiered she'd have no time for anything resembling a personal life. "Nice knowing you," he said, without seeming to care, and he'd taken his sex skills elsewhere.

Stacey said, "Deb doesn't know what she's talking about."

"If you're not dating, why aren't you?" An outside observer might have thought Ellen was expressing sisterly concern, but Stacey recognized the sound of a trap being set.

"I'm too busy."

"If you're gay, this would be a good time to come out of the closet. I could break the news to Mom and Dad. They'd be fine with it."

"I'm not gay."

"It's really okay if you are."

"That's either very touching or very condescending of you to say, but I am not attracted to women."

"Yeah? When was the last time you had sex with a man?"

To Stacey's regret, Ellen knew that Stacey had stayed a virgin till college and lost it to the first guy she'd met who had been as desperate as she was to insert Tab A into Slot B and get the sex experience over with. She knew this because Stacey had made the mistake of telling Ellen the whole story during Christmas break in her freshman year, over drinks at Ellen's student apartment in Toronto. Back in the days when Ellen was pre-med, not yet a physician. When Stacey thought she could trust her sister and confide in her, and before she'd figured out they were locked into a lifelong game of one-on-one.

"That reminds me," Stacey said, "how's post-partum sex going for you? A character on *The Benjamins* is a new mother and there was some debate in the writers' room about how soon after childbirth a woman can or will have sex. Your thoughts on that?"

Never one to pass up a chance to brag, Ellen said that she and Hugo had waited six weeks after the birth of their eldest, but only four weeks post-delivery of the twins. She also delivered a five-minute, jargon-filled mini-lecture on the subject, and closed with, "How can the writers not know this kind of basic information? Or do you only hire people who are uneducated?"

Five minutes later, Stacey parked the car near the trailhead. "There she is," Cooper said, when Stacey got out. She was ready for him — before she'd picked up Ellen at the hotel, she'd spent a half hour at home practising a friendly, no-stakes, casual attitude. So as not to let on that she'd felt absurdly gleeful when Cooper had answered her email about booking two places in the tour with the words, "Awesome. Should be a good time." What a girl she was being, to think that tossed-off reply indicated Cooper might like her. She needed to man up and cool down.

She said hey to Cooper, and introduced Ellen to him, with no trace of longing on her face or in her tone. The small talk as the three walked toward the group of cyclists already gathered was innocuous. They chatted about bikes and equipment, and Stacey took in the sight of Cooper's hairy but not too hairy forearms, and his tree trunk–like neck, endearing despite its thickness. She marvelled at the small but unmistakable thrill she felt ripple through her in Cooper's presence, and she made sure to hide that thrill. She was a sphinx.

"Let's get you girls your bikes," Cooper said, and led them to a trailer where good old boy Riley was holding court, flirting with two thick-thighed women. Cooper said, "Hey, Riley, look — it's Stacey from that TV show retreat we did at Haven. She's come for the bike tour with her sister. Ellen — meet Riley."

"Hey," he said. "Welcome back." It was obvious he didn't remember Stacey, but she didn't care. He returned to his conversation with the two women. One said, "For sure I recognize you from that beer commercial with the bear!" He bowed his head in false modesty and copped to the role. Stacey felt Ellen look him over, felt her check out his dyed blond hair and his drawl, and probably begin to compose an anecdote about this outing that she would tell Hugo later, about how L.A. was so full of vapid, empty-headed aspiring actors, and Stacey hung out with these narcissist pea brains daily; what a wasted life she lived.

Cooper picked out two bikes, adjusted them to their heights and preferences, and provided helmets, cycling gloves, and water bottles. When they'd signed a waiver and handed over some cash, they were ready to go.

Before the group set out, Riley climbed up on a rock and gave a hammy spiel that sounded like the bike version of the talk he'd given before the hike at the retreat. He covered safety and park etiquette and said that the trail had two branches. Those who wanted more of a challenge should follow him at the fork, while riders in search of an easier time should stick with Cooper.

Ellen said to Stacey, "Who are we going with? Stoner dude or dimple guy?"

She'd noticed Cooper's dimple? All the more reason for Stacey to pretend she hadn't. "I haven't biked for a while, so I'll hang back and try the easier trail. But go with Riley if you want, and we can meet back here afterward." Please go with Riley.

"No, we'll stay together. Go ahead, I'll follow you."

They joined the back of a slow-moving single-file queue of bikers lined up behind Riley, whose bike had a pole attached to it from which waved a jaunty flag imprinted with the Hike, Bike, Love logo. Cooper, at the end of line, had the same flag on his bike.

Ellen said, "So what's with the Love in the company name? Will they hug us when the ride's over?"

Stacey was about to tell her that Love was Riley's (apparently real) surname, which she knew from reading the bios on the company's website, when Cooper's voice yelled from behind, "Hey, watch out!" and a dreadlocked cyclist zipped past her on the right, grazed the top of her exposed forearm with his handlebar, and kept going.

A ribbon of pain wove through her skin. She cried out, stopped her bike, slid off the seat, and just missed contact with another rogue cyclist, who sped by too close and too fast, hurtled past the queue of riders in front of her, and disappeared down the trail, chased by shouts of disapproval from the group.

"Are you okay?" Cooper said.

Stacey looked up from her arm, which was missing a long, narrow strip of skin and was bleeding dramatically — several red rivulets wended their way through her freckles — and into his concerned face. "What the hell was that?"

He was off his bike, and had pulled a first-aid kit out of his saddlebag. "You got tagged by some hotdogging punks who think they own the trails. Let's take a look at that cut."

"It's not deep."

He tore open a packet containing an antiseptic wipe, took a firm but gentle hold of her arm, and dabbed at the blood. "We'll clean it up and see."

Stacey looked away from her arm and fought off an alarming sensation of light-headedness. "Have you got any ink on you?" she said. "With some cross-hatching, this would make a bad-ass tattoo."

Cooper smiled, but Ellen, still astride her bike, moved her sunglasses up onto her forehead, eyeballed the damage, and said, "It's nothing to worry about, just a mild abrasion." And when Cooper gave her a questioning look, "I'm a doctor."

He let go of Stacey's arm, like he was going to hand her over to the expert, but Ellen said, "Keep at it, you're doing fine. Stick a few adhesive bandages on the widest part and she'll be good to go."

Stacey said, "Ellen also teaches medicine, which might explain why she's treating you like an intern right now. *I* appreciate what you're doing, though. Thank you."

Cooper applied a Band-Aid to the cut, then another. "You're welcome, and I'm sorry you got hurt under my watch. After your partner tripped and fell on the hike at Haven, too. How's she doing?"

"What partner?" Ellen said. "I thought you weren't —"

"Cooper's talking about Ann Dalloni."

"Oh."

"Ann's fine."

"Good." He closed up his first-aid kit. "You sure you want to keep going?"

Stacey glanced at Ellen. Her sunglasses were back down over her eyes, her feelings masked by a neutral expression she probably used when speaking to her cancer patients.

"I'm fine to ride," Stacey said. "I *want* to ride. Let's go."

Cooper grinned, said, "That's my trooper," and squeezed her shoulder briefly. He hopped onto his bike, and they were off down the trail.

The scrape stung like hell whenever a puff of breeze or a ray of sunshine hit it, which was every second, but as long as Cooper approved, and shoulder-patted her if she suffered in silence, she'd be quiet, and happily so.

Two hours later, in the car on the way back to town, Ellen said, "Well, that was interesting. Not much of a workout, but interesting."

"I'm glad we did it." Stacey was glad they'd ended up getting a private tour from Cooper after the rest of the group decided to take the more difficult route with Riley and leave the gimp behind. Glad she'd been able to keep up a decent pace on the easier path, ask semi-intelligent questions about cycling, the trails, the types of people who come on the tours, and the scenery, and make Cooper laugh a couple of times, all while lapping up his attention and not seeming to flirt. Though the day's performance — including the parts when she'd had to juggle her dual roles as taciturn younger sister and jovial good sport — had tired her.

Ellen said, "I think he likes you, that guy."

Stacey wanted to ask what guy, but she couldn't play that dumb, they had only spent time with the one. "Cooper? He was just relieved I wasn't maimed or threatening to sue. Injuries can't be good for the company's reputation."

"Do you like *him*?"

Yes, she did, after spending the afternoon in his living, breathing, smiling, talking, calm company. "He seems like a good guy."

"So why don't you date him? Or is he too many levels of social strata below you?"

"What? You think I'd only date TV people? They're almost all slimeballs. And what's with you pushing the dating agenda anyway? Do I seem unhappy to be single?"

"You should be thinking about settling down one of these years and having kids. My kids should have cousins."

"The world does not need any more freckled redheads."

"Okay, forget my kids. Date him for your own sake. People aren't meant to live alone. They're supposed to pair up and mate."

"Says who?"

"It's the natural order of things."

"I've never been a believer in that science mumbo jumbo." When Ellen frowned at this, Stacey said. "I'm joking. And anyway, I think Cooper has a girlfriend." Unfortunately.

"I give up. Do what you want."

"I will."

"Good."

"Uh-huh."

After a minute, Ellen said, "Are you coming for lunch with Mom and Dad, or are you going to use that phony work excuse and leave me alone with them?"

"I can't come, I really do have to work."

"Figures." Ellen took her phone out, and started to text. She was probably saving a life remotely. Or telling Deb and Grant she'd meet them back at the hotel in thirty minutes.

When they were back on the Pacific Coast Highway, Stacey said, "That bike ride has got me thinking. I might propose a new arc for one of the young characters on *The Benjamins* — get him to take up biking, start wearing his hair in dreadlocks, hang out with some bike thugs, then accidentally kill someone when he's out riding recklessly on a trail. Or injure someone and get into trouble for it. What do you think? How would that be for a compelling storyline?"

She didn't mention that if she were to pitch that arc for Mark, the teen rebel on the show, and get it signed off by all concerned, she could suggest Topanga Canyon as a location, hire Cooper as a consultant, and have an excellent excuse to see him again. Or was she being transparent — had Ellen seen through her already, and would Ann and Jenna?

Ellen hadn't answered, was still busy with her phone.

"I said how's that for a storyline?"

Her thumbs still moving, Ellen said, "Sounds good."

Stacey thought so, too.

18

The next morning, Stacey still had Cooper on her mind. On the drive in to work, she relived their time together on the trail, analyzed — like a lovestruck teenager — what he'd said and done for signs that he liked her, and thought about the best way to propose the new biking storyline for the show so she could see him again. But she wasn't so far gone that she broke her work routine: as usual, she was alert and composed at her desk at 8:00 a.m.

Not as usual, Bonnie appeared at her door at 8:05 and said hey.

"You're here early," Stacey said.

"I wanted to catch you before you get buried in meetings. Can you spare me a minute?"

Bonnie had been Ann's hire, her first choice for supervising producer/senior writer on *The Benjamins*, by virtue of their shared history — Bonnie had worked on two of Ann's previous shows. But Stacey liked Bonnie, despite her Ann affiliation. She was talented and quick, and for a writer, she was reasonable, not too flaky or full of herself.

As she had with everyone on staff, Stacey had tried to befriend Bonnie, to make her an ally. Until the retreat, Stacey would have said they got along well enough, but since then, Bonnie had become even friendlier. One week they'd chatted about coffee preferences (Bonnie had a weakness for mocha Frappuccinos), and the next they moved on — via casual conversations on the short walk into the office from the parking lot, or while washing their hands in the women's restroom — to the topic of Bonnie's personal life.

Stacey had learned that Bonnie's live-in boyfriend was a writer on a hit sitcom who refused to lift a finger around the house; that her parents had split up after thirty-five years of marriage because her father was dating a fake-titted, fake-lipped party girl who was Bonnie's own age; and how Bonnie felt about that, and about men and intergenerational dating, as a result. All information Stacey stored away for the day when it might come in handy. Like every other human-interest factoid she absorbed and took note of.

Bonnie sat on the edge of Stacey's visitor's chair. "I won't keep you long. I wanted to run some thoughts by you that I'm going to raise in the writers' room this morning, see what you think. Pre-discuss them."

Ann's was the opinion usually sought on writers' room matters, but Stacey wasn't about to turn down a chance to get more involved. "I'm all ears," she said.

An hour and a half later, Stacey entered the writers' room right behind Jenna. "I love your scarf," Stacey said of an excessively long piece of gauzy fabric printed in varied shades of green that Jenna had wrapped six times around her neck in what might have been an attempt to look fashion-forward and jaunty. It looked stupid.

"Thanks!" Jenna said. "The colour brings out my eyes." She widened her eyes to demonstrate. "How are you? Good weekend?"

"It *was* good. On Sunday, I did an off-road bike tour with your friend Cooper." Stacey looked around for Jordan, a young staff writer she'd selected as the carrier for her idea that the Mark character take up mountain biking. She'd chosen Jordan because he self-identified as a skateboarder — he had the hair, the clothes, the shoes, and the board that he rode through the office and around the lot. If anyone on the writing staff could get excited about an extreme sport, he could. She staked out a seat near his end of the table, and removed her jacket. "I had a little mishap on the trail though," she said, and Jenna, bless her theatrical nature, exclaimed so loudly when she saw Stacey's arm — which still looked abraded, oozy, and colourful — that she drew the whole room's attention. "Oh, my God," she said. "What happened?"

Stacey took the floor and made a short, funny story out of the brush-by with the punk cyclists, Cooper's first-aid efforts, and Ellen's "I'm a doctor" comments.

Jenna said, "I hope it doesn't scar. You should put some vitamin E cream on it. I have some at my desk. I'll go get it."

"Thanks." How considerate Jenna was being. What could she be after? Stacey stashed that question away to mull over later, and turned to Jordan. Ann had just walked in, episode 10 discussion was about to begin — Stacey only had a minute to use her powers of persuasion on him. Under cover of the general conversation, she said to him, "You know who the punk kids on the bikes reminded me of? Mark Benjamin. I could so see him hanging out with stoner mountain bikers. Couldn't you?"

"Totally."

"We should sit down later and toss that idea around, see what we can come up with on it."

"Love to," Jordan said, like he was grateful Stacey was speaking to him. Good. One objective down for this meeting, one to go.

When the competitive banter that marked every morning's start had died down, Bonnie said, "So, I was thinking about the Nate and Julie relationship at yoga last night."

She was referring to Ann's wish-fulfillment story line, a romance between the Nate character, played by Ryan, and his aunt by marriage, a well-preserved fifty-year-old character (played by a forty-four-year-old actress in fitness-magazine-cover shape).

One of the writers, a smartass named Todd, had been tossing whole almonds from one of several snack bowls set out on the table into his open mouth, hitting his target two out of five tries. Between tosses, he said, "If it involves those two doing the downward dog together, I vote no. Let's not nauseate the viewers."

At the other end of the table, Ann frowned.

"That's exactly what I've been thinking," Bonnie said. "Not about yoga, but about the ick factor. Enough with the steamy older woman, younger man sex scenes — isn't it about time Nate wakes up, repulsed, and realizes he's screwing an old bag?"

Todd, who was in his late thirties, and so therefore still thought of himself as twenty-eight, said, "I'm with you there. A stud like Nate can pick up a busload of girls just by flashing those abs and that grin, so why would he stay with Julie? It's not like he's seeing her for her money."

Michelle, the executive story editor, said, "He's not exactly flush. His parents have him on a tight leash for cash. We established that in the pilot."

Stacey checked the wall clock and tried to estimate how long Ann would stay quiet while Bonnie and Todd trashed her opportunity to live vicariously through Julie, who, in the tradition of avatars, was taller, thinner, better-looking, and sexier than Ann had ever been, Ann being more of a Hillary Clinton type, body-wise. Okay, and brains-wise and balls-wise.

Not two minutes had passed when Ann hit the table with her hand, a signal she intended to speak. The room went quiet, except for Todd's chomping noises, and Ann said, "What have you people been smoking? The Nate and Julie relationship has been fully charted up to episode 15, and affects the arcs of at least four other major characters. You're not proposing we change the direction of that storyline just because somebody in this room has a personal problem with her over-the-hill divorced parent dating a bimbo, are you?"

Todd swallowed audibly, and Bonnie's face darkened. Before she could sputter out a retort, Ann said, "Back me up here, Stacey: you who has every theme and variation of the storylines stored in that file cabinet brain of yours — tell these people they're crazy to think we can make that big a plot shift at this stage."

Stacey looked up from her laptop screen, made sure not to make eye contact with Bonnie, and addressed the room. "Ann's right." She inflected her voice with calm reason. "We can't break up Nate and Julie yet. There are too many plot threads underway that depend on them being together, implausible couple or not."

"Thank you," Ann said. "See, folks? Now can we move on?"

"But" — Stacey spoke slowly, like she was thinking out loud — "what we *could* do in this episode is have Nate deal with feelings of disgust" — Ann scowled — "or doubt, anyway, about Julie's age, and overcome them. That would address Bonnie's concern about verisimilitude, but still keep the affair alive, and help position Nate as the mensch Ann would like him to be."

Ann: "Not a mensch so much as a sensitive, open-minded guy who can see past the small impediment of Julie's chronological age."

Todd scoffed, but Bonnie said, "I like that, Stacey. Having Nate question the appropriateness of the relationship would work as a reality check — as if we're posing the question viewers would be thinking, and answering that question. We could also have Rachel ask him what it's like to date someone older, and that could foreshadow her loss of virginity to her teacher in episode 12."

Stacey held back a bravo for Bonnie's delivery: she'd sold the idea as freshly hatched. Rather than as a pre-discussed, pre-planned tactic.

The other writers spoke up with suggestions, the intern took notes on the master log. And when Ann gave Stacey an inquiring look, she shrugged back as if to say, why not give Bonnie a bone?

19

Ann's Journal

Journal, journal in my laptop: am I always angry, or only when I write in here? Rhetorical question.

Major Piss-Off #1: that the second retinal specialist I saw today agreed with the first and had the audacity to predict that I'll be legally blind within two years, give or take a calendar quarter. But my vision's no worse today than it was two months ago, so why should I believe them, or the third doctor I've got lined up to see? I may outlast them all. I will.

Another thorn in my side today: Bonnie. Where does she get off having not just ideas, but ideas that don't mesh with mine? Doesn't she remember who signs her paycheque? Okay, it isn't me, but she should remember who got her hired to begin with. And that snake Stacey was right behind her, don't think I didn't notice.

I notice EVERYTHING. Too bad I can't retain it all anymore. Today I completely blanked out on the name of Stacey's assistant, the little gay guy with the tight shirts and the black-framed glasses. I remember it now, of course. His name is Topher. Like the actor from *That '70s Show*. And like the little brother in that Dave Eggers book *A Heartbreaking Work of Staggering Bullshit* (what it should have been called). My mind is a fucking gold mine of information, it really is. I should donate it to the Library of Congress when I'm done with it. Or to the Museum of Film and Television.

But when I reached for Topher's name in my mind today — nothing. The cupboard was bare.

Aging sucks. It sucks that my vision is going, it sucks when younger people are grossed out to think I might have romantic or sexual yearnings — yearnings I've never acted upon, I might add — for someone other than my ancient and lately decrepit-looking husband. And it sucks to feel those same young people breathing their naked ambition down my wrinkled neck.

Back off, pushy little strivers. Back the fuck off. I'm not dead or blind yet.

20

Jenna's friend Brooke had organized the mini-reunion of their high-school crowd a year before, the reunion that Jenna had gone to out of curiosity, and to show off her then-fame. And now Brooke had reconvened the group, along with a hundred and fifty more people, at her wedding. Jenna had RSVP'd well in advance that she'd attend, because it would be fun to see everyone again, and because she still thought she had the best career. Except it turned out Brooke had become an important executive — a vice-president or a director of something — at an internet company, and she was marrying a guy, also successful, whom she'd met in business school. At Stanford.

And now Jenna was at a swanky manor house venue on a clifftop in Malibu, and the day was not going so well. From her spot at the bar in the reception hall, she looked through enormous picture windows at a gorgeous view of the sunset, in front of which Brooke and the groom were being photographed; at the rows of beribboned white chairs in which the guests had sat to witness the tasteful ceremony; at the clouds of white tulle and drifts of white flowers artfully placed around; and at the many decently attractive women — more than she'd expected — walking around in pastel coloured dresses.

Brooke looked good, too — as good as she could, given the raw material she had to work with. She'd chosen her gown, a Vera Wang, well. It worked on her big-tits-no-waist-or-ass body type. She and her parents had paid big money for that dress, and for the refined and sophisticated atmosphere that made Jenna feel like she was choking, or would have made her feel like that if she hadn't been pouring Prosecco — not champagne, unfortunately — down her throat.

The day hadn't been a total disaster — Brooke's parents had thanked Jenna for coming as if she'd done them a favour by showing up, and Brooke's younger brother claimed to have followed her career and seen all her movies, which was nice to hear, if hard to believe. Also nice was that Brooke's mom looked impressed when Jenna introduced Andrew as her boyfriend, like Andrew was a catch. Andrew who had come along as her plus-one because the groom's uncle was a client of his law firm, what a small world, and while she stood around waiting to be adored, he could network.

He was networking right that minute, talking to a middle-aged man with a jowly face. "Have you met Steve Morgenstern?" he asked Jenna.

Jenna turned it on and said hello to the man she thought must be the uncle from the law firm but no, it was someone else Andrew knew. So, what did she care, except that the guy was looking at her in a way that could be called appreciative. Unless he was leering. Yes, she'd love another glass of wine, thanks.

She dropped out of the conversation — they were talking about the goddamned Lakers now — and watched one of the groomsmen across the room, a guy she'd noticed during the ceremony. He was good-looking, in a dark-haired, light-eyed way, and he was flirting with a not-very-pretty bridesmaid, one of Brooke's work friends. A part of Jenna wanted to tell the bridesmaid not to fall for the groomsman's lines, and warn her that hunks with bedroom eyes couldn't be trusted. Didn't everyone know that? Or did people think that kind of guy was attainable because women characters they saw on TV landed them? Women characters played by actresses as beautiful as the guys. As beautiful as Jenna.

Someone came up behind her and touched her arm, said her name.

She turned to face Cooper, and beamed at him. An admirer at last, or at least someone who wanted to talk to her. "You look amazing," he said in her ear, and she said thanks and hugged him. She could smell his cologne — a scent that triggered mental images of the beach, bonfires, and the front seat of the car he'd driven in high school — and feel his heartbeat through his shirt, and was that a T-shirt underneath it? Shit, she'd gone in too close if she could tell how many layers of clothes he was wearing. She should maybe let up on the wine. Dinner hadn't been served yet.

She pushed off from Cooper's chest, swayed briefly on her heels, and righted herself.

"Whoa there." Cooper held her steady for a second — his hands on her waist — and eased her onto a bar stool. "Are you all right?"

"I'm fine." She didn't slur her words or talk too loud. She didn't sound drunk at all. "Lovely ceremony, wasn't it? Brooke looks so happy."

"Yeah, but all these weddings are starting to look the same. This is the fourth one I've been to this year."

"I know. You'd think we'd reached marrying age."

Cooper smiled, but not with his eyes. "So, are you next? Did you catch the bouquet?"

"Brooke hasn't thrown it yet." And Jenna would make sure she was nowhere near the toss when it did happen.

Cooper gestured toward Andrew, who was still talking to Steve Morgenstern. "Is that your guy?"

What was with the cheap shirt Cooper had on? It had felt stiff to Jenna's touch, and was creased with fold marks as if he'd bought it at a Walmart on the way out to the wedding and put it on in his car, along with the cheap matching tie. "Yeah," she said, "that's Andrew, in the navy suit. He's an entertainment attorney. I moved in with him last month."

"Cool. He looks —"

"Rich?"

"Well, yeah." This time, Cooper's eyes smiled too. "Rich and settled. And like a grown-up."

"That's because he *is* a grown-up."

"I'm not. Sometimes I feel like I graduated from high school two years ago, not ten. Don't you?"

No, she didn't. Or did she? Jenna searched around in her fuzzy mind for high-school memories. She remembered hours spent getting ready for school, hours of boredom in class, and oh, yeah, hours of sex with Cooper. He'd been so horny when they'd dated, so hot for her. Every single day, he'd wanted to get her alone and naked, and fuck her, every which way.

"Every which way," she muttered. Cooper leaned closer and said, "What?" and she smelled the cologne again. She couldn't name it, but the scent was so familiar, like hearing a song that she'd forgotten she'd once been obsessed with.

Andrew came over then and kissed her bare shoulder. She introduced him to Cooper, who said, "I'm a high-school friend of Jenna's. I've known her since before she became famous."

"I'm hardly famous," Jenna said.

"I'm also the guy who led hikes at the retreat Jenna organized a while back."

Andrew said, "You led hikes? What are you, a park ranger?"

A flicker of amusement — or was it irritation? — lit up Cooper's face for a second. "No, my business partner and I own a bike shop in Topanga Canyon. We run hikes and mountain bike rides out of it."

"A bike shop?" Andrew's smile was shark-like. "You make a living doing that?'

"We get by." Cooper turned to Jenna. "That was an interesting bunch of people out at Haven that weekend. How're they all doing?"

"Some of them are a little crazy. And some are a lot crazy. But they're doing good."

Andrew gave her a disapproving look, Jenna didn't know why — because of her grammar?

Cooper said, "How's that girl Stacey? She came out with her sister and did a group bike ride a few weeks ago, did she tell you?"

"Yeah. And I saw the nasty cut she got during that ride." To Andrew, Jenna said, "Some punks scraped Stacey's arm when they rode by, and tore a strip of skin right off."

Cooper shifted his weight. "Yeah, that was unfortunate. Was she pissed about it?"

Jenna decided to play with him. "I've never seen her so angry."

Cooper winced. "I should have called her afterward to follow up, see how she's doing."

Jenna placed her palm on Cooper's chest, felt the edge of his undershirt again. Why was she touching him? And how could her glass be empty again already? "I was teasing. She wasn't pissed at all. She joked about it."

"Still, I should call her. Or email her."

Andrew said, "Stacey's single, if you were wondering."

And Cooper's skin colour, from his neck to his hairline, changed from tan to embarrassed, right before Jenna's eyes. What the hell? Did he like Stacey? And if he did, how did Jenna feel about that?

Cooper said, "*Is* she single?"

Crap, he did like her.

"Yeah, she is," Andrew said. "Right, honey?"

"I think so."

Andrew said, "Stacey's also a mover and shaker, business-wise, if that makes a difference to you." He pulled out a bar stool and sat, the better to disguise the height disadvantage he had compared to Cooper, Jenna thought. A mean thought. She looked around for Cooper's volleyball player girlfriend, for someone who resembled the woman she'd seen in his Facebook pictures. She said, "Did you bring the girlfriend tonight?"

"No."

Andrew said, "Didn't rate a plus-one on your invitation?"

"I did, yeah, but Petra and I broke up a few months ago. I'm here alone."

Double crap. He liked Stacey *and* he was single. But that was okay. Stacey was welcome to Cooper, and Cooper to Stacey. Fuck them both. They could fuck each other, and Jenna wouldn't give a fuck. Hahaha. She said, "There's plenty of bitches and hoes where she came from / Don't you know, don't you know."

Another dirty look from Andrew. "Easy there, Jenna," he said. Like he was her father.

"Those are rap lyrics. From a Young Jeezy song," Jenna said. "Or maybe one of T.I.'s."

Cooper smiled. "I knew what you were saying." He set his glass down on the bar. "I should go congratulate the happy couple. Good seeing you both." He left them and melted off into the crowd.

Andrew said, "He's tall, that guy."

"Six-three."

"Did you ever fuck him?"

Fuck, fuck, fuck, every which way. "No, we were just friends."

Two women over by the dance floor were looking at Jenna and whispering. Probably talking about who she was — *that actress*. Or was her dress tucked into her thong at the back? She looked quickly over her shoulder. She was good, everything was where it should be.

Andrew said, "You look stunning tonight, by the way."

"Why, thank you. You're looking handsome yourself." It was amazing what expensive, well-tailored clothes could do for a man's silhouette. How much they could hide and smooth over.

Andrew nuzzled her neck, and though she didn't like PDAs generally, she closed her eyes, lifted her chin, and let him do it. He said, "Maybe we should leave early. Slip out and go home, go to bed. Let the bride be the star of the show without every man here looking at you instead."

Across the room, she saw Cooper pat the groom's shoulder and kiss Brooke on both cheeks. Had he told Brooke she looked amazing too? "We can't leave yet, it's too early. People would notice and think I'm rude."

"Okay, but let's try to go right after dinner."

"Deal." Jenna straightened up, picked up her clutch, and rubbed the back of her neck with her free hand, like she had a kink in it. "I'm going to find the ladies' room, and hope there isn't too long a line for it. Meet you at our table in a bit?"

Andrew waved at a middle-aged man who was crossing the floor toward them. "Hurry back, now."

NOVEMBER

21

Back in the day, Jenna had seen an episode of *The Hills* when Lauren Conrad was supposed to be an event planner, and she walked around a big party space filled with celebrities and rich people who were probably just extras pretending to be rich, and she talked into a headset the whole time and carried a clipboard. How old and tired was that setup? And how sad was it that Jenna had the same props on now, for a real-life job, not an acting gig, at the viewing party? Had she turned into one of those here-today-gone-tomorrow reality-show girls? That would be tragic. Though she did feel sort of important. What had Stacey called her when she strolled up to the entrance, looking stylish in a beautifully cut coat over a crisp shirt, narrow pants, and to-die-for shoes, and carrying a Gucci handbag? The Keeper of the List, that's what.

Stacey asked Jenna how it was going, who had arrived, and who important had yet to show up, and when Jenna told her, she said Jenna was doing great, she was so good with people.

Stacey said, "I was a Keeper of the List in my time, years ago. You have to be tough but fair to do the job properly. And have nerves of steel. You might want to lay low on the charm front, and access your inner bitch. It'll be a stretch for you, I know, but you can do it." She lowered her voice. "Any time you're stuck for a cold reply, just ask yourself what Ann would say, and you'll be fine."

Stacey had laughed then, and said, "Now, where's the bar?" though Jenna didn't think Stacey drank. And if anyone deserved alcohol right then, it was Jenna, after spending three hours on setup with the event planners and restaurant staff, and taking Ann's nagging phone calls about how things were going, and was everything on schedule and did the fans show up, and please add this and that network and studio person to the list and don't make her spell the names, Jenna should know them by now, and make sure they get the VIP treatment at the door. Did Ann have to be such a boss every minute, and act like she thought Jenna was useless? She should be more like Stacey, and relax, because Jenna was coping fine, thank you, and acing this assignment. Better than Lauren Conrad would have.

Here was Andrew. He tossed his car keys to the valet, slung his access-badge lanyard around his neck, and walked past security and over to her. Inviting significant others to share in the celebration had been Stacey's idea, and how could Ann argue with that? Though Jenna had a feeling Ann would have preferred that her husband stay away — she'd told Jenna once that he cramped her style at industry parties and she hated having to look after him when she should be working the room. Jenna knew what she meant, so she'd tried to discourage Andrew from coming, since Jenna was the Keeper of the List and wouldn't be able to talk to him much, but he thought he should come to support her. She'd only invited him so he wouldn't be hurt if he found out other people's partners were there, and it was one of those situations where each person feels they're doing the other a favour and no one is happy.

Andrew kissed her on the cheek and knocked her headset off balance. She had spent ten minutes adjusting it so it wouldn't flatten her hair, but she didn't show her irritation. She said, "Why don't you go get a drink? The producers are up on the second floor and the cast is arriving soon. I'll see you inside later."

He looked around at the searchlights, the banners with the *Benjamins* name and logo hung on the walls of the building, the photo backdrop on the red carpet, the photographers and cameramen, the line of fans waiting to get in. "Big crowd, nice setup. Break a leg. I'll see you inside."

If Jenna weren't on display and on camera, she would have scowled at Andrew's back. She did not need to be told to break her leg. She adjusted her headset, pressed on the earpiece, and heard the chief event planner, who was stationed inside at command central, in front of a rack of monitors, say: "The cast is approaching, the cast is approaching. The first limo should be at the door in two minutes, I repeat, two minutes." Wonderful. In two minutes Jenna could stand by and watch the actors being photographed and longed for and screamed at, and she could feel even more washed-up than she already did.

22

The live viewing party for episode 7 of *The Benjamins* had been Stacey's idea, a way to generate fan excitement, get the cast out in public looking pretty, build some goodwill and buzz. Naturally, Ann had taken over almost as soon as Stacey proposed it, and insisted on hiring her PR people and event planners — teams she'd worked with for years, who knew her preferences in food, wine, flowers, and wait staff, and who would always see her as the big boss, and Stacey as the assistant who'd made too good.

To break up the logjam Ann built around the event, Stacey suggested that Jenna be the in-house point woman on it, since she had done such a good job on the retreat. And since Stacey had decided to cultivate Jenna, make her an ally. Like Bonnie, and everyone else Stacey had ever worked with.

To that end, Stacey had made a point, in recent weeks, of throwing a friendly comment Jenna's way once a day. By the time the planning for the viewing party got to the detail stage, they were getting along so well Jenna just had to be comparing Stacey's laid-back, sunny supervisory style to Ann's imperious Queen Shit manner, with Stacey coming out the preferable alternative. Didn't she?

When the white limos the cast rode in arrived, Ann and Stacey were standing on the bar's second-floor deck, surrounded by producers, writers, senior production staff, and some suits, all at a safe remove from the well-lubricated, mostly female fans, median age twenty-three, who thronged the bar's lower level. They had assembled thanks to the organizing efforts of carefully chosen TV bloggers and recappers who had shown *The Benjamins* love since the pilot had aired.

At the sight of the cars, the fans screamed as if rehearsed, and they screamed louder when the cast members alighted, all dressed in white. Another of Stacey's ideas had been to not only have hair and makeup done for the cast, but to costume them for the party. Ryan rocked a tank top with jeans, the better to show off his guns, abs, and glutes; Vanessa sported an off-the-shoulder top that exposed her supple young skin; and Lucy, who played Arielle, Stacey's teenage alter ego, was pretty in a cotton eyelet mini-dress.

The costume designer had also done well by Wendy, the forty-four-year-old who played Ann's avatar, a fifty-year-old MILF. She was tricked out in a fringed minidress with spaghetti straps and high-heeled bondage sandals, in keeping with her status as the character fans loved to hate. The remaining principal cast members were also attired in character — the older actors in elegant white linen, the middle-aged ones in crisp white shirts and jeans, and so on.

Stacey said, "The cast looks good."

Ann said, "Especially Ryan. And listen to the fans."

"You'd almost think they'd been paid to scream like that."

"They haven't, have they?"

"No, no. They're bona fide."

Ann said, "I love that dress on Wendy. Oh, to be that thin again."

Stacey repressed an eye-roll; Ann had never been that thin.

Rob the producer bumped Stacey's shoulder. "Good evening, ladies," he said, and got a curled lip back from Ann, who was touchy about being addressed as a lady, in the tiresome retro-feminist way of her generation.

"Hey, Rob," Stacey said. "Having fun?"

He smelled like he'd already had a few drinks. "Yeah, it's a great party."

"Is your wife here with you?"

"No, she had to take the kids somewhere."

Or she hadn't been told that spouses were invited.

"What about you?" he said. "Did you bring a date?"

"No. Ann's husband is here, though. Have you met him before? He's the guy with the white hair at the end of the bar on this level — see him?"

They both looked over, and caught John staring down the shirt of a female bartender while she bent over to scoop up ice.

Ann said, "What's taking him so long?" and Rob and Stacey's heads swivelled back in unison toward the action on the main level below.

Rob pointed to the bar entrance, where the cast was filing in, to the accompaniment of camera flashes and a loud pop song. He said, "Jenna's right in the thick of it down there, isn't she?"

Jenna, headset askew, appeared to be trying to talk sense to a pair of women who wanted to climb over the velvet rope.

Ann said, "She's doing a good job. She could really go places, given the proper guidance and training. She gets distracted easily, but I've really brought her along since she started."

Stacey said, "If dealing with the mob at this party doesn't turn her off the production side of the business, I don't know what will."

Rob cleared his throat loudly, like he had a gob of phlegm — or gall — to choke down before he could speak. "What about Jenna's potential as an actress?" he said. "She's got real talent. She's like a diamond hidden away in our vault that we should take out more often, so we can see her sparkle."

Holy shit. Stacey knew Rob liked Jenna, but she hadn't thought he'd go so far as to debase himself with tortured metaphors and heart-on-the-sleeve-ness. The question was, how to turn Rob's weakness into her strength?

Ann scrunched up her face, said, "What?" and to John, who had torn himself away from the bartender, and was holding out her drink, "Finally."

John was the kind of over-sixty guy who Stacey thought looked better with white hair — his was full, and wavy — than he had when he was young and his hair was dark. He was Bill Clinton to Ann's Hillary. "One mojito, as ordered," he said.

Ann said, "What took you so long?"

"I was having a delightful conversation with the bartender. She's doing a master's degree in anthropology at UCLA, she told me. Who would have thought I'd meet an academic at this party?"

"Don't be an imbecile, John. Everyone has a master's degree these days, they're a dime a dozen. Stacey has one."

"Well, what do you know?" John said, and bestowed a roguish grin on Stacey.

Rob was still around, his face a picture of disappointment since his big bold move — the suggestion he must have worked toward for weeks, and gotten liquored up to make — had been ignored. Stacey almost felt sorry for him. But when she brought up the subject again, it was to goad Ann. "Could you excuse us for a second, John? Rob was talking shop, and Ann and I have left him hanging — I believe he just made a plea to cast Jenna on the show."

Ann took a big slurp of her drink. "Is that what you were talking about, Rob? Forget it. I don't want Jenna to leave me in the lurch to do a guest spot. The answer is no."

Rob threw Stacey a plaintive look before wandering off, but she had nothing for him. The mighty Oz had spoken.

She leaned over the railing and watched the actors make their way to the autograph-signing stations set up below. From her vantage point, the cast appeared to glow — all that bronzed skin, in white clothing, under the bluish lights — like Tolkienesque elves. "Doesn't the cast look lovely?" she said, and felt a momentary surge of maternal affection for the family she'd created. As if they were really related, and to her.

"Mm-hmm." Ann clasped her hands over her belly, and burped.

John cocked a craggy eyebrow at Stacey. "Do you really have a master's degree, Stacey?"

Ann said, "For God's sake, John, don't flirt with Stacey. You're old enough to be her father." The same way Ann could be Ryan's mother.

Stacey went to the restroom and touched up her lip gloss and her I'm-having-a-good-time face. When she came out, she stopped at the bar and ordered a Perrier from the bartender John had ogled, a woman with a sleek body, long, expensively coloured blonde hair, and a pretty face. Stacey put her age at a well-maintained forty. An engraved nametag pinned to her fitted shirt identified her as Shevaun.

High-pitched screams and moans wafted up from the main floor, accompanied by staggered flashes of light from cellphone cameras going off. Stacey said, "Cute young actors are such a big draw for female fans, aren't they?"

Shevaun passed over Stacey's drink. "They only love those guys because they don't know anyone like them. They don't know what vain, self-centred jerks they can be."

Ah, a cynic. "You in the business?"

"Used to be. Do you work on this show?"

"I'm one of the producers."

"So you know the people standing up here?"

"Most of them."

Shevaun did a head nod in the direction of a fit-looking man in an expensive suit down the bar several feet. "How about that guy?"

Stacey said, "That's Andrew Medway, an entertainment attorney." He had introduced himself earlier. "He's with that pretty girl Jenna who's working the door tonight. She's also an actress."

"Okay." Another head gesture, this one toward John, on the opposite end of the bar. "How about that older man in the bowtie? Who's he?"

"John Nelligan. He's a history professor at Pepperdine. That's his wife at the railing, Ann Dalloni. She's the co-creator of this show."

Shevaun snuck appraising glances at John and Ann. "So he's well-off."

Stacey didn't know who or what she was dealing with here. Shevaun could be a gold digger, an escort, a drug dealer, an aspiring blackmailer, or she could be looking for a job. But did it matter what she was after, if Stacey could steer whatever kind of trouble she represented in Ann's direction, for the hell of it? "His wife makes a good buck, yeah."

Shevaun wiped the counter of the bar with a cloth in one smooth motion, and wiped any recognizable emotion off her face at the same time. "I was just curious. You meet all kinds in this job."

"I'm sure."

Shevaun's phone must have buzzed then, because she pulled it out of a pocket, turned away from Stacey, read a text, and shook her head and smiled, as if she couldn't help but be amused. A sequence of actions that John, alone again at the end of the bar, followed up on by raising his glass to her.

Interesting.

Stacey took out her own phone and made a note in it of two words: sugar baby. That concept would make a good storyline for the show, for the Derrick character. She went back to where Ann stood, surveying her subjects. "God, it's hot in here," Ann said. "Can't someone turn on the air conditioning?"

Stacey was about to fuck with Ann and pretend that the room wasn't warm, when Lori Painter joined them. Lori was the network executive who had greenlit *The Benjamins*, and who held their futures in her sinewy hands.

"Ann! Stacey!" She bestowed a rotating beauty-queen grin on them both. "Congratulations! On your numbers and on this party. I smell a hit!"

Stacey thanked her, and commenced with the suck-up small talk. "We're stoked about the twenty-two-episode order. We were so happy to hear that news."

"Though it wasn't unexpected," Ann said. "My shows always get a pickup."

"We've got high hopes for *The Benjamins*," Lori said, and asked Stacey to point out who was who in the cast.

Stacey had a feeling Lori hadn't seen an episode since the pilot, so she reminded her who the main characters were and sketched in the primary storylines. She kept it short and sweet for fear of outlasting Lori's attention span, but Lori sustained an expression of wide-eyed interest the entire time Stacey spoke. Stacey adapted the expression for her own use and was reflecting it back when Lori said, "This show is tracking so well I can't wait to hear more about the spinoff ideas Ann mentioned at dinner last week. You two make such a great team!"

Spinoff ideas? The only spinoff idea Stacey knew of was her own closely guarded one, for a fish-out-of-water teen drama that would send the Arielle character to a snobbish boarding school in Kentucky horse country. But she hadn't fully fleshed out the concept yet, nor had she breathed a word about it to Ann, or to anyone else.

Stacey said, "We can't wait either!" and glared at Ann, who shrugged in reply.

When Lori had moved on, her fifteen-minute obligation to the party having been met, Ann said, "What time is it? Shouldn't the screening start soon? And where's John gone? It was a bad idea to invite the spouses. Your bad idea, I recall. Do I have to go find him now?"

Stacey reached out and clasped Ann's wrist. "Don't run off. Let's talk a minute." She might have failed to keep an edge out of her voice.

Ann looked down at Stacey's hand. "Let go of me."

Stacey released her grip. "Sorry." She clenched and unclenched her hand at her side. "What's going on, Ann? You met with the network and didn't tell me about it? And since when are we thinking about spinoffs?"

"Don't be so dramatic. I had dinner last week with Angela at Tavern. Lori happened to be there with someone else. She stopped by the table to say hello, we talked about the ratings, and Angela said, 'Wait till you hear about the spinoffs Ann's developing.' She was trying to pimp me, that's all. You know how agents are."

Could Ann be telling the truth? Not likely. But possible.

Ann said, "The screening should have started ten minutes ago. What's the point of hiring event planners if they can't execute a plan?" She pulled out her phone, and held it up close to her eyes. "And why is it so damned dark in here?" She handed the phone to Stacey. "Text Jenna for me. Tell her to get the screening started."

Stacey said nothing. She took the phone, texted the message to Jenna, and glanced over at the bar. John was talking to Shevaun again. She handed the phone back to Ann.

Ann said, "What's wrong with you? Are you sulking now? Just because you misconstrued Lori's little remark?"

Stacey wanted to say that sulking — along with other behaviours usually associated with spoiled children — was more Ann's thing than hers, but she held back. Like always. "I'm tired. It's been a long day."

"Tell me about it. Try being my age and working the hours we do."

Fuck Stacey's life. Ann was never going to quit with the complaints and bitching, never. She'd be bitching on her deathbed. No, she'd be bitching on Stacey's deathbed, because the high-octane vitriol that fuelled Ann would keep her going forever.

Stacey said, "I may head out soon. As fun as this has been."

"Okay, go. Go! Be like that."

Evenly: "I'll go when I'm ready."

"You know what, though?" Ann said.

Patience, that's what Stacey needed to draw on. And stamina. Deep stores of both. "What?"

"I did take a meeting with Lori without you, and one of the things we discussed was spinoffs."

Stacey looked into Ann's sickeningly self-satisfied face. "And why did you do that?"

"Because I felt like it. Why shouldn't I take meetings without you, any time I want? Who *are* you, anyway?"

Stacey turned away and caught sight of Jenna below them, off to one side of the room, leaning against a wall. Rob was with her, speaking into her ear, but she was intent on her phone screen.

Ann must have seen her, too. She said, "Let's face it, all you are is yesterday's Jenna, a nobody trying to work your way up. You may be good with spreadsheets and numbers and budgets and all that shit, but you'll never be me, no matter how hard you try. And I think it's time you faced that, and stopped trying to climb over me to get to some imaginary peak you think is the top."

Forget patience. The only way to clear the growing obstacle in Stacey's path that was Ann was to remove it.

Ann said, "Sorry if I'm being too blunt. I could blame it on the alcohol, but there's been tension building between us for a few months now, and isn't it better to clear the air, get things out in the open?" She had the nerve to nudge Stacey here, like they were pals. "You know, before things get ugly?"

It was Stacey's turn to speak, it seemed. To match Ann's frankness with some of her own. "You want blunt? How about this: I get that you're being a total prick right now, but what else are you saying? Do you want to dissolve our partnership?"

"What? No. Why would I want that? Our agreement suits me fine, as long as you accept that your role will always be a subordinate one."

"Oh, right." Stacey's sarcasm was so heavy she risked having it come off as sincerity. "How could I forget?" She slapped her forehead. "You're the boss, and I'm the lackey. Now and forever."

"Exactly." Ann's phone buzzed. She held the screen up close to her face again — really close. "What does this say?"

Stacey looked over Ann's shoulder, read the text. "It's from Jenna. The screening will start in two minutes."

And, Stacey realized, her own campaign, to take Ann down, would begin in one.

23

After the episode had screened, the cast had signed auto-graphs and posed for a hundred photos each, and the delirious fans had left, still squeeing, Jenna helped an under-the-influence Ann and her equally drunk husband into their town car and waved them off. The viewing party was finally over.

Jenna had told Andrew to go home earlier — no reason for him to suffer through the whole event — so she was alone for the drive back to his house. Alone to think about how the evening had gone, to wonder how much she had contributed to its success — a little more than a little, she thought — and to decide not to tell Andrew what Rob had said, about how his attempt at getting her a part on *The Benjamins* had failed.

Rob had stood too close, and reeked of alcohol — how unfair was that, that while she'd worked hard and stayed sober, everyone else had drunk their faces off at the open bar? — when he'd cornered her during a text message exchange she was having with Ann, who would not leave her alone about getting the screening started, when that task wasn't even on Jenna's Keeper of the List job description.

Rob said, "Look, I tried, I really did. Because someone as talented and beautiful as you are deserves a chance to shine." He laid his hand on her bare shoulder and ran his index finger down her arm in a creepy way that made Jenna squirm and shake him off, though she tried to do it without shuddering.

Rob said, "Ann flat-out wouldn't go for it. Stacey might have, but not Ann, and she calls the shots."

"Thanks for trying, Rob, but you shouldn't worry about me. I'm not even sure I want to act anymore."

"How can you say that?" He sounded genuinely upset, like she was wasting something special, rather than being no different from a hundred other actresses. "Your time will come, I know it. One day you'll get the attention you deserve."

"You're sweet to say so," Jenna said. "And thanks for sticking your neck out for me. But I have to go." She held up her phone. "I can't keep Ann waiting if I want to keep the job I've got."

She'd acted like it was no tragedy if her acting days were done, like she was relieved she no longer had to endure casting calls and auditions. Like she didn't want to be treated as a brainless pretty face and clotheshorse anymore.

She stopped off at an In-N-Out on her way home, gorged on a double cheeseburger, threw it up in the restroom, and drove home.

When she walked in, Andrew was watching a basketball game on his giant TV. "How'd the rest of the party go?"

"Fine." She kicked off her shoes, poured a big glass of wine, drank half of it, refilled the glass, and sat down next to Andrew on the sectional.

He squeezed her shoulder. "You looked cute in your headset, carrying a clipboard."

"Cute?"

"And competent. That's my girl down there, I wanted to tell people. The cute and competent one."

Jenna snuggled in closer, placed her hand on Andrew's junk, and after a few minutes, started stroking his dick through his sweats, brought it to life. She might as well fall back on plan B.

24

Ann's Journal

What a night.

Pulled off a successful viewing party — check.

Dismissed Rob's asinine request to cast Jenna and therefore deprive me of my assistant just when I've got her well-trained on my coffee and food preferences — check.

Drank a little too much and told Stacey where to get off — check. No regrets there, she deserved to be taken down a peg. She can go sulk in a corner now and get out of my face.

On the minus side, how abhorrent was the dirty-old-man act John put on with that soft-porn actress moonlighting as a bartender? I hate him. At this moment, he is walking around the house singing, like an old-timey drunk. Takes one to know one, but still: HATE.

And did Lori Painter have to spill the beans about our meeting last week? Way to break confidence there, Lori. I guess now I'll have to go over her head with my besmirch-Stacey campaign. Like to Lori's boss, the guy who owes me big-time since I saved his skin a few years ago, when I single-handedly hauled the network out of the basement on the strength of my shows.

Yeah, I'm going to call Marty, and suggest we get together for a cozy chat to talk about old times. I'll remind him how important I am, and how integral to the network's success. And when he's taken that in, I'll tell him I want Stacey out and gone.

25

A table read of episode 12 was scheduled for 10:00 a.m. on the Monday following the viewing party, which meant that Jenna had to be at work at 8:30 to prepare for it. She made sure there was the right number of labelled copies of the latest draft of the script, she arranged for coffee, juices, water, and Ann's favourite croissants to be brought in, and she had the large, bare room where the reads were held set up with tables and chairs in the proper formation.

Everything and everyone was in place when she looked around that room at 9:55, except for Ann. Was Jenna supposed to call and ask if she was going to be late, and whether they should start without her? She imagined how that would go over. She took her seat, a few feet back from the rectangular arrangement of six tables. In the unimportant-person section of the room, away from the actors, who lounged in their chairs like they owned them.

At 9:58, one of the studio execs checked his watch and whispered something to Stacey, who leaned back and asked Jenna if she knew where Ann was. When Jenna said no, Stacey thanked her, and spoke to the exec and to Brendan, the episode director. Jenna couldn't hear what was said, but Brendan laughed a little, and Stacey turned around and winked at Jenna. Stacey was so much nicer and more normal than Ann, and so much easier to deal with. Stacey who might have agreed to cast her, Rob had said, if it were her decision alone.

At 10:04, Stacey put her fingers in her mouth and whistled. "Let's get started," she said, but her words were overrun by Ann's booming voice — it entered the room before she did.

"My apologies for being late," Ann said. "The traffic, my driver — I won't bore you with the details." She wore dark sunglasses, and was weighed down by a coat, her briefcase, her handbag, and a bound script she held in her hand. She took her usual seat at the top of the rectangle and put down the script. "Where's Jenna?"

Jenna stood. "Right here."

"Then help me with my things. Chop, chop." Some asshole laughed at this, and Jenna helped Ann offload her shit like she was her goddamned maid.

"Now that I'm here, we can begin for real," Ann said. She had a sly look on her face that Jenna recognized: she was about to insult someone, and pretend it was a joke. "You weren't going to go ahead without me on Stacey's say-so, were you? Never settle for second best, that's my motto."

The asshole laughed again. Jenna snuck a sympathetic peek at Stacey, who, if she was pissed off by Ann's put-down, didn't show it. Ann handed the read over to Brendan, and it began.

26

Topher had come into Stacey's office just before the table read, closed the door behind him, and told her that his friend Jeremy, an aspiring screenwriter who waited tables at Farmshop, had seen Marty Woods having a breakfast meeting there with Ann, that morning. "Which I'm sure you already knew about," Topher said. "I'm just telling you in case you didn't."

Stacey hadn't known that Ann was meeting with her pal, the president of the network's entertainment group, but she thanked Topher for the tip — "I love that there's a secret spy network of waiters in this town. There's a screenplay idea right there!" she said — without letting on that she hadn't known, or that the news gave her a panicky feeling in her chest. And when Ann blamed her late entrance at the table read on traffic, Stacey did not exchange an "oh no, she didn't" glance with Topher. She didn't react much to Ann's assertion of dominance, either, not beyond a small shake of the head meant to indicate amused tolerance of Ann's outsized ego. This was not the time or place to reveal her new gloves-off attitude toward Ann. Or that she'd begun to plot a solution to their incompatibility problem.

Stacey wanted a work divorce — to sever the partnership and dissolve the production company, but retain full custody of *The Benjamins*. This objective, though simple, would not be easy to achieve. Barring death or sudden incapacitation, Stacey was certain Ann would not exit the company willingly, nor would she cede control of the show. Not without destroying it first, out of spite.

In the days and nights since the viewing party, Stacey had briefly considered being direct with Ann. What if she simply said, no subterfuge, that it was time they parted ways? Now that they'd stopped walking together — ostensibly because of Ann's knee problems, but really because they couldn't stand each other — why hang on to a company called Two Women Walking?

The problem was that while Stacey could conceivably tamp down her rage against Ann, act civilized, face facts, and negotiate terms, the idea that Ann would entertain any approach that would erode her power base by even an iota was too incredible to contemplate for more than a few minutes.

What made more sense, for now, was for Stacey to play a longer game, to continue to create alliances and build up support with people who mattered, both within the company and outside it — and hope that Ann would hoist herself soon enough on the petard of her increasingly erratic ways.

If Stacey did unseat Ann — no, *when* she did — who would be on her team? She tallied the room's inhabitants, viewed them through a friend-or-foe filter. Like she'd put on truth vision goggles that allowed her to penetrate the disguises worn by the aliens gathered at the table, and see their true, reptilian forms underneath.

The actors, who could have been expected to present a facade at all times out of habit, were the most transparent: the veterans followed their scripts closely, had already flipped ahead to their scenes, and could be seen mouthing their upcoming lines, silently rehearsing. The younger ones texted on their phones under the table while they waited for a scene they were in. And the guest cast members — this week, there were five — tried hard to look like they belonged, but were clearly nervous. Stacey saw pit stains, at least one shaking hand, and nervous hair twirling going on among them.

Brendan, the director, also fidgeted. He had an iPad on the table in front of him, and when he wasn't typing notes in it, he arranged and rearranged his keys, his phone, his water bottle.

INT. JULIE'S BEDROOM — AFTERNOON

(JULIE, NATE)

NATE AND JULIE ARE IN BED, POST-SEX. NATE IS LOST IN THOUGHT. JULIE LOOKS SATISFIED.

                JULIE
That was the bomb. That thrumming thing you did with your fingers? You don't have to do it every time, but once in a while, oh, yeah!

                NATE
                What?

JULIE REACHES UNDER THE SHEETS FOR NATE'S PRIVATES.

                JULIE
I'm telling you to keep UP the good work.

There were a couple of laughs at this exchange, and a few groans, and Ryan raised his hands above the table and did a jazz hands gesture that added to the hilarity.

Could Stacey count on any of the actors? Most were friendly suck-ups when she saw them, and some, like Peter, might support her long-term, and not be merely self-serving. The rest would stick by whoever could employ them. Same for the director and assistant directors.

Who else, then? Bonnie, as writer of the episode, occupied a prime position at the table, and she was a picture of concentration: her eyes narrowed behind her reading glasses when she looked down at the page, her eyebrows raised in two question marks when she watched the actors speak their lines.

She definitely had potential to be a floor-crosser, and was worth the cultivation efforts Stacey had made so far. At the next jokey line, Stacey laughed helplessly — so funny! — and leaned across the table to give Bonnie a high five, which made her grin big. Creative people were such pushovers for praise. Soon Stacey would ask Bonnie to work with her on the boarding-school spinoff. She might be enticed to help develop it, if Stacey sent a few more compliments her way and listened to more complaints about her slobby boyfriend.

Stacey considered the four executive producers at the table. Three were Ann's long-time hires, men in their fifties who had never liked Stacey, and felt displaced by her. She'd been trying for years to win them over, and she'd never get more from them than the grudging acceptance they granted her, coupled with a desire to see her fail. If Ann were out of the picture, Stacey's next move would be to cut them loose.

The fourth executive producer was lovestruck Rob. He might align himself with Stacey over Ann, given the right opportunity.

He was majorly deluded to be pining for Jenna, but with some adroit manipulation, and if she favoured Jenna, Stacey could get him on her side. Though did she really want to take steps to change the downward slope of Jenna's career trajectory? Maybe, if to do so would help destroy Ann.

Next to Rob sat Gideon and Nicole, the studio execs. They were cagey, masters of reserved enthusiasm. Their clothes were always better pressed and more fashion-forward than what anyone in a production office would wear, and they never spoke when a nod could communicate their approval of a casting decision, or a scene. What did they really think of Ann behind their masks? They'd been enthusiastic about her reputation when they'd agreed to produce the show, but they were twenty years younger than Ann at least, maybe twenty-five, and Stacey wouldn't be surprised if they were tired of Ann's diva routine. The key to getting in their good graces was to deliver good numbers and keep the drama onscreen, not on-set. It wouldn't hurt to friendly up to them, too, and try to find a way inside their walled minds.

EXT. SIMON'S HOUSE — MORNING

(SIMON, MARK, RUTH)

MARK IS PASSED OUT POOLSIDE ON A CHAISE LOUNGE WITH SUNGLASSES ON, AND HIS PANTS UNDONE. HE'S DROOLING. SIMON STANDS ABOVE HIM, COFFEE MUG IN HAND.

　　　　　SIMON
　　　Mark. Wake up.

MARK SNORES.

> SIMON

Mark, wake up! We need to talk.

MARK TALKS IN HIS SLEEP, LAUGHS LIKE HE'S STONED.

> MARK

It's how big? No way. Show me. SHOW ME.

RUTH COMES OUT OF THE HOUSE IN A TENNIS OUTFIT.

> RUTH

Hey Dad.

> SIMON

Look at your brother. What are we going to do with him?

> RUTH

He's sleeping in. It *is* Saturday Aren't kids allowed to sleep in on weekends?

> SIMON

Not when they come home drunk and stoned at 5 am, they're not. Mark, wake up!

> RUTH

Did he piss himself this time?

SIMON LOOKS CLOSER AT MARK'S PANTS.

> SIMON

Oh hell. I don't think so.

> RUTH

Well, that's something.

RUTH SPOTS ANOTHER BOY PASSED OUT ON A CHAISE LOUNGE FACING THE OTHER WAY.

> RUTH

Who's that?

The other boy was Mark's drug-dealer friend, the one who would introduce Mark to mountain biking in the next episode. As per plan, Stacey had hired Cooper on as biking consultant a few weeks before, and had had the pleasure already of seeing him at a meeting, unfortunately in the company of assorted producers and crew.

She had a second meeting scheduled with Cooper and the location manager for the next day. She'd been looking forward to it — the appointment date and time had glowed at the back of her consciousness, like a hidden Easter egg — since she'd booked it a week or so before. But now that a takedown of Ann had become her primary goal, should she deny herself the indulgence of seeing Cooper? No. Soldiers were allowed to enjoy carnal pleasure before being sent off to war, weren't they?

And so, if the scenarios she'd envisaged with Cooper worked out, would she.

27

When Jenna stood up to leave after the table read, Ann commanded her to pull up a chair and wait while the exec producers, the studio execs, the director, and the writer stayed behind to review how the read had gone. Everyone else scattered, including Carly Horton, who Jenna watched saunter out of the room as if she didn't have to be back on-set or in makeup or wardrobe or in her trailer learning her lines. As if she had no idea how lucky she was to be a series regular on a hit network show, even if she had to wear a bikini or strip down to her underwear in every single episode.

At the exec table, Stacey said, "I thought the lines on page 5 about what Mark's been up to came off as expository. Can we be less obvious about laying pipe there?"

Ann didn't have her script open in front of her. "What lines? In which scene?"

Bonnie: "I know what you mean. I'll rework them."

Ann: "I said, in which scene?"

Gideon: "The one on page 5. I'm with Stacey. That bit rang false to me too."

Ann slapped the table with her hand, hard, which made Jenna, sitting next to her, flinch. "Are you people deaf?" Ann didn't shout, but damn close. "I asked which fucking scene you're talking about."

Jenna wondered if she was expected to answer Ann's question — which had been already answered twice, hadn't it? — but Bonnie spoke up. "The fucking scene we're talking about is the kitchen scene between Julie and Simon. The scene on page 5 of the script."

Ann said, "Thank you, Bonnie. Was that so difficult, people? And yes, those lines should be reworked, freshened up. They sound stale. Okay, what else?"

If any glances were being exchanged about Ann's attitude, Jenna did not want to look up and intercept them.

The reason Ann had asked Jenna to wait around for the post-read meeting was so that Jenna would drive her in a golf cart across the studio lot back to the production office, and listen to a dictated task list on the way.

The first thing Ann wanted was for Jenna to rearrange her meetings for the next morning. "I'll be out till eleven or twelve," she said. "I have a doctor's appointment."

Since when did Ann make her own appointments? It must be for something she didn't want Jenna to know about, like fillers or lipo. Both of which Ann should have used long before now, in Jenna's opinion. "If you're going in for a cosmetic procedure," Jenna said, "don't believe it when they say there's no down time."

"What?"

"Like those lunchtime lipo sessions that are advertised all over? I know someone who had one and she couldn't leave her house for a week afterward, what with the pain, and the bandages, and the bruising."

"I'm not going for liposuction. I'm seeing an ophthalmologist."

"Oh, okay. When should I reschedule your meetings for?"

"Sometime later than tomorrow morning, what do you think?"

"Sorry," Jenna said, though she wasn't. "But I don't understand how I can change the meetings without throwing off the production schedule. You're already booked solid for the rest of the week."

Ann didn't say anything for a minute. Then, "So, don't change the meetings. Go to them in my place."

"Me?"

"Yes, you. Is there anyone else in this cart?"

"You mean like go and take notes and report back to you on what happens?"

"Yes, but I'd also like you to represent me: say and do what I'd say and do."

"I don't know if I can do that," Jenna said, but she could. She pictured herself made up and costumed to look like Ann, in a fat suit and a wig. Jenna as Ann swept into a roomful of people and demanded that the meeting get started immediately, what the fuck were they waiting for? She could play that part all right.

Or she could go into the meetings and be so smart and nice that she would get her foot one step farther in the door. In *a* door.

"Yes, you can. Don't do that fake modesty thing and underestimate yourself. It's annoying as shit. I'll brief you beforehand. And I want you to help me organize a Thanksgiving dinner; I'm having some friends over in a couple of weeks. Call the usual caterers, get me some menus, and let's go over them. While you're at it, order me in some lunch, too. I feel like a Cobb salad today. Okay?"

Okay.

28

On her way out of the building after the table read, Stacey walked past Gideon and Nicole, who stood outside, their heads close together, speaking quietly. Stacey put on her sunglasses, and was about to set off on a walk across the lot when Gideon said to wait up, they'd walk with her.

They fell into step, one on each side of her, and Stacey said, "The read sounded strong overall, didn't it? I love how the tension is tightening with the introduction of the stalker storyline for Nate."

Gideon said, "I wanted to ask about that. About later in his arc, when he hires someone to teach him self-defence."

"Hey, have you been reading my outline? I love it!" Stacey read impassivity on Gideon and Nicole's poker faces, and adjusted her positive attitude, dialled it down a notch. "It's going to be good when the bodyguard gets between Nate and Julie and disrupts their relationship."

Nicole said, "What form of martial arts are you planning to have the self-defence instructor teach?"

"We haven't decided yet. The bodyguard character doesn't show up until ep 20. Why?"

Gideon said, "We were thinking that kickboxing might be a good choice."

"We can check that out for sure. And I want to look into Krav Maga — the Israeli self-defence program. I've heard it's pretty intense."

"I'm sure it is, but kickboxing might be better. And you know who does kickboxing? Lori Painter. It's her fitness thing."

"In that case, kickboxing it will be." After Stacey confirmed that Lori was still into it. Just in case Gideon and Nicole were trying to throw Stacey under the bus. Doubtful they were, but no harm in checking. "And thanks for that tip. Nothing makes me happier than keeping Lori happy. Except keeping you two happy." She laughed so she wouldn't look like too much of an ass-kisser. While still being one.

Gideon placed his manicured hand on Stacey's arm. "That's why we like you, Stacey. Aside from the fact that you have a deep comprehension of the word 'budget.' We like that you *get* things. And that you take our notes."

Stacey be nimble, Stacey be quick, Stacey jump over the candlestick. "Yeah, Ann really knows how to bring the drama, doesn't she? To the show and in real life. She's such a character." To love or hate, take your pick.

They were nearing the building that contained the studio offices. "Glad we had this talk," Nicole said. She and Gideon identi-smiled, and they split, leaving Stacey to increase her walking speed and add two more supporters to her list.

At 8:55 the next morning, Stacey bounded into the post-production suite for an editing session like she couldn't wait to hang out in a darkened room obsessing over minutiae, and said good morning to the editor and her assistant, whose names Stacey knew, though Ann didn't. Brendan and Todd came in, and the only person missing before they could start was — again? — Ann. Or so Stacey thought until Jenna showed up and said, "Ann isn't coming in this morning. She has a doctor's appointment, so she told me to sit in for her. If that's okay."

A second's pause while the room waited for Stacey to speak. "It's more than okay, we're happy to have you," she said. Though why the hell hadn't Ann told Stacey she'd be out of the office? And why had she pushed Jenna into the deep end of the pool? "Come sit by me, and I'll take you through it."

Jenna sat in the chair next to Stacey, a notebook and pen in her hand.

"Is Ann okay?" Stacey said. "Her appointment's not for anything urgent?" She could only hope.

"No, she's just seeing an eye doctor."

All right then. And too bad.

The edit went fine. Stacey was patient with Jenna — she explained what they were doing and why, and made sure to ask her opinion about which take she thought worked best or how many seconds of a shot to use, though Jenna had nothing insightful to contribute — she had not armed herself with Ann's unrelenting confidence in her own judgment, nor assimilated Ann's eye for detail and artistic vision.

After the edit, the next meeting on Stacey's schedule was with the set designer, across the lot. On her way there, Stacey asked Jenna if she was coming to that meeting too.

"Ann wants me to," Jenna said. "Do you want a lift over there? I can get a cart."

"Thanks, but I'd rather walk. It only takes ten minutes, and I rarely get a chance to walk during the day anymore since Ann busted her knee."

Jenna fell into step beside her. "You might have to change the company name soon — from Two Women Walking to One Woman Walking, One Woman Being Driven."

Stacey didn't mind Jenna's little joke. One Woman Walking would suit her just fine as a company name. Or Last Woman Standing.

She quickened the pace a touch and Jenna kept up, without showing any strain, and she had on ankle boots with heels, too. What a difference it was to walk with her instead of Ann. To walk with someone who was in good shape. Agile, even.

"What do you do to work out?" Stacey said.

"Some yoga, some Pilates. But I'm getting bored with both of them. What about you? You run, right?"

"Yeah, but I'm going to try kickboxing. Have you ever done that?"

"No, I haven't."

"I'm looking into it for research purposes, for the storyline about Nate and his stalker, and I heard about a women-only mixed martial arts gym in Studio City." The gym that Stacey had found out Lori Painter went to. "There's a beginner's class on Tuesday nights. You want to come with when I go check it out next week? Learn how to fight?"

"Next Tuesday night?"

"You should come. It'll be fun. And it's not like anyone else in the office is in good enough shape to give it a try."

Jenna hesitated before taking the bait, but only for a second. "Okay, sure," she said. Her phone chimed and she took it out of her bag. "It's Ann." She read a text. "She's still at Dr. Gottsdotter's office, she should be here by one o'clock."

"What's the doctor's name?"

"Gottsdotter." Jenna held out her phone for Stacey to see. "Like God's daughter, I guess, only Swedish or whatever. Why, do you know him? Or her?"

"No, it's just an unusual name." An unusual name Stacey had heard before.

Another chime, another text. Jenna read it and sighed.

Stacey said, "Let me guess: she wants you to order her in some lunch?"

"And take pics of the new set and send them to her, plus I have to deal with the messages and emails and scripts that will have come in while we were in the edit. I'll be busy."

"Ann likes to crack the whip, that's for sure," Stacey said, and didn't break her stride. Why would Ann be seeing a renowned retina specialist like Gottsdotter? Stacey knew of the doctor's reputation because she hadn't always ignored her parents' dinner table mutterings and meant-for-two private conversations. Over the years, she had acquired and retained some base knowledge about both their specialties, and about whose careers they respected and envied.

What if Ann had a career-ending eye condition? How convenient would that be? Though with Stacey's luck, Ann's problem was something routine like cataracts, and she was demanding a second opinion from the best doctor in L.A. out of her misplaced sense of entitlement.

Stacey said, "Do you want me to ask Topher to cover your desk for the rest of the morning? He won't mind." He *would* mind, but if Stacey got him involved, she could get more access to Ann's business, have him do a little spying. A plan she should have thought of and put into place earlier.

"Thanks, I can manage. And I'm sure he has plenty to do for you."

"Okay, but if I can help by filling in for Ann in some other way, let me know." Empty words, but worth saying if they made her look helpful and caring.

They turned a corner, and Jenna said, "Actually, there is one thing you could do, if you have a few minutes to spare."

"Sure, what is it?"

"The network publicist set up phone interviews with *Entertainment Weekly*, *E! Online*, and *TVLine* — they're looking for teasers and spoilers for the next few episodes. Ann was supposed to talk to them, but she keeps putting off making the calls, and I'm running out of excuses to give the publicist. Would you mind being interviewed instead?"

"Not at all. Have the publicist hook me up and I'll take care of that today." Would she ever. She'd do the interviews, be funny and clever, get her name out there in connection with the show. What a good day this was turning out to be, with Ann away. And she still had the location meeting with Cooper that afternoon to look forward to.

"Can I get you another drink?" Cooper said later that night, and though Stacey had been drinking mineral water, and should have been at home working, or working out, or both, not sitting in a hipster Santa Monica bar gazing into Cooper's ordinary yet oddly mesmerizing brown eyes, she said, "Thanks, I'd love a single malt, on the rocks." She pulled out her phone to fake-check her messages rather than stare stare stare at Cooper while he walked over to the bar to get their drinks, and while her body heated up with lust or desire — something acquisitive, anyway — at the sight of his ordinary yet oddly stirring gait. She was so fucked. And could only hope she would get fucked, by Cooper, tonight.

It had been Cooper's idea to go out for drinks. He suggested it in Topanga Canyon, after the location meeting. Six people showed up from Two Dubs to see and assess the proposed site, which made it difficult for Stacey to engage Cooper in any enjoyable way. She couldn't bask in his presence — not with so many people around, so many tasks on her mind. Not when she was wearing her work hat.

The meeting had just ended when she stepped away from the group to take a phone call from Topher about a problem with the house set — there'd been a leak, some small water damage, repairs were necessary. While she listened to Topher, the others dispersed and headed off to their cars. Not Cooper. He stayed put a respectful ten feet away, and stood, legs akimbo, looking out over the canyon, his eyes shaded by a baseball cap. He waited for her to finish the call before asking her out, though she didn't know that was what he wanted to do. She thought he wanted to talk further about the site, or about his consulting role.

"Sorry about that," she said, when she'd hung up. "And hey, well done today. The location is perfect. And you were so solid on the mechanics of shooting here. Have you done film work before?"

"No. It just made sense to think ahead about some of the logistical issues, like parking and power supply."

"You made me look good for hiring you — so, thanks for that." The quasi-hug she initiated brought her close to him, allowed her to brush against his hard chest with her hand.

"You're welcome. And thank you for paying me to come out here and act like I know what I'm talking about." His mouth was near her ear, his cheek pressed against her hair. She fought an impulse to lay her head on his shoulder, and she stepped back. "It's a pleasure doing business with you." Shit, that was lame. She sounded like a madam in a brothel. Or a hooker.

If only she could forget about trying to come up with flirty talk that didn't sound cheesy, and just ask him if he wanted to come over to her place later. So she could kiss him long and deep, press the length of her body against his, and they could fuck, in an indolent, golden-lit way. There'd be none of that clichéd crashing open of doors and knocking over of furniture that signified passion onscreen. No, they'd be naked and smooth-skinned and she'd stroke his delts and his biceps, and he'd be a skilled lover who would make her eyes roll up into their sockets in ecstasy.

She might have come right out and invited him over on the spot if she were sure he'd be down for some slow fucking. But she wasn't sure. He seemed at least a little wholesome, like he thought romance should precede sex, and would think her whorish if she wanted to dispense with verbal foreplay. And that was a good thing — his lack of sleaze compared to the creeps she dealt with on a daily basis was part of his allure.

"We should go for a drink," he said. "Celebrate my first-ever consulting job. What time do you let yourself off work? Or does the boss ever take a break?"

It was four o'clock. She had a shitload of shit to do at the office, people waiting on her for approvals and decisions. Taking two hours out of her day to do the location scout had already put her behind schedule. But would Clear-Eyed Wholesome Cooper be willing to meet up for a drink after dark, at ten?

He *was* willing — he looked pleased when she suggested it, and they agreed to meet in a bar near her condo so she wouldn't have far to drive after coming in from Manhattan Beach. A bar situated so that she could easily ask him up to hers after their second drink if she wanted to.

Now, it was eleven, past her bedtime, and they'd covered all the preliminary conversational topics: she'd asked how business was going at Hike, Bike, Love, he'd mentioned Jenna in a pleasingly indifferent manner — "I saw her and her boyfriend at a wedding recently," he said. "How's she doing at work?"

Fine, Stacey had said. Jenna was doing fine.

Cooper came back to the table, drinks in hand. Stacey had shown up for this not-a-date in the clothes she'd worn all day — jeans, motorcycle boots, and a hundred-and-fifty-dollar T-shirt under a long cardigan — but Cooper had changed his clothes since the canyon. He'd replaced his hiking attire with a close-fitting navy polo shirt, straight-leg jeans, and boat shoes, and he was hatless. His upper body was showing, and so was his lack of interest in fashion trends.

She thanked him for the scotch and took a sip, felt the alcohol shock her system. All she'd eaten that day was some tofu and seaweed salad at two o'clock, and she so rarely drank that she'd be buzzed in a few minutes. But Cooper was worth loosening her grip on herself for a few hours. And she'd only have one drink.

He gestured to her phone. "You still dealing with work stuff?"

She put the phone away. "There's always something. But I'm glad I came out tonight. It's good to spend some time in the real world once in a while, see normal humans in action."

Cooper raised his beer bottle. "To normal humans."

"Like that couple across from us," Stacey said. "Check them out. But don't turn around. Come sit beside me."

He got up from his chair and slid in next to her on the wooden bench against the wall, so that his thigh, warm and solid, touched hers. The long narrow room was crowded, and the noise level high. The couple sitting across from them — the guy wore a rib-bon-trimmed fedora set at a jaunty angle, the girl worked a pixie haircut that showed off her bone structure — were deep in conversa-tion. No way would they have noticed or heard anything said across the aisle. But Cooper turned in toward Stacey, and said, "What about them?" so low and close that she felt his breath on her cheek.

She knocked down another mouthful of scotch. "The guy's going all in. Look how he's squared his shoulders to face her full on, and his legs are wide open. He's presenting his genitals to her."

Cooper laughed. "Presenting his genitals? Like a baboon? What kind of girl is going to respond to that?"

"I didn't say it was a smart thing to do, just that he's doing it. And see how he's leaning toward her, and staring at her mouth? His body language couldn't be clearer. But she's not buying it, not so far. She's hidden her boobs behind that scarf and sweater she has on, and her legs and ankles are crossed under the table. She's barred entry."

Cooper's mouth was at Stacey's ear again, his nearness making her crazy. She had to have him that night. Within the hour.

He said, "She's smiling, though. She likes what he's saying despite the dumb hat. And look — she's taking off her sweater."

Fedora was still talking, Pixie Cut had removed a layer, and now she was stroking her clavicle with her be-ringed fingers.

Stacey said, "He must have a silver tongue. He's either telling her a fascinating story, or charming the clothes right off her. What do you think?" "I think you're the one with the silver tongue. I bet you could talk anyone into anything."

She was about to say she'd always thought her superpowers resided in her hair, when — enough with the preamble. She said, "Can I talk you into coming up to my place? Right now? To fuck me?"

His face was in close-up next to hers. The apples of his cheeks lifted in a smile. "Yes, you can," he said. He drained his beer in one long draft and stood up. "Let's go."

29

In the three weeks since her "date" with Cooper, Stacey had seen him several times — for a drink and sex, for coffee and sex, for sex in the shower. And now that she was seeing him at home, there was no need to take precious hours out of her workday to hang with him on location. So on the Tuesday before Thanksgiving, the day the mountain biking scene was being shot, he was in Topanga Canyon with the crew, and she was at the office.

Her eleven o'clock meeting was with Louise, the costume designer, to approve wardrobe for episode 12. Unfortunately, Ann was also present.

At eleven-twenty, the efficient Louise wheeled out the last rack of clothing in her array. "And finally, we come to Julie. For the family brunch scene, I like her in this dress." She held out a short lavender-coloured bandage dress with a criss-cross bodice and a flippy skirt. "Its body-conscious silhouette expresses Julie's heightened feelings of sexuality since she's been sleeping with Nate, and the flared skirt conveys her new sense of playfulness."

Stacey said, "It's very pretty. Is it Hervé Léger?"

"You have such a good eye, Stacey. Yes, it's from next spring's ready-to-wear line."

Ann said, "You're sure it's not too young a style? We don't want her to look like mutton dressed as lamb."

Stacey said, "I think she can carry it off. And it'll contrast nicely with what Louise picked out for the other women in that scene."

"Okay," Ann said. "Just give Wendy some advance warning so she can fast or do a cleanse or whatever before she has to wear it. What's next?"

Stacey counted the remaining hangers on the rack. Five outfits to go. Could they possibly get through an entire meeting without Ann being disagreeable, without any verbal pushing and shoving? What a refreshing change that would be.

Louise was holding up the next garment when Stacey's phone buzzed in her hand, with an incoming text from Cooper:

Your actor Joey was fooling around on a bike with the stunt rider and he wiped out and hurt his ankle. It doesn't look too bad but I thought you'd want to know.

No, no, no. An on-set injury to Joey could spell all kinds of trouble. For storylines, and continuity, and reshoots, and Joey would have to be coddled, and insurance claims made, and explanations given to the studio. All of which Stacey would have to handle, when her plate was already overfull.

Another buzz, another text from Cooper:

Sorry. I should have kept an eye on him.

Cooper didn't need to apologize — his job was not to babysit Joey. Before Stacey could text him back, her phone buzzed again, this time with an email, at the same time as Ann's phone, sitting on a table in front of them, chimed.

"Go ahead if you want to check that," Louise said to Ann.

Ann let her phone lie. "I don't have my reading glasses on me. And doubtful it's urgent. You can continue, Louise."

Stacey had already opened the message, sent to them both from Steve Heller, one of the producers loyal to Ann.

Joey hurt his right foot/ankle trying a bike stunt. It's swollen and he's in pain. I've sent him to get it X-rayed & checked out and I've shut down shooting for the day. But I have to wonder whose stupid fucking idea it was to put Joey on a bike.

What a lovely email. And how typical of Steve, to try to assign blame for what had clearly been an accident, the fault of no one except possibly Joey. What was worse, any minute now Ann would react the same way.

Ann said, "Stacey, you're being rude to Louise — she's waiting to tell us the hidden meaning the leather pants draped over her arm will communicate when Julie puts them on, and you're ignoring her."

Stacey put down her phone. "I'm sorry, Louise. I just found out there was a mishap on location — Joey has turned his ankle. I should make a few calls, find out more details. Can we take a break so I can deal with this, and get back to you in ten minutes?"

Louise said yes, of course, and Ann said, "Is that what the chime was on my phone? A message about this so-called mishap?"

"Probably. Steve sent us both the same email."

"Read it to me."

"I just told you what it said."

"I asked you to read it to me. Do I have to say please?"

Louise murmured that she'd be right back and retreated into the hallway. Stacey silently cursed Ann, and read Steve's email aloud.

When she was done, Ann just about crowed. "I know exactly whose stupid fucking idea it was. Yours!" Because she had somehow found out that the biking storyline had been Stacey's idea to begin with, and not Jordan the skater-writer's. And now Ann was going to hop onto the chair back and yell cock-a-doodle-doo.

30

Jenna drove up to the soundstage entrance at noon. Ann had asked her to be waiting outside at 12:20 with a cart or a car, but to hell with that. If Ann was going to make a set visit, Jenna would show her face too, increase her profile. And get a reminder of what being on-set felt like.

She'd tried to invite herself along to the costume meeting earlier that morning, too, because who had the best sense of style and fashion knowledge on the lot? She did. But Ann hadn't gone for it; she'd said she was perfectly capable of approving costumes without any assistance, including Stacey's.

Assorted crew guys were scattered around the set used as Julie's office when Jenna walked into the sound stage. Wendy, the actress who played Julie, sat in a director's chair off to the side, being touched up by hair and makeup people. The producer and director were hunched over a monitor, and Ann stood in the middle of the set, facing Ryan, who was dressed in his character's usual look: a plaid shirt and jeans. Ann was talking to Ryan and gesturing. A scruffy-looking AD and a boom mic guy leaned against the set wall and looked on.

Jenna came in close enough to hear what was being said, but something about the uneasy set of Ryan's shoulders — the way he leaned back at a slight angle from Ann, who was all up in his face — made Jenna take cover in a dark corner, where she couldn't easily be seen.

"Here's what you do," Ann said. "Start by running a finger down her arm, nice and slow. Like this." She picked up Ryan's hand with her own, placed it on her shoulder and traced a slow wavy line with his index finger on her skin.

Jenna put herself in Ryan's place, and imagined a male producer or director using her finger to trace patterns on his arm. That would be kind of skeevy.

Ryan laughed, uncomfortably. "You think?"

"That opening move will get the juices flowing in our female audience for sure," Ann said. "And you should follow it up with the old one-two of cupping her head in your right hand while going in for a love bite below her left ear. "

"A love bite?" Ryan said, and looked around, as if for help or rescue. But no one other than Jenna appeared to be paying attention to the scene he and Ann were playing; everyone else was involved in their own conversations.

Ann said, "Try it on me, so I can be sure you know what I mean. And your shirt should be open. Let's see that magnificent chest."

Ryan reached for his shirt front and slowly — reluctantly? — undid one snap, then two.

"All the way." Ann reached with two hands and ripped the shirt edges apart, like a drunk cougar mauling a male stripper at a club. Or like an executive who had forgotten what the company policy manual listed as grounds for sexual harassment charges.

"Go ahead," Ann said. "Show me what you're going to do."

Ryan smiled, shrugged, visibly took a breath, put his arms around Ann's black-clad bulk, cradled her head with his right hand, and holy hell, was his mouth actually on her neck now?

An ear-piercing shriek of a whistle made Jenna wince and Ryan jump off Ann like he'd been caught making out with his girlfriend's little sister. The whistle had come from Wendy, who strode over and said, in a teasing tone, "Ryan, you naughty boy! Everyone knows I hold exclusive spit-swapping rights with you. How dare you try to cheat on me with Ann?"

The AD and boom mic guy laughed, so did hair and makeup, and Ryan — whose face had expressed a lightning round of emotions in the past few seconds, including confusion, dawning realization, and gratitude — recovered, jokingly apologized to Ann for getting carried away, and promised Wendy he'd never do it again.

"I'll let the director take over here," Ann said, and turned to leave.

Jenna didn't stop to think. She stepped back, scooted down a narrow passageway and out of the building, ran to the golf cart, and drove it up to the door seconds before Ann emerged looking stormy.

"Hey, Ann," Jenna said, all innocence. "How'd your meeting go?"

"What the fuck are you talking about?"

"Didn't you have a costume meeting today?"

"Good point." Ann pulled out her phone, and handed it over. "Get Louise on the phone for me."

Jenna kept one eye on the road as she scrolled through Ann's contacts, found and called Louise's number, and handed back the phone.

"Louise?" Ann said. "I've changed my mind about that bandage dress for Wendy. It's too pretty. Put her in something slutty and trashy instead, would you? Something more vulgar. That's the look we want to go for." She put down her phone, sat for a minute, and said, "You know what I'd like to know? How that twat Wendy got her talent deal with the network. How many cocks has she sucked?"

Jenna said what she might have said if she hadn't seen the scene on the soundstage. "I thought you liked Wendy."

"I never *liked* her. I found her useful as an asset. But assets have a way of depreciating, some more quickly than others." She looked at Jenna. "You're still holding strong though, aren't you? You're still providing value?"

"I'm trying to." She drove up to the production office building. "What can I get you for lunch?"

31

Stacey had given vague answers to anyone who asked what she was doing for Thanksgiving, and implied that she was going out of town to meet up with relatives, when she intended to spend the holiday weekend the same way she had for the last few years, holed up in a secluded inn near La Jolla. There, she could run twice daily on the beach and up and down the cliff paths, subsist on yogourt and salad, avoid 2,000 calorie turkey dinners, brood, rail against fate, and develop her quash-Ann game plan.

Brooding and railing were on the agenda because Joey's sprained ankle had turned out to be a torn ligament that might take months to heal. And in the twenty-four hours since the injury, Ann had told anyone who'd listen that Stacey should be blamed for the accident, which made Stacey feel like Ann had won a round, even if only half the people she'd spoken to believed that Stacey was at fault.

On the Wednesday before the holiday, Stacey had her bag packed and waiting in the car so she could leave straight from work. At noon, she told Topher he could take off a few hours early, and she was thinking about following him out the door when she got the phone call she'd half-expected for a few weeks — the call to notify her that Pauline had died during the night.

"I'm so sorry to hear that," she said to the attorney who'd called, the man who was managing Pauline's affairs. "May I ask what time she passed?"

"The time of death was four fifty a.m."

When Stacey had been awake, and working in bed. Yet she'd heard nothing — no death rattle, no keening cries from Buddy, no curtains flapping in the wind because a window had suddenly blown open. Pauline had died without any sign of her passing. Almost as if she'd never lived.

The attorney said, "I'm calling in regard to Mrs. Robertson's dog. It's our understanding that you've agreed to adopt him. How soon could you pick him up?"

A few hours later, after Stacey had cancelled her reservation at the inn, she collected Buddy and a box of his belongings from Pauline's condo. The dog walker who'd stayed behind to arrange the transfer said Buddy had been subdued and mopey all day, but he got up willingly enough when Stacey came in and wagged his tail ever so slightly, and he didn't hesitate in her doorway. He walked right in and embarked on a sniffing tour around the living room, into her bedroom, and through the bathroom.

Stacey filled his water dish and set it on the floor in the kitchen. "There you go, Buddy," she said. "There's your water." He came over, lapped at it, and looked up at her as if to say: *Now what?*

"How about we go for a walk?" Stacey said. "Clear our heads, get some air." They'd walk up and down Ocean, see the sunset, then come home and mourn together — Buddy for Pauline, and Stacey for a time when beating Ann at her own game wasn't her primary goal.

32

Ann's Journal

I'm in my study with the door closed, writing to myself —
how's that for a heartwarming holiday picture? John has
gone out to buy some Armagnac for after dinner, which
had better not be a euphemism for him seeing some girl
on the side. I warned him the last time that I won't toler-
ate that kind of behaviour anymore, and I meant it.

Our friends will be here in an hour, and Rosa will
serve us the feast I ordered, and wine will be con-
sumed, and conversation will flow, though if anyone
suggests we go around the table and say what we're
thankful for, I may have to pick up the carving knife
from the turkey platter and lodge the blade in someone's neck. Except that I couldn't hit that small a
target, not with my fucked-up eyesight, not anymore.
If I ever could.

Anyway. This isn't going to be a pity party, so
when the topic shifts to politics, or the civil rights of
the downtrodden — before you go slavishly clean the
kitchen, fetch another bottle of wine for us, will you,

Rosa? — I will not interrupt whoever is jawing on in order to announce my eye diagnosis to the assembly.

No, tonight I'll do what I usually do on Thanksgiving — drink too much and stuff myself with food, which will taste good, not like ashes in my mouth. If I have to go blind, I'll go blind in style.

I won't tell anyone else that my vision is deteriorating apace — just as the doctors predicted — either. I had a bad moment on-set yesterday, when I fell prey to maudlin thoughts about all the beautiful things in the world that will soon be lost to my sight, including Ryan, my little Ken doll. I may have made an ass of myself over him for a few minutes there, but I snapped out of it.

This week's lesson: there may be certain outcomes I can't control, but I'll keep an iron grip on those I can, because I ain't done yet. There's plenty of hell yet to pay.

Hey Joe, get me a steaming cauldron I can cackle over and dance around, will ya?

God, I'm clever. Who else can pull off references to *Singing in the Rain* and *Macbeth* in the same one-liner? No one. My wit and wisdom are wasted on today's television audiences, I tell you. Wasted.

Though if Stacey were here, she'd say, "No one gets those outdated references anymore. *Singing in the Rain*? What are you, eighty?"

Hey Joe, better get me a tarantula after all.

33

Over the Thanksgiving break, Jenna flew to San Francisco to suffer through a meal with Andrew's judgy family, professionals with money who didn't hide what they thought of actors. "So many young people must go to Los Angeles every year chasing fame," Andrew's mother said. "And so few of them find it. What a waste."

Sitting at the Medway table, Jenna felt like the uneducated Valley girl she was, though afterward Andrew told her not to put herself down, that she was movie- and TV-smart rather than book-smart and there was nothing wrong with that. And when she took him the next day for a turkey dinner at her parents' house in Van Nuys — where the menu included green beans with canned french-fried onions, a marshmallow-topped sweet potato casserole, *and* nasi goreng — he was a big hit and friendly to everyone, even her embarrassing Indonesian cousins.

She told Kerry all this the week after, on the drive up to Ann's house, which Ann wanted decorated for Christmas. When Jenna had mentioned that Kerry was an interior designer now, and had staged houses for sale — here, she'd put up some pics of the staged rooms on Tumblr, weren't they stunning? — Ann told her to go ahead and hire Kerry for the job. This way Ann could look like a generous benefactor helping another underemployed actor, and get her house tricked out in the bargain.

Jenna snaked her car up Outpost Drive, her hands tightly gripping the wheel. She hated driving on the hill roads; there was always some jerk on her tail trying to go too fast. She said, "It could have been a worse holiday break, but there were too many family functions for it to be any fun. I would have preferred to go to Cabo or somewhere hot, lie around in a bikini, drink cocktails, and give thanks for a boyfriend who can pay for a five-star hotel."

"So get Andrew to take you somewhere like that for New Year's. We're going to the St. Regis in Kauai after Christmas. You should come! We could do girls' days at the spa while the boys play golf or surf."

"Andrew doesn't surf, I do."

"Even better. I'll get mud wraps, you can surf with some ripped Hawaiian dude you meet on the beach, Andrew and Eric will golf, and everyone will be happy when we meet for drinks and dinner at night."

Jenna turned onto Mulholland and a jerk in an SUV roared past them. "I'm not sure I'm ready for a couples vacation. I'm still getting used to living with Andrew."

"How long till he puts a ring on it? You expecting a Tiffany box under the tree this year, or what?"

"I hope not."

"Why not?"

"I'm not ready to settle down." She wasn't ready to settle, she meant. Though Andrew might be ready. Maybe she *should* start hinting about a Hawaiian trip, and distract him from any ideas about holiday proposals.

Jenna pulled into Ann's driveway and Kerry said, "Shit, this place is big. The decorating budget just doubled."

Jenna punched in the security code to open the electronic gate, drove around the curving driveway, and parked at the rear of the house, in front of one of four garage doors. "Ann said we're supposed to go in the back door. It should be to the left of the garages, and it should be red."

"There it is." Kerry pointed. "And does that door call out for a big honking wreath or what? Hold on, I want to take some pics." They got out and Kerry held up her iPad. She'd taken two shots with it when they heard a car coming around the driveway. It swung into view, revealed itself to be a five- or six-year-old Audi driven by a blonde wearing sunglasses, and stopped.

Kerry said, "Are we expecting anyone?"

"I don't think so. Ann said it's the maid's day off."

"That's no maid."

The woman sat and stared at them for a few seconds, then edged the car closer, powered down her window, and said, "Hi. I think I must have the wrong house. Is this number 4175?"

Jenna said no, this was 4195, and the woman said okay, thanks. She executed a tight three-point turn and took off.

Kerry said, "Is it just me, or was there something fishy about that chick?"

"What do you mean? She was looking for a house down the street."

"How'd she get through the gate without knowing the code?"

"It must not have closed after we drove through."

"She looked familiar, too. Like maybe I've seen her in something. Or worked with her before."

"Who haven't you worked with?" Jenna tried the door. "Hey, it isn't locked." She walked in, with Kerry behind her.

"Hello, hello," a male voice called. "I'll be right down."

Jenna, startled, dropped the keys on the floor.

Kerry whispered, "I thought no one was supposed to be here."

"Me, too." Jenna raised her voice. "John, is that you? It's Jenna, Ann's assistant. Ann asked me to come over with my decorator friend?"

Kerry pointed to herself and mouthed the words "my decorator friend?" and Jenna stifled a giggle.

John walked out onto the glass-partitioned second-floor gallery that overlooked the foyer. He had on a dress shirt worn tails out, pressed jeans, and were those Birkenstocks on his feet? "Jenna?" he said. "What on earth?"

Jenna explained about the holiday decorating assignment. She introduced Kerry and asked John if he would prefer they reschedule; they'd only come this afternoon because Ann hadn't expected anyone to be home.

He stood at the top of the stairs and looked out through the wall of windows while she spoke. One of his age-spotted hands rested on the railing, and the other held what looked like bourbon, in an Old-Fashioned glass. At two o'clock in the afternoon.

Had he heard what Jenna had said? Should she repeat it, or should she turn around and walk out? A phone — his phone — chimed. He glanced at it and said, "Come along and do what you have to do. I was on my way out anyway." He turned on his heel and walked down a corridor. Jenna heard a door close, then nothing.

Kerry waggled her eyebrows in a way that made Jenna want to laugh again, and said, "This foyer is nice and large." She held up her iPad and framed a shot on its screen. "It might be a good place for the tree. Does Ann want more than one?"

"Probably. She's turning her usual holiday party into a *Benjamins* one so she can expense everything, and she wants it to be lavish."

"Okay, got it. I'm going to walk around and make some notes."

More movement upstairs, and John reappeared, with shoes on and a jacket, in a hurry. He trotted down the stairs and said, "I'm leaving. You can let yourselves out and lock up?"

Jenna said yes, and apologized again for disturbing him. He grunted in reply, and walked through a passage that must have led to the garage. She heard another door open and close, then the muffled sounds of a car starting up and driving out. Goodbye.

Kerry was standing in the middle of the enormous living room that spanned the width of the house. "Is he gone?" she said.

"Yes."

"You realize that we came this close to catching him entertaining that hooker, or mistress, or whoever the hell she was — the chick in the Audi."

"She can't have been a hooker, come on. Maybe she was a masseuse. Or a personal trainer. Or someone coming over to sell him, like, a closet system."

"A closet system?"

"Or whatever it is people make a home visit to sell. Window coverings?"

"If she was coming here for a legit reason, she wouldn't have turned tail as soon as she saw us, now would she?"

Jenna sank into a chair. "You're right. And shit. I don't want to cover for John, but I don't want to tell Ann what we saw either. She's definitely the kill-the-messenger type."

"Tell her we came over, and he was here, but he left right after we arrived. I wouldn't mention Blondie. If this isn't his first rodeo, he's already concocted a story for why he was home when he wasn't supposed to be."

"Okay, but we can't tell anyone else about this. Including our guys."

"I won't tell a soul. Not because you asked me, but because I want to hit this decorating job out of the park and use it to get some others. You think Ann will allow *InStyle* to come in and photograph the place once I've made it look pretty?"

Jenna had only agreed to try kickboxing because Stacey asked her to, and so she could earn brownie points. But she liked the classes. When she did the kicking and punching drills, she felt strong, and tough, even in the girly gym with the beginners. Three weeks in, she was thinking she might come more often, on her own, and move up to the next level, which covered self-defence techniques and partnered drills.

So, she should have been more focused in class after her visit to Ann's house with Kerry. But she was distracted, wondering how Ann would react if she found out that John was cheating on her. Ann had been acting psycho enough lately; Jenna did not need news of an affair to set her off further. What she did need, for self-protection purposes, was to become tighter with Stacey, who she had started to think of as Sane Boss.

After class, when Jenna and Stacey sat down in the gym reception area to decompress and cool down, Jenna said, "What a great workout tonight! I loved the music."

"Never underestimate the force of a driving pop song."

"But it was weird; during the bag-punching drill, I was thinking about the show."

Stacey wiped her face with a towel. "Who did you imagine you were hitting?"

"I didn't want to punch anybody, but I was thinking about the Julie and Derrick characters, how Julie is sleeping with Nate, and every marriage on the show is in trouble."

"Dysfunctional relationships *are* what nighttime soaps are all about." Stacey looked amused. "You thought about that in class?"

"I guess I've become invested in that storyline."

"That marriage gets worse before it gets better, too. We're going to keep Derrick in the dark about the affair until at least ep 16, and then have him meet a wannabe sugar baby who he starts seeing after he finds out Julie's been cheating on him."

Jenna was no sugar baby — she'd paid her own way until recently, hadn't she? — but she could easily play one. Why was she even thinking about that, though? She wouldn't get a chance to audition for that part or any other.

Stacey seemed to expect a reply. What had she said last? That the Derrick character would start fooling around, too. Jenna said, "So I'll have to wait a while if I want a happy ending."

"You'll have to wait till the show ends, which I hope won't be for years." Stacey bent down and loosened the laces on her sneakers. "But why were you thinking about that storyline in particular? Does Ann talk a lot about the Julie and Nate relationship?"

Time to sing. "She did go off about Wendy the other day after she'd been on-set. She wanted to know 'how the fuck that twat Wendy' — her words, not mine — ever got her talent deal with the network, and how many people did she have to blow for it." Jenna took a moment to let it sink in that she was giving Stacey some solid intel here. "You know how Ann can be when she gets in a mood."

Stacey sat up. "Yeah, there's never a dull moment with her. Though lately I wonder if there's something new going on in her personal life. A reason that she's become so — I almost want to say *unstable*."

So Jenna wasn't the only person who thought Ann was a nutbar lately. "Maybe at her age, the problem is hormones — a lack of estrogen. She should eat more soy. But she hates healthy food." Jenna got up. Her work was done, her points made. "Ready to go? Where'd you park?"

"Right in front. Where did you?"

The door to the studio opened, and in walked a slim woman in workout clothes, her hair tied in a high ponytail. Jenna recognized her from the viewing party VIP list, and was trying to remember her name when the woman said, "Stacey? What are you doing here?"

"Hey, Lori. We've just done a class." Stacey looked from Jenna to Lori. "Have you two met? Lori, this is Jenna Kuyt, an actress who's been doing some behind-the-scenes work for us at the office. Jenna — Lori Painter from the network."

Lori said, "Hi, good to meet you," to Jenna, as if they hadn't met before, which was annoying, but Jenna said the same back, and asked what class Lori was taking.

"I'm at level two, and I love it. After a long day of meetings, these workouts provide me with a real outlet for pent-up aggression. Not that I have much." She did that jokey thing where she contradicted what she'd just said by nodding and mouthing the words, "Oh, yes I do." "But I didn't know you did martial arts, Stacey. How long have you been at it?"

"We've only been coming for a few weeks. We're going to incorporate kickboxing into one of the storylines on *The Benjamins*, so I wanted to get a feel for it firsthand. I talked Jenna into coming with me, and she's way better at it than I am."

Jenna said gee, thanks, that she was still learning, and that she liked it too.

"Great to see you here," Lori said. "I should get into class."

"Knock 'em out," Stacey said, and turned to go. She was holding the door open to leave when Lori said, "Let's talk soon, Stacey. You can catch me up on your plans for the show. I hear you've got some killer episodes coming up."

Did Jenna hear Stacey utter an enthusiastic "yes" under her breath and see her do a mini fist pump on their way out? Maybe not. Stacey sure seemed happy, though. And God, she was *so* much less moody than Ann.

34

Stacey lay in the crook of Cooper's arm and played with the hair on his chest. Which was a suckily domestic, couple-ish thing to do, but she thought she should try out — for research purposes — a short cuddle session, to get a feel for how other people lived. Everything was material, and who knew? One day she might want one of her characters to have sweet, vanilla sex with the last nice guy in L.A., and lie around with him in bed afterward. When that day came, Stacey would know what she was talking about when she picked apart the script. As long as, in the now, neither she nor Cooper got any ideas about being romantic or committed.

There'd been no thought or talk of seeing each other over Thanksgiving, for instance, or of meeting each other's relatives. Though Cooper *had* enthusiastically embraced Stacey's new roommate as soon as they were introduced. "Who's the puppy?" he said. "Who's the puppy?" And for a good ten minutes, he played a tug-of-rope game with Buddy that they both seemed to enjoy.

Cooper's phone rang on the bedside table closest to Stacey. She picked it up, saw Riley's name, and passed it to him. He pressed ignore and put the phone back down, but the five-minute limit Stacey had imposed on cuddling had been reached, so she rolled off him.

"How was your Thanksgiving?" she said. "Good food? Any family tension?"

"It was peaceful. My parents were all over my brother's two little kids, and my sister brought her boyfriend from Seattle that everyone likes." He patted his flat stomach. "And I didn't eat too many carbs, though my mom makes the best mashed potatoes and homemade dinner rolls. They're addictive."

"Uh-huh."

"I had to cover for Riley on Saturday and Sunday though. Dude decided at the last minute to go away for the weekend and left me to run two bike tours alone. I had to call someone in to man the shop while I was on the trails. Kind of a piss-off."

Stacey examined his profile, his unlined forehead. He didn't look or sound upset. Was he really angry, and just good at hiding his emotions? Or was he as laid-back and unperturbed by everyday aggravations and petty shit as he seemed to be, with his apparent indifference to the spotlight, his willingness to step back into the wings of any drama?

Stacey said, "Maybe he was calling you to apologize."

"When?"

"Just now. On your phone."

"Oh yeah. Maybe. But probably not. I saw him this morning, and he thanked me for covering for him, but he didn't say he was sorry."

He was so unbothered.

"I'm curious," she said. "How angry were you at him? So angry you wanted to tell everyone you know, including me? So angry that you're now contemplating revenge?"

He turned on his side to face her. "Come on, who'd think about revenge after a small thing like that?"

She almost said that having to work with Ann would make anyone consider desperate measures, but no. It was one thing to have allowed Cooper to see her orgasm face in daylight. It would be another to confess to having plotted several scenarios to wreck Ann's career and reputation. She said, "Don't evade the question. How pissed were you?"

"Not even halfway to a level where I would want to punch Riley in the face."

"So, you could be roused to violence, under the right, extreme circumstances."

"I don't know. I've never hit anyone in my life, but I'd like to think that I have it in me to fight if the situation called for it. If someone attacked me and I had to protect myself, or protect someone else."

Good answer. Stacey might have said the same thing about herself, might have admitted that she only fantasized about making Ann go away when Ann threatened Stacey's livelihood. She might have confided that in Cooper if he meant more to her than a walk on the tame side, and if she thought she could trust him. If she thought she could trust anyone.

Stacey went into work earlier than usual the next morning. There was a 6:00 a.m. call for a family brunch scene at the Benjamin manse, to be shot on a soundstage across the lot, and she wanted to stick her head in, and show herself, to friends and enemies alike, as unbowed and unbroken since Joey's accident. Also as in charge and involved. Ann would not be present, either. Stacey had checked her schedule, and Ann was not due in till ten.

The sun had just risen when Stacey drove into the studio parking lot at 7:00. The offices were still dark, but shit was popping on the soundstage. She pulled on her cloak of congeniality, and worked the room. She glad-handed cast, crew, director, and writer, made lively small talk, and put on a convincing portrayal — if she said so herself — of a beneficent leader, there to show support for the troops.

She was standing near the craft service table talking to Joey, who was on crutches, when Ryan, in costume for the scene, came over, poured himself a coffee, and stood by with the cup in his hand, like he wanted to speak to one of them. Doubtful he was waiting for Stacey — she and Ryan hadn't spoken since the retreat, and hadn't exchanged more than three sentences then. She wrapped it up with Joey and made to step away, but Ryan followed her. "Hey, Stacey. Got a minute?"

"Sure. How you doing? You look well-rested for so early in the morning."

"Thanks. You, too."

He did look good, but jittery. Bright-eyed. Could he be high?

He said, "I wanted to talk to you alone. Could we maybe go find a private corner?"

"Okay." What could this be about? Had he broken his promise not to have sex with Vanessa until she was legal? She'd seen pics on Just Jared of Ryan out on the town with some other young actress, so she'd thought he and Vanessa were done. Shit, this had better not be a plea for more lines, more scenes, a bigger story arc.

Coffee cup in hand, Ryan led her down a hallway, and stopped to lean against a wall near an exit door. Where no one but Stacey could see him rub his cheek a few times and run his fingers through his standing-on-end hair — both would have to be retouched before his scene — or hear him say, "Some weirdness happened on-set last week. With Ann. Did you hear?"

She shook her head. She hadn't heard. And why not? What was the point of fostering loyalty in the ranks if she didn't get reports on episodes of Ann's bad behaviour? Provided that's what Ryan was talking about. "What happened?"

Ryan lowered his voice so that Stacey had to move closer to hear him. He said, "We were shooting a scene from episode 12 — the scene where I have sex with Julie in her office, with the door locked?"

"Yes, I know it."

"We were blocking the scene with the director and the AD. I didn't even know Ann was here watching. She marches on-set, and starts telling me how and where to kiss Julie, like at what angle, and on which exact spot on her neck, and where to put my hands. Then she says I should expose my chest and she pulls my shirt open."

The dirtbag — had Ann lost her mind? It wasn't easy to maintain an air of puzzlement rather than devilish enjoyment at hearing that Ann had screwed up royally, but Stacey did her best. "Was she trying to direct you?"

"Kinda. But after I said I'd see about giving her suggestions a try, she said, 'Try it now. On me. So I can be sure you know what I mean.'"

If Ann kept this kind of shit up, and in front of witnesses, she could cut the ripcord on her own parachute. "I see."

"Yeah."

"Were the cameras rolling? Did anyone get this on tape?"

"No."

Damn. "So, what'd you do? Close your eyes and think of England?"

"What?"

"Sorry, I shouldn't kid around. Did you take your shirt off and make out with her?"

"I didn't know what to do, and the director and AD weren't saying much, so I put my arms around her, and started to, like, kiss her neck. Then Wendy stepped in, and made a joke about how she has exclusive make-out rights with me, and people laughed, and Ann walked off set, and that was the end of it."

This incident must have been what caused Ann to mutter darkly to Jenna about Wendy, to ask who she'd blown to get her talent deal. Stacey made a mental note to check the writers' room logs to see if Ann had snuck in any future humiliating plot developments for the Julie character. Ann could be counted on to do something like that. Stacey said, "So, in the end, no real harm was done?"

"I guess not, but it was awkward. And creepy, to be honest."

She could imagine how creepy it would be for a pin-up like Ryan to have a woman his mother's age pull casting-couch stunts on him. "Excuse me for asking, but why are you telling me this?"

He hunched up his shoulders. "I thought you might talk to her, ask her to back off. I'd speak to her myself, but I don't want to hurt her feelings, or insult her."

Stacey was sure he didn't want to get fired from the show either.

His trademark grin put in an appearance for the first time that morning. "You could be subtle about it. Tactful. You're good at that."

"I don't know, Ryan. I feel for you, but you've put me in an uncomfortable position." And mightn't she prefer that Ryan bring a sexual harassment suit against Ann? Not against Two Women Walking, though, she wouldn't want that. "Don't get me wrong: I appreciate what it took for you to come to me with this. Let me think about what to do." If anything, except let the incident fester.

He wielded the grin again. "Thanks, I owe you one."

Soon everyone would.

DECEMBER

35

Ann had asked Jenna to pick up lunch for her from Joan's on Third on her way into work, which added a half hour to Jenna's morning drive, when Ann could easily have had her driver pass Joan's on *her* way in. Whatever. Jenna picked up the high-fat, high-calorie salads Ann requested, and now that it was lunchtime, Ann wanted Jenna to sit with her while she ate, so Ann could talk to her with her mouth full.

"I have two topics to cover," Ann said. "First, the Christmas party. Wait, where's my fork? And could you pour me a glass of lemonade?"

Jenna sometimes wondered if Ann got a kick out of being served by Jenna specifically, or if she just liked being waited on, period. She fetched Ann's fork and lemonade anyway, closed her nostrils to the pungent smell of blue cheese in the potato salad, and prepared to take notes.

Ann issued last-minute instructions to be passed on to the caterer, the valet parking service, and the jazz quartet, and asked Jenna for an update on the party RSVPs. "Start with who's coming from the show."

Jenna read the names on the list. Principal cast members, executive producers, staff writers, and production department heads were all accounted for. "And me," Jenna said. In case Ann had had any thought of not inviting her.

"Invite your designer friend, too. That way, she can freshen up the decor for the party and not charge me another arm and leg to do it."

"I thought you liked Kerry's work."

"I did. It's surprisingly tasteful, but it was expensive. Invite her. She'll come. It's the least she can do after I let magazine people in to photograph the house and gave her the credit."

In Jenna's opinion, Ann was as much or more of a publicity whore as Kerry. And a credit hog, too. But she said, "Okay, I will."

"What about Stacey? Is she coming?'

"I read out her name already."

"Fuck. Who else have we got?"

Jenna ran down the list of studio and network execs who had responded, and named the higher-ups who hadn't. "And no plus-ones this time, right?"

"Right. Why should we pay for them to eat and drink? Though I'll get John to put in an appearance as host. If we're speaking that day."

Did Ann know about John's girl on the side or not? Maybe Ann did know, and didn't care. Maybe they had an open marriage.

"All right, next topic. Is the door closed?"

Jenna turned and looked behind her, the way Ann was facing, in view of the closed door. What the hell? "Yes."

"Good. Because what I'm about to say is strictly between us. Do you understand?"

She *did* know about John's affair.

"I understand."

Ann put down her fork, pushed away the plate of food, and swivelled around in her office chair to look out the window into the parking lot. This must be important.

"I've been thinking," she said. "About my future, and the future of Two Women Walking, and the future of *The Benjamins*. And your future."

Had Ann read her mind? Did she know that Jenna had thought about having a sit-down with her agent to talk about the upcoming pilot season, to ask if there was any point in putting herself out there for it, or should she just give up on acting, now and forever? Jenna looked at her nails. She was due for a manicure. And she should book a pedicure while she was at it, and when was her next waxing appointment? Hold up, Ann wasn't speaking; she had taken a dramatic pause. She still sat in profile — patchy hair, double chin, protruding belly and all — and gazed out the window. What had she said? Something about the future.

A big fat tear slid down Ann's cheek.

Oh, God, now what? "Are you okay?"

Ann pulled out a tissue from the box on her desk and wiped her face. "No, I'm not. How could I be when I'm going blind?"

"What do you mean? I thought your eye problems had cleared up."

"That's because I let you think that." Ann dried her tears and spilled the story on her condition: she had something called wet macular degeneration. The specialists she'd seen had told her there was no cure. Her eyesight had already deteriorated by 50 percent, and she could only expect more impairment in the months and years to come.

"I'm so sorry," Jenna said. No wonder Ann had been such an asshat lately. "What will you do about your work? How will you keep on? Will you have to retire?"

"Not if I can help it. Not till I'm good and ready." Ann swivelled back to face her desk. "I'm not going to stop running this show. Or any new shows I develop."

"You're going to develop new shows?"

"I can't squander my gift. I was put on this earth for a reason: to entertain the masses."

It was wild how highly she thought of herself. "What about Stacey? Does she know about this? She could pick up some of the slack. She's so organized, she's on top of everything."

"NO. Stacey doesn't know, and I don't want you to tell her. As soon as she finds out, she'll use my infirmity as an excuse to wrest the show away from me. Fuck that noise. I'm going blind, not dying. And I'll still be in charge. With the help of my trustworthy friends. Like the producers I can count on, the guys who have been with me for years, the ones who aren't self-serving, over-ambitious traitors."

Here she went again with the paranoia about Stacey. Jenna almost rolled her eyes, as a test to see if Ann would notice, to gauge exactly how blind she was, but she didn't risk it.

Ann said, "I hope I can count on your help, too. How does the title of associate producer sound? I'd like to make you one. I'd like you to become my eyes."

That last bit sounded scary, like a scene from a horror movie. For a disorienting few seconds, Jenna pictured herself lying unconscious on an operating table, like in *Minority Report*, while a gowned and masked doctor plucked her eyes out of their sockets and inserted them into Ann's head.

But she liked the sound of the associate producer title. How good would that look on her IMDB profile? And on business cards she could have printed. "What would it mean for me to become your eyes? What would I do?"

"Come with me wherever I go and tell me what you see. We'd be a team."

Yeah sure, a team. More like Jenna would be Ann's caregiver. Though if she were Ann's eyes, she'd be able to influence Ann's decisions. Steer them in ways that worked in Jenna's favour. She didn't know how yet, but if she agreed to this, the odds were good she'd find a way to get what she wanted. "This would be a promotion, right? You'd pay me more?"

Again, Ann seemed to size her up with a look. She wasn't blind yet. "Of course. Give me a week or two to put through the paperwork, and we'll make your new title official and get you an increase."

"Let's do it then," Jenna said. "Let's give it a try."

36

"Don't look now," Kerry said to Jenna in Ann's living room, on party night, fifteen minutes before the official start time, "but is that the blonde chick from the Audi setting up the bar on the terrace?"

Jenna waited a discreet ten seconds, then peeked out the window wall at the woman in a cater-waiter uniform — white shirt and black pants — positioned at the cloth-covered table outdoors. "Crap. It *is* her."

Kerry adjusted a vase of hydrangeas on the mantelpiece. "You'd better fasten your seatbelt. Looks like it's going to be a bumpy night."

Ann walked into the room, her beaded caftan rustling with every movement. Jenna thought she looked terrible — her heavy makeup aged her a good ten years, she had on a new pair of glasses with round frames that made her look like an owl, and her hair was spiked straight up, in a misguided attempt to create volume and height out of straw. Or maybe to play up the owl theme.

"Did I just hear an allusion to *All About Eve*?" Ann said. "What century have I walked into?"

Jenna said, "Kerry and I were playing Name That Movie Quote," and she did not react to the ha-ha-nice-save face Kerry made behind Ann's back. "You look good, Ann. Very festive. I love those green glasses. Are they new?"

Ann growled, "Who the fuck do you think you're talking to?" and, after an awkward pause, Kerry said, "I know! *Taxi Driver*. 'You talkin' to me?'"

Jenna laughed, hiding any sign of her desire to strangle them both.

Ann peered at her through the ugly glasses. "Where can I get a drink around here?"

The closest bar was outside, where John now stood, talking to the blonde bartender. "I'll get you one," she said. "What would you like?"

"A dry martini." The doorbell rang. "Kerry, be a good girl and get me that drink. And if you see my husband, haul his ass into this room. Jenna, go to the door and greet our first guest. What do you bet it's Stacey? It would be just like her to come early."

Kerry tipped an imaginary hat so that only Jenna could see, said, "One dry martini coming up," and headed out to the bar; Ann took up a hostess-y position leaning against the mantel; Jenna went to the door, which had already been opened by a caterperson, and greeted not Stacey, but one of the producers.

It *was* going to be a bumpy night.

37

Stacey kept no written or digital record of her battles with Ann, but she knew exactly where they each stood on her mind's score sheet, and, on the night of Ann's party, to her dismay, they were tied. Every time Stacey pulled ahead — when Ann crossed the line from eccentric to crazeballs in public, or when Stacey cemented a bond with a former Ann acolyte — Ann hustled her way back into the game. By getting good press in a high-profile media outlet, or by earning good reviews and ratings for an episode she had taken a solo writing credit on. By hosting a fancy, no-expense-spared employee party at her vast sprawl of a house in the Hollywood Hills, a party that would make her look generous and big-hearted.

Stacey could never pull off an event like that — her condo wasn't big or stylish enough. Besides, she'd never understood the point of seasonal decoration. She had no interest in filling her home with extravagant displays of colour-matched flowers.

Resentful of the party or not, Stacey still had to show up, so she bought a new dress that showed off her legs, and new shoes of a height and style that arthritic, broken-down Ann could never wear, and she spent more time than usual getting ready. She'd walk into Ann's house looking glam, and search for ways to score bonus points while she was there.

The party was in full swing when Stacey arrived. She greeted Ann with the curt civility that had become their new norm, made the rounds inside saying hello to the people who mattered — in this setting, everyone — and stepped out onto the terrace, where tall propane heaters had been set up to encourage outdoor lounging. She saw Ann's husband John over by the infinity pool, holding forth to a captive Bonnie, whose expression of polite interest was splitting at the seams. Stacey would go over and rescue her in a minute, after she picked up a drink.

Well, look who was tending bar — Shevaun, the social climber from the viewing party. Stacey said, "Perrier in a martini glass, please. And hi again. You worked the viewing party we did in Hermosa Beach, right? I'm Stacey, one of the exec producers on the show."

Shevaun cracked a cautious smile. "I remember you, sure. The show's still doing well, I hear. Congratulations."

"Thanks. How's bartending treating you?"

Shevaun slid the glass of Perrier over. "Not bad, but I'm giving it up soon. I'm working on a career change." And without meaning to, Stacey guessed, Shevaun glanced across the terrace at John. His back was turned to them, but his shock of white hair shone under the white fairy lights like an unholy halo.

Stacey smiled. If Shevaun was working on securing John as her sugar daddy, Ann was bound to find out, get incensed, and be humiliated. She wished Shevaun luck with her new venture, and went over to hang with Bonnie. Within two minutes, she'd subtly pressured John into winding up his anecdote, complimented its lame punch line, tolerated him looking her up and down, and pulled Bonnie away on the pretext they had a pressing business matter to discuss.

"Thanks for saving me," Bonnie said, when they'd sat down on two poolside lounge chairs. "That guy is toxic. He reminds me of my father, in all the worst ways."

"Yeah, I picked up the SOS message you blinked with your eyelids from twenty feet away."

Bonnie raised her glass. "Here's to avoiding lecherous old farts."

Stacey clinked glasses and listened to Bonnie's acidly funny observations about every partygoer within view. She watched Shevaun turn her bartending duties over to a co-worker and slip into the house via a side entrance that John had skulked through a few minutes before. Stacey laughed at Bonnie's latest quip, and saw a light come on, then quickly go off, in a second-floor room. Could the not-so-young lovers really be as stupid as to tryst in Ann's own house, during Ann's own party? Stacey couldn't have asked for better bad behaviour if she'd spiked their drinks with aphrodisiacs. Or written them a script.

The best part was that she could not be more innocent of the goings-on — not only had she not orchestrated tonight's rendezvous, she was out in the open talking to Bonnie while it happened, where any number of people could see her having a good time. Or she was until her phone buzzed with a text from Jenna:

Help. Ann's losing it. Kitchen.

Stacey excused herself. She walked, not ran, through the guests on the terrace, and into the big open living room, just in time to see the back of a long-haired blonde woman, in a coat over black pants, go out through the front entrance. Cue the door slam. An odd tableau presented itself in the rest of the room — people stood frozen in clusters, pretending to chat, while the jazz quartet played on from the glassed-in gallery above the main space. Stacey passed by Ryan, who muttered, "I told you she's crazy." She made her way to the kitchen and opened the door just in time to hear Ann scream at top, hysterical volume, "Get out! Now! And don't come back!"

Such melodrama.

Another setup awaited her inside the kitchen — Ann stood behind a marble-topped island, leaning heavily on her hands, like a black-skirt Italian mama about to roll out some pasta dough. A wooden block that bristled with heavy-duty knife handles sat close to her right hand — very Chekhov's gun.

John faced Ann across the island. His normally red face was redder than ever, a cowlick of white hair veering off from his head at an oblique angle. His tie was crooked, one shirttail was out, and the other — cliché alert — was sticking out of his open fly. Cowering in the breakfast nook were two women in chef's whites holding metal baking sheets laden with mini-cupcakes decorated in Christmas colours, and Jenna, whose distressed eyes implored Stacey to do something, and fast.

John's voice shook with rage, but at least he kept his volume down to a hissing level. "Don't tell me what to do and where to go. Who the hell do you think you are?"

As entertaining, if way over-the-top, as this scene was, Stacey didn't want to see it continue. She signalled to Jenna to take the kitchen staff out the back way. She exited through the door she'd come in and faced the living room crowd, which had grown in the few minutes since she'd left it.

Stacey turned to the two closest people, who were Jenna's friend Kerry and Peter, the actor. "The party's over," she said. "Pass it on."

Peter and Kerry quickly and quietly passed on the message. The jazz quartet continued to play as the guests began to move out slowly, and Stacey went off in search of Jenna. She found her at the door that led to the garage. She was helping the catering staff pack.

"The party's breaking up," Stacey said. "We should go, too. Let Ann deal with her marital troubles in peace."

"I can't leave the caterers here alone. And the valets, and the musicians. I'll see them out, then I'll go."

"I'd stay with you, but I think Ann would prefer me gone. You're sure you're okay here?"

"I will be. Thanks for coming when I texted you. I didn't know what to do or who to call." Jenna looked behind her, saw no one, and dropped her voice to a whisper anyway. "One minute I'm helping her play hostess, and the next she catches John screwing that bartender upstairs, and all hell breaks loose."

From the kitchen, Stacey heard John yell, "You're damn right I'm leaving," and the sound of footsteps coming their way.

"Quick," Jenna said, "in here." She pulled Stacey into a powder room and closed and locked the door.

"Gee, I'm flattered, Jenna," Stacey said, "but —"

Jenna shushed her, and they waited, quiet, looking at each other through the mirror above the sink. More footsteps, muffled now, could be heard coming downstairs, and in the hallway outside the powder room, followed by the sound of a car starting up and driving away.

Jenna said, "Stay here. I'll go see if the coast is clear," and slipped out. Stacey applied some lip gloss. She checked her phone and read a text from Bonnie:

WTF is going on? Most dramatic holiday party ever, or what?

Stacey laughed out loud.

Jenna came back and reported that John had left and Ann had gone outside by the pool. Stacey resisted making a crack about Ann drowning her sorrows, or just plain drowning, and told Jenna they'd speak later. She spent twenty minutes working her way through the crowd in the valet parking line. She dismissed the incident as nothing to worry about to everyone she saw, and assured the sometimes concerned, sometimes avidly curious faces turned toward her that Ann wasn't feeling well, was over-tired — and who wouldn't be, with her schedule?

Once in her car, she took off her shoes and drove barefoot down the hill road to Franklin. She was headed home, but at the first side street, she pulled over and texted Cooper a booty call. She brought up her Twitter feed on her phone and looked for any sign of rogue tweets reporting the incident. A couple of the actors tweeted actively about the show and had become unofficial, unpaid show publicists. They probably knew better than to bite the hand that created them, but Stacey refreshed the feed repeatedly anyway. Because how cool would it be if Ann's tantrum and marital spat became news? So cool.

38

When the last party guests had left, and the catering truck and the valet parking van had driven away, Jenna almost walked out without saying goodbye to Ann.

But she couldn't when it was only eleven o'clock, and Ann sat alone in the dark on the terrace, gazing away from the house — the scene of the crime — and out at L.A. And when it didn't look like John was coming back, not tonight. And when the combination of your husband being publicly caught cheating and you going blind would destroy and depress most people. It might even destroy and depress the indefatigable (Jenna had looked up the word) Ann Dalloni.

She opened one of the glass doors and stepped outside. "Ann? Everyone's gone, and I'm about to go."

Ann turned her head to the side, showed her profile. "Come, Jenna. Come sit by me. Be my witness."

Jenna came. "I'm here." She'd sit and listen for a few minutes, no more. "How are you doing?"

"What a stupid question. I'm livid with rage. At everyone. Including you, if you're going to pity me."

"Sorry." God forbid Jenna should try to be considerate. What did Ann want? That Jenna be livid too?

"I've been thinking about what happened, and why. You do realize this is all Stacey's fault, don't you?"

"What? How?"

"Stacey set John up with that bartender; she made it happen. It's part of her evil plan to destroy me."

Jenna took a breath and a beat. "I know you're upset. But it's hard to believe Stacey would do that." Evil plans seemed more like Ann's specialty.

"So, she's won you over too, has she, with her fake friendliness, her bogus concern for others? That's all an act; she's as cold-hearted as they come. I know how determined she is. I recognize her killer instinct. The day I took Stacey under my wing was the day she started plotting to ride my coattails all the way to the top. Talk about *All About Eve*."

What do you say when the boss you're trying to be sympathetic to about her personal problems acts like a paranoid freak? How about: "You think life is imitating movies now?"

"I think you should look closely at Stacey some time when her guard is down. Look and see how dead her eyes are. Dead like the eyes of a sociopath."

"And yet she seems so nice on the surface."

"Nice? Hah, I say. HAH!"

Should she divert the conversation by asking Ann about John, and whether their fight was major, or did they do this kind of thing all the time? That didn't seem like a safe topic for discussion either. There were no safe topics. She said, "I should get going. Andrew is waiting for me at home. He worries when I'm out driving late at night."

"I hope you're not thinking of marrying that guy. Give him a few years, and he'll cheat on you, too. If he isn't fucking around on you already, it's only because someone like Stacey hasn't put temptation directly in his path."

What? Andrew had more reason to fear being cheated on than Jenna ever would. It was time for Ann to stop with the crazy talk, take a downer, and go to bed. "Can I get you anything before I go?"

"No. I'll walk you to the door." Ann pushed herself up and out of the chair. "All I want is to wake up tomorrow and find out that everything that's happened in the last six months was a bad dream, like on *Dallas* back in the day. Remember that? Of course you don't." She straightened her clothing and took a first step. "Now, if I were to wake up and find out Stacey went for a six a.m. run and got hit by a car, that would be good news too."

"Ann, please — don't say that."

"On third thought, it might be better if I didn't wake up at all."

Jenna checked Ann's face — she had on a demented smile. Was she trying to be funny, or was the reference to death a cry for help? A montage played in Jenna's mind in which she went home to sleep, and got a phone call the next morning from Ann's hysterical maid, the one who had come in and found Ann's lifeless, bloated body face-down in her bed. One pale, fleshy arm hung over the edge of the mattress, and a suicide note that blamed Stacey, scrawled in Ann's big blind handwriting, lay on the bedside table.

No. Her imagination was overactive, it always had been.

They walked into the house — that is, Jenna walked, and Ann shuffled, slow-mo, behind her. In the foyer, Jenna said, "You were joking back there, right? I don't want to leave and find out later you did something crazy."

Ann made a dismissive *pfft* sound. "If I do something crazy, I'll make sure you're the first to know." She opened the door. "Now get out, so I can double lock the door, and load my gun in case John tries to come back. I'll shoot him right in the dick if he does — that'll show him."

Jenna turned back in the doorway. What a heavy load Ann was, in every sense of the word. "You don't really have a gun, do you?"

"Of course not. Go home."

Jenna got into her car. She checked her phone and found two missed calls from Kerry and a text from Stacey:

Did you make it out alive?

She texted back that she had, messaged Kerry that they'd talk later, and drove home. After she'd downed two tequila shots, she sat down with Andrew in the living room and told him what had happened.

He laughed when she finished. "That's a great story." He pulled out his phone and opened his browser. "Have any of the gossip sites picked up on this yet?"

"I hope not. Ann would hate that. And I don't like being caught in the middle between crazy powerful Ann and sane but less powerful Stacey."

"You should side with the person who's going to come out on top. Back the winner."

Like she was doing by dating him?

"How do I know who will win?"

"Let's think about that: Ann's got the pedigree, but if she's been as inconsistent as you say lately, maybe she's already in decline, and Stacey's the horse to back. Or neither may survive — the network may be close to firing both of them. And that's if they decide to pick up the show for next season."

"What do you mean? *The Benjamins* will get a second season pickup for sure. It's had so much buzz, and the numbers have been good."

"Not guaranteed-renewal good. And the season is far from over."

Jenna picked up a throw pillow from the couch and hugged it. "If only I could get a good part on a good show, and get the hell out of there."

Andrew reached for her hand and held it. "You want to quit, go ahead. I've got you covered."

So she could become a Real Housewife? No thanks. Her phone vibrated on the coffee table and Kerry's name showed on the screen. "I should talk to her." She got up, said into the phone, "Was that a shitshow or what?" and went upstairs.

39

tacey was scheduled to see Ann for the first time since the Christmas party on the following Monday, at a 10:00 a.m. casting session for a young actor to play the Arielle character's love interest in a multiple-episode arc.

When Stacey walked into the meeting room, she was greeted by Judy, the casting director, who had been at the party but did not refer to how it had ended, not in front of her two assistants, who busied themselves with coffee, water, muffins, and call sheets. Instead, Stacey engaged Judy in small talk about that morning's traffic, though Stacey had missed it, having been in the office since seven-thirty.

She said cheery good mornings to the producers who trooped in a few minutes later, to the director of the episode, to Bonnie, representing the writers, and to Lori Painter, who came in with Gideon and Nicole. What a treat to have both studio and network present to approve the casting of a small part. Which meant what, exactly? Nothing good. And that there might be fireworks.

Last in was Ann, her head held high. Jenna preceded her up the aisle and guided her to a seat at the front of the room like she was escorting her elderly grandmother. What was this now?

Judy called the session to order, reminded everyone why they were there, and introduced the first of three candidates she had narrowed down from a field of would-be TV hotties.

Guy number one was blond and blue-eyed, with a gym rat build. Stacey's first impression: he looked too cocky to play the poet jock who would tenderly take Arielle's virginity.

When he'd read through the sides with a casting assistant, Judy asked him about his credits (a Nickelodeon kidcom, guest spots on a couple of teen-centric CW shows) and his other talents — he was a musician, weren't they all — and he was thanked and sent away.

"Any top-line comments before I call in the next one?" Judy said.

"I like his voice, that sexy breaking thing he had," Ann said.

"He was pretty," Stacey called out from her seat at the back of the room, and a few others murmured agreement. "Maybe too pretty?"

Someone said he was awfully Aryan-looking, Rob the producer said he had the right build for football, and Bonnie said she'd have trouble believing that that kid, with those blond tips, was any kind of poet.

Judy said, "Let's move on." Ann whispered a question in Jenna's ear, Jenna whispered back an answer, and Ann nodded.

The next actor was shorter and slimmer than the first, and had a mop of dark curly hair and hazel eyes. His read of the sides was charming and quirky, to go with his nose ring and tattoos — a prominent one of a bird or a bat on his neck, and a full sleeve of ink on his right arm. Not a look you'd expect for a sensitive jock role, but maybe he was trying to stand out from the pack. Or Judy could be pushing him for reasons of her own — she sometimes put the candidates she favoured in the second position, Stacey had noticed, rather than in last.

"Too Jewish?" someone said, when he'd gone.

"He's not too pretty, I'll say that. Not sure I'd buy him as a jock, though."

"Did he read as gay to anyone else? Or was that hipster I felt?"

Ann said, "The main vibe I got off him was geek, with a capital G."

Lori Painter turned in her seat and gave Ann an incredulous look. "Geek? With the nose ring and those tattoos? Really?"

Jenna did her Boss Whisperer routine again in Ann's ear, and Ann said, loud enough that Stacey could hear: "Why didn't you tell me that, then?"

To the rest of the room, Ann said, "I meant that he seemed like a geek pretending to be a bad boy. When what we're looking for is neither."

"If you say so," Lori said, heavy on the sarcasm, and Stacey might have chalked up a point against Ann if she weren't processing what it meant that Ann's vision was clearly failing, big-time.

Actor number three looked biracial — half-black and half-white. He wore his hair in a buzzcut, and had killer cheekbones and gorgeous blue-green eyes. Could Ann see his eyes, Stacey wondered, or was his face a blur? And how on earth would Ann keep positioning herself as the Queen of Television Drama, chief arbiter of all things, if she couldn't see?

Number three's build was lean and athletic. He'd be believable as a basketball player or a running back, he read well, and he had a contagious, relaxed laugh. He would have been a shoo-in except that his look was so similar to Arielle's — he could be her brother, or her cousin.

When he'd left the room, Nicole said, "Nice find, Judy. He's adorable." Stacey said, "Yeah, I liked him too," and Bonnie said, "Smokin'!" and fanned herself with his resumé and photo.

Gideon said, "I'm not sure his look is a good fit with the rest of the cast, though. What do you think, Stacey, Ann? Is this character supposed to be like or unlike Arielle?"

Ann said, "Both: he's supposed to be sensitive like her, and jockish and popular, unlike her."

"Should he resemble her physically though? Regarding that last actor."

How much did Stacey love it when someone else challenged or needled Ann? It was like being given a gift.

Ann said, "We could go either way in terms of how similar or dissimilar he looks. But I like number one best anyway, so who cares about number three?"

"I do, actually," Lori said, and Gideon and Nicole said they did too, and there was a moment's uncomfortable silence during which even Jenna was quiet.

With some difficulty, Ann rose to her full height, which was 5'4" in flat shoes, and said, with a forced laugh in her voice, "What, are you guys ganging up on me now?" No one responded. "Stacey — where are you?"

"Right here," Stacey said, without getting up.

"Which candidate do you like? Don't go all sycophantic now and say number three."

Stacey relaxed her body language for the benefit of the sighted people in the room — let them see how unruffled she was. "I thought number two brought something fresh to the party," she said, with a nod to Judy. A pat on the back, an acknowledgement of effort made, was always a good idea. "And either one or three could do the job, and appeal to the teen fans, each in his own way. As usual, Judy has brought us strong candidates to choose from."

Judy bowed her head in acknowledgement of Stacey's comment, but Ann said, "I should have known you'd waffle," and sat down.

Stacey heard one or two murmurs — could someone have objected to Ann slamming her? — then Lori said, "Thanks for your input everyone, and thank you, Judy, we'll get back to you. Ann and Stacey, can you stay behind for a minute?"

Everyone but Stacey and Ann got the hint and left, including Jenna, though not until she'd whispered to Ann that she was going.

When the door had closed behind the last person out, Lori said, "Ann, I love you to death, but you have *got* to ease up on the public spatting. With Stacey, and with everyone else. That was outrageous."

Ann said, "How about we ease up on studio and network attending a routine casting session? What happened to you approving cast members *after* we've chosen them?"

Lori rubbed her right temple like she had a headache. A headache named Ann, Stacey hoped. Lori said, "Let's cut to the chase. Who do you want for the part, Ann?"

"The first guy."

Lori looked at Stacey. "Who do you like?"

There was only one correct answer. "The last guy."

Lori said, "Me too. And Gideon and Nicole feel the same way. So number three it is. Unless you have a big problem with that, Ann. And I mean a huge problem."

Wait for it: Ann said, "Ninety-nine problems, but that isn't one."

Stacey almost laughed. Whatever her other failings, Ann had some big balls to paraphrase Jay-Z on the subject of bitches to Lori.

When Lori had left, Stacey said, "Ann, are you having trouble seeing things?" Because why not just ask?

"Only when I have to look at you," Ann said.

Stacey might have sunk to her level and said something equally childish if she hadn't felt a text coming in on her phone from Lori. A text that said,

We should talk. Meet me at kickboxing tomorrow night?

40

Ann's Journal

Fuck everyone and everything.

Fuck my eyesight for being so bad so that I could barely make out the faces of the actors in the casting session today, every salient detail of their appearances wiped out by the shape-shifting black amoeba-like blob that appears more and more frequently now in my field of vision.

It's not present at this moment, admittedly. But I've got my font size on my documents zoomed up to seventy-two points. How much longer till I can't read the words on the screen anymore? At least I can type without looking at the keyboard. Most of the time.

And fuck Lori Painter for doing her impersonation of a high-school vice-principal, reaming me out like I'm some kid. She's a kid. After all the effort I've put into my Make Stacey Go Away campaign with the higher-ups, Lori still thinks she can treat me that way? FUCK HER.

I'll make a few more calls and spread more sedition around before the Christmas break. And I'll get

I-rue-the-day-she-was-born-in-stupid-parochial-Canada Stacey fired and blacklisted, once and for all.

If it's the last thing I do. Come hell or high water. Do or die.

You get the idea.

41

Stacey had skipped kickboxing class the past few weeks. She'd told Jenna she was too busy with work, but encouraged her to keep at it and to definitely try the higher-level class, the intermediate one that Lori Painter took. So when Stacey arrived at the gym the night after the casting session, she wasn't surprised to see, through the glass studio door, that Jenna was in the class with Lori and they were sparring partners. According to Stacey's plan.

She had thirty minutes to kill before the class would end. She changed into exercise clothes, beat up a punching bag in an empty studio for a bit, showered, changed again, and waited in the reception area.

"Hey girls," she said, when they came out. "Good class?"

Lori was red-faced and sweaty-haired. "Great class." She fist-bumped a glistening Jenna, who looked ready for her close-up, like she'd been sprayed with fake camera-ready sweat. "Thanks for partnering with me tonight, Jenna. And for helping me take my mind off work for an hour."

"I had a blast too." Jenna turned to Stacey, and for a second she seemed to be trying to send Stacey a mute message — of explanation, for the Seeing Eye Assistant act at work? But Stacey gave her no opening. They could talk later.

"I'm gonna go, and shower at home," Jenna said. "See ya!"

She trotted off, and Lori said, "She's cute, isn't she?"

"Yeah, and she can act, too. She'd be a good fit for that bodyguard role we've got coming up on *The Benjamins*, actually." Stacey said this as if the thought had just come to her. "I should give Judy a call, get her to include Jenna in the casting mix."

"You should. She might be right for it, and I'll bet she could use a break from being Ann's shadow. That was a little weird, wasn't it, yesterday? All the whispering?"

"Yeah. But hey, no ever said working with Ann was boring."

Lori stared at her for two full seconds and said, "I want to shower, but have you got time to go for a drink afterward, at the juice bar downstairs?"

"Love to."

"Give me fifteen minutes."

Stacey spent the time while she waited skimming some of the more intelligent TV sites for recaps and comments related to *The Benjamins*. She also reviewed her top-three speculations for why Lori had called their meeting: to say that the network had decided to fire Ann and put Stacey in sole charge of the show; to hear Stacey's pitch for the Kentucky boarding-school idea; or to ask Stacey if she was gay and would like to date. Okay, the first was wishful thinking, and the third was unlikely. It had better be, or she was in for a rough half hour.

When they'd settled in at a table in the juice bar, Lori got right down to dancing around her issue. "I know this is irregular, but I wanted to talk off the record about what's being said at the network about you. Let me start by saying I'm in your corner. You're bright, super-organized, co-operative, and I have to love a showrunner who delivers a quality product on time and on budget. So full marks for those things."

"Thanks," Stacey said. She'd keep any sign of the mounting dread she felt off her face if it killed her.

"No problem. Now, how can I say this? I'm going to blurt it out." She took a fraught pause anyway. "Ann's been telling anyone who will listen that you're bad news and you're bringing down the show. She wants you fired."

Stacey could not show any emotion that could be interpreted as anger, or frustration. And she couldn't say what she was think-ing, which was, *Are you fucking kidding me?* She said, "I don't understand."

"It's clearly a defensive move on Ann's part. There have been whispers about her peculiar behaviour lately. I mean, that bizarre shit at the casting session, and did I hear that she got handsy on-set with an actor recently? With that Ryan guy?"

Stacey bit her lip. No comment.

"Whatever her demons are, she seems to be trying to deflect them onto you. She says you're poisoning the well, and that if you're gone, all will run smoothly again. Which I know is not true. But unfortunately for you, she has such a long, successful track record, and so many friends in high places, that people are inclined to take her side over yours."

Stacey shook her head like she was puzzled, and not filled with rage, nor with an infuriating desire to start crying, like a cranky child. "I don't know what to say." She really didn't. "I can't defend myself, and I don't want to slag her either."

"That's because you're an honourable person."

Honour had nothing to do with the urgent pressure she felt to contain her feelings. Later, when she was alone, she could scream and beat her chest with her fists. Later, she could fire her agent for not having caught wind of Ann's machinations and warned her about them. Not to mention that traitor Jenna, after everything Stacey had done for her. She'd be near the top of the list of people Stacey would deal with. "I appreciate you telling me this, and I know you're in an difficult position, but what's going to happen? Will I be fired?"

"It's too soon to say. The execs above me want to see how the show does when it comes back after the holiday hiatus, and if it's still got legs, how long they are. And frankly, they want to see if any more complaints emerge about either of you. Or if there are reports of blow-ups on-set, or scenes like at Ann's Christmas party. There's a low tolerance for bad public behaviour these days."

Stacey slid off the high stool she was sitting on, and picked up her bag. She needed to get outside before she dissolved into a puddle of water on the floor. When she had to be considered the good witch in this scenario.

"Thanks for the heads up, Lori." She touched Lori's shoulder like she was a good sport. Like they both were. "I need to think about this, about where I am and where I want to be, and what I can do, if anything, to salvage my reputation."

"I wish I wasn't the bearer of bad news. Or bad rumours. I don't want to overstate the rumblings I've heard — maybe nothing will come of this, and it will all die down."

"And maybe the sun won't come out tomorrow. I have to go."

Stacey walked out of the juice bar with her head held high, and did not collapse as soon as she got into her car, did not lay her head on the steering wheel and sob. She started the car, turned off the car stereo and her phone, and drove fast, thinking only of her route, and the road, and how to navigate through the traffic, and how soon she could get home and figure out what to do.

She pulled into her parking space twenty-eight minutes later, and was so focused on getting inside the sanctuary of home that she didn't see Cooper come out the building's front door and start down the walk toward her until he called her name: "Stace?"

What was he doing here? They hadn't arranged to meet.

He loped toward her with his long strides. "Hey."

"Hey."

He said, "I had to deliver a bike in the Palisades, and I called to see if I should drop by, but your phone was off. So I stopped in and had the concierge call up, but no answer." He came closer and eyed her face. "Are you okay?"

She didn't mean to, she shouldn't, it would only show weakness — but she stepped forward, buried her face in his fleece-covered shoulder, closed her eyes, and let him hug her, just for a minute. She said, "What time is it?"

"Nine-fifteen, nine-twenty."

She looked into his kind eyes. "Why don't you come up for a while?"

They went up the elevator, and she told him she'd had a tough day, with too many meetings to sit through and egos to manage, nothing worth talking about. He said that sucked, and asked her if she wanted a foot rub or a neck and shoulder massage. She did not, thanks, but she said she could use a good, hard fuck.

He laughed a little and said he'd see what he could do about that. If she was sure that's what she wanted.

After they'd done that, behind her closed bedroom door (so as not to confuse the dog), and showered — Stacey's third of the day — she changed into a sleepshirt, put her hair up in a messy bun, made some herbal tea, and lounged with him on the couch, with Buddy curled up at their feet.

Cooper flipped channels on TV between nature shows and an extreme sporting event, and talked about his day. About the tours he'd booked, and the two seven-thousand-dollar road bikes he'd sold, and about his younger sister, who'd announced she was engaged, and how hearing her news made him feel like he was supposed to start acting more like a grown-up, but he wasn't ready, not yet.

She let his quiet voice wash over her, and she imagined herself fired from *The Benjamins*, unemployed for months, then hired on as a second-string executive producer on a third-string cable drama. She pictured herself photoshopped into the album of Cooper's life — into visits with his family, barbecues and birthday parties, nights out with Riley and whatever bimbo he was seeing, a vacation with his gang to a timeshare in Tahoe to ski, and — no. She wasn't ready to give up everything she'd worked toward, and live that ordinary, under the radar, rinse-and-repeat kind of existence. She'd sooner die.

Or kill someone.

"Look at those cheetahs," Cooper said. "I've got to get to Tanzania one of these days, or Kenya. Have you been?"

"No."

"Wouldn't you want to? A full-blown safari's on my to-do list. Along with surfing in Australia."

Kill not just someone, but Ann. That was the so-obvious-she'd-almost-missed-it solution to Ann as insurmountable obstacle in her path: kill her.

Stacey sat up. Goosebumps had risen on her arms among the freckles. How would she do it?

Cooper pointed at the TV, at a cheetah ripping into the stomach of a live gazelle. "I love cheetahs, but shit, that's brutal."

She wanted to be alone. She wanted Cooper to leave, so she could plot a murder. A real-life one, not for a TV show.

She slowed down her breathing, opened her mouth, and yawned big. Cooper caught on right away. "I should be going," he said, "let you get to sleep."

"Sorry. I'm pretty tired."

He got up and collected his keys and sweater and shoes. She walked with him to the door and kissed his shoulder. Now go.

"I'll call you," he said.

She said yeah, okay, thanks for coming over, closed the door behind him, and began to plan.

42

On the last day of work before the year-end break, Jenna brought a cappuccino — in a china cup, with two chocolate pistachio biscotti arranged on the saucer — into Ann's office, set it down on her desk, and, without thinking, said, "So are you ready for Christmas?" Whoops. Not the best question to ask, under the circumstances.

But Ann said, "Yup. And I'm looking forward to it. I'm going to eat well, dig into my stash of prescription drugs, drink the rare wines I've been saving for the right occasion, and wallow in my solitude. How does that sound?"

Um, like the worst Christmas ever? "Like you deserve a good rest."

Ann encircled the saucer with her hands and touched the biscotti. She picked one up, took a bite, and sent crumbs flying across the desk. Lovely.

"The truth is," she said, her mouth full, "I couldn't do much work if I wanted to. My eyesight has gotten a lot worse."

It was sad, what was happening to Ann. Not Jenna's problem, but still sad.

Ann swallowed the bite she'd been chewing. "What do you think, Jenna? Am I just fucked?"

"No, you're not. There's that voice recognition software I read about, so you could still write. And the text-to-speech software that would allow you to hear documents you'd normally read. And I can continue to be your eyes and describe what you can't see: people, and takes —"

"And wardrobe and makeup and hair and scenery, and every other thing that appears on a TV screen? Let's not sugar-coat this: the outlook for life as I know it is pretty bleak."

Jenna didn't say anything, because there was nothing to say, no bright side to look on, no silver lining she could think of. She couldn't even say well, at least you can get fat now.

Ann said, "This whole situation sucks a huge amount of dick, but I'll tell you what the worst part is."

Jenna hoped Ann wouldn't say the real tragedy was that she couldn't see that cocky, in-love-with-himself Ryan anymore — he wasn't half as handsome as he and Ann thought he was.

"The worst part is that while I decline and fall, Stacey can only rise. She's waiting for me to stumble as we speak, so she can swoop in and finish me off." She bit into the second biscotto. "I almost tripped over her little dog today. Don't tell me she didn't send him out into the hallway when I was walking by in the hope that I'd fall and break a bone."

"Buddy is so cute! I like it when she brings him to work."

"Cute? Nothing about Stacey is cute. She's like a troll under a bridge in a fairy tale. Or a demon trapped inside a haunted house in a horror movie."

The hate-on Ann had for Stacey was too strange. "If you ask me, Stacey's the last thing you should worry about," Jenna said. Quietly.

"Mark my words: if she wants to take my place, she'll have to do it over my dead body."

And here they went again with the dark thoughts. Jenna put her hands on her hips, and adopted the tone of an annoying school teacher she'd once played on a crappy tween show: "Promise me you're not going to do anything stupid over the break."

Ann stood, plucked the seam of her pants out of her ass crack, and picked up her bag. "Do us both a favour and don't talk to me like that ever again. I'm calling it a day. Did you order the car for five o'clock?"

"Yes, I did. I'll walk you out." Jenna swept the crumbs on the desk into a napkin with her hand and picked up the half-empty cappuccino cup. "And all kidding aside, you'll be safe at your house?"

"You bet. I've got an alarm system, and security guards on car patrol in the neighbourhood that I pay through the nose for. And I've got weapons."

"Weapons?"

"A baseball bat that I keep under my bed. If John tries to come home for the holidays, cap in hand, I can bash his head in."

At least she was joking now. Or trying to joke.

"What about you, Jenna?" Ann said. "What are your plans for the next two weeks? Lovey-dovey time with your boyfriend? Some ethnically flavoured family festivities?"

"We'll see my family for Christmas, and then, remember, I told you? Andrew and I are going to Kauai for New Year's with Kerry and her husband."

"Are you expecting a proposal over the holidays? I bet you are, no matter how many times I tell you marriage is a fool's game."

"I'm not expecting anything. We only moved in together a few months ago."

Ann said, "Just be ready with an answer, that's my advice. In case he decides to go sentimental on you and propose."

Maybe Ann *would* be okay, and come to terms with her depressing shit, and continue to put down everyone she knew. Maybe she would retire because she had to, and Jenna could stop feeling sorry for her, and stop being her assistant. There was a happy thought.

Jenna helped Ann into her car and went back inside to tidy up her desk. She was about to leave when her cellphone rang, with a call from Tasha, her agent. "Jenna! Where are you?"

"I'm closing up shop at the Two Dubs office; we're about to start a two-week break."

"Are you going out of town?"

"Not till after Christmas, why?"

"You got called in for a part. It's not the best timing, but they want the casting done before the New Year, for filming in January, and they asked for you specially. Can you do a first-pass audition tomorrow morning? For Judy Wexler."

"Judy's the casting director for *The Benjamins*."

"That's what they want you for. The part is, let's see — 'a self-defence instructor slash bodyguard, female.' They've sent sides over, it's for a five- or six-episode arc in the back half. I don't remember — have you done much action, or studied stage combat, anything like that?"

Jenna told her about the kickboxing and said she was definitely down to do the audition. Tasha promised to email her the sides, and Jenna sat back down at her desk. Was this real? Her cellphone chimed — Tasha's email had arrived. Jenna turned on her computer, accessed her email, printed the sides. It *was* real. But how had this happened? Who could have asked for her to come in? Rob? Judy, who'd looked irritated when Jenna whispered in Ann's ear? Ann herself? Could this be her idea of a Christmas gift? No way. Ann had indicated on one or two occasions since Jenna had known her that she had the ability to think about someone other than herself, but not lately, not since she'd become preoccupied with her eye/husband/Stacey problems.

That's who was behind this: Stacey. Jenna picked up her bag. She'd walk down the hall to Stacey's office to say thanks, then call Andrew, tell him the good news, and try not to sound too excited.

43

Stacey was in her office when Jenna knocked on her door at five-twenty. "Come in," Stacey said, "but give me a minute to finish this thought."

Jenna bent down to pet Buddy. Stacey typed a last sentence in an email and clicked send. She wasn't angry at Jenna anymore; she'd been extra-nice to her since deciding to remove Ann from the planet, because she had an idea that Jenna might help her do that, though exactly how was still to be determined.

"There, done," Stacey said. "What's up?"

Jenna looked happy. "I'm headed out, but I wanted to say thank you so much for setting up the audition for me tomorrow for the bodyguard part. It was you who arranged it, right?"

Fucking right it had been, and fucking right Jenna should be grateful. And fork over some information in return. "I might have dropped a word or two in someone's ear on your behalf — mainly because you're ideal for it — but if you land the part, it'll be your skills and talent that got you there."

"You're too kind to me."

No, she wasn't. "Don't thank me till you've signed a contract. You know how quickly things like this can fall apart."

"I know. But I'll be ready, and I'll give it my best shot."

"I'm sure you will."

"One question," Jenna said. "Does Ann know about this?"

"I don't think so. Hasn't she already left for the break?"

"Yeah, about twenty minutes ago. But someone could call her and tell her, if they wanted to."

"How about we wait to tell her until after Judy puts you on the shortlist? When it's more of a *fait accompli*."

"A what?"

"A done deal."

Jenna seemed to think about that one for a minute before she agreed, as Stacey had known she would. Stacey said, "Are you still going on vacation? Ann's not keeping you on call to wait on her over the holidays?"

"No, she's given me the whole time off, and I'm going to Kauai for New Year's."

"Sounds like fun."

"But I'm a little worried about Ann. I think she'll find it hard to be alone for Christmas."

Stacey looked at an imaginary message on her phone, the better to hide her interest in Ann's doings. "Because of the split with John, you mean."

"And because of the whole going-blind thing," Jenna said. Having apparently forgotten that Stacey had not been told about Ann's impairment.

Stacey could work with that, and show no surprise. "Progressive conditions are difficult to deal with. And for this to happen to someone who defines herself by her work — it's a real shame."

"And it seems so random. I mean, sixty-two is old, but not *that* old. And I'd never heard of this wet macular degeneration thing before Ann got it. Had you?"

So that's what Ann had. "Yeah, but my father's an eye doctor."

Jenna said, "Sometimes I wonder if Ann might be so depressed that she'll do something drastic. Like try to commit suicide." Her large eyes got larger, like she was acting out shock.

Stacey suppressed a snort of disbelief. Self-loving, self-worshipping Ann would never intentionally end her life. Not while Stacey was still alive to be tortured, anyway. But if Jenna thought suicide was a possibility, so might others. Stacey said, "Ann is so strong and full of life that I can't imagine she would harm herself." She took a thoughtful pause. "Though she has had some big setbacks lately."

"I know, right?"

"Does she have holiday plans that you know of?"

"She said she's going it alone with her wine and her pills."

And there was Stacey's light-bulb idea, courtesy of Jenna: she could somehow force Ann to overdose, and set the stage so it looked like suicide. The thought of pulling off that scenario sent a current through Stacey that made the scar on her forearm itch. She scratched it, and said, "I wouldn't worry. Ann's a tough cookie, and resourceful. You should concentrate on your audition: kill it, then enjoy the holidays."

"I will. Thanks for listening, Stacey. And for putting a word in for me."

"You're welcome. My door's always open. Except when it's closed." She smiled to signal that she was joking, sort of. "Could you close the door on your way out, actually? I'm going to be here a while longer."

"Sure. Happy holidays!"

"You, too."

Stacey flew to Toronto on December 24, checked into a hotel, and saw her parents, sister, brother-in-law, and nephews for one dinner and one morning gift-giving session. The gifts she gave were expensive, the ones she received thoughtless: a Body Shop gift basket and a Jamie Oliver cookbook — really? She flew back to L.A. on December 25.

When she walked in her own door around six that evening, Buddy came running to meet her. The dog walker had taken him overnight and brought him back late in the day. She put down her bag, hugged him hello, and got down on the floor and tussled with him for a few minutes, the way Cooper did, the way Buddy liked.

"I'm home, condo and dog, I'm home," she said. She wondered, for an instant, if she were going crazy. Nah. Her morals might have slipped, what with her blithe disregard for the Thou Shall Not Plan a Murder commandment, but her sanity was all there. Her mind actually felt sharper than ever now that she had a mission to complete. And it wouldn't be a murder so much as a mercy killing. A way to put Ann out of her misery and make the rest of the world less miserable at the same time.

She was about to take Buddy outside when her landline rang. Her parents, calling to make sure she'd got home safely? Not likely. Probably a telemarketer, hoping to cash in on Christmas cheer. She walked over and looked at the call display. John Nelligan, it said. What could he want from her? She picked up, said hello.

"Stacey? It's Ann."

"Hi Ann." Stacey kept her voice cool. "Merry Christmas."

"Same to you. Am I interrupting a holiday gathering, or can you talk for a minute?" She sounded strangely reasonable.

"I can talk."

"I've spent the day thinking about what's been going on at work recently, and I believe I owe you an apology."

This ought to be good. "How's that?"

"Let's face it, Stacey: our partnership has been strained in the last few months, and I'm largely to blame. I've had some personal problems, with my health and my marriage, and I may have taken out some of my frustration and anger about them on you. If I did, I'm sorry."

Not much of an apology. But could Ann possibly be sincere, and want to reconcile?

Ann said, "Are you still there, Stacey?'

"Yeah, I'm here." Wary, but there.

"Are you available tomorrow afternoon? I'm hoping you can come out to my house to meet, away from the office. I think you agree that it's time we went our separate ways business-wise, but let's see if there's a win-win way to do that without getting our managers and attorneys and agents involved."

Stacey could imagine what Ann's idea of a win-win situation was — Ann take all, her blindness be damned. But an invitation to the house would provide Stacey with the opportunity she was looking for, if she played it properly and didn't appear too eager. "You've caught me a little off-guard," she said. "I agree that it's time we move on, but I'm not sure it's possible for us to sit down and speak calmly about it." Shit. Had she sounded too negative?

"All I suggest is that we give it a try," Ann said. "We've worked together long enough, we can do that much. Don't you think?"

Stacey gave out a small sigh of capitulation. "Okay. Let's meet, and see how it goes."

"Thank you."

"I could come over at two o'clock tomorrow. How would that be?" Two o'clock would give Stacey plenty of time to refine her script, rehearse her moves, and pick up the props she needed.

"Two o'clock is fine. I'll see you then. And thank you, Stacey, for being so understanding."

Thank you for being so understanding? The Ann that Stacey knew would never be so polite and considerate. She must have her own underhanded agenda for the meeting, but that was okay. When it came to dirty tricks, the student was about to school the master.

44

"So, how'd the audition go?" Jenna's mother asked. Her dad came in from the living room, where he'd been watching TV, and said, "What's this? You're gonna be in another show?" Her sister turned off the water she was running and said, "Give us the punchline: did you get it?"

Jenna looked at the expectant faces turned toward her and wished she hadn't started telling this story. She'd sworn, months before, after a few rejections too many, that she would stop telling anyone when she tried out for a part. The fewer people who knew, the fewer people she would feel embarrassed in front of when she failed. But, lulled by the holiday spirit in the TV commercials she'd seen all afternoon and stupefied by the carbs in the delicious Dutch Christmas bread she'd eaten one thin slice of, with butter, she'd gone this far in the telling; she couldn't stop now. And the audition had gone so well, the feedback had been so good, that it would be beyond unfair if this job fell through.

She said, "I don't know yet. I have a callback on the day before we go to Hawaii."

"You're going to get it," her mother said. "I have a good feeling about this."

The doorbell rang. Her sister went to answer it and Jenna resumed peeling carrots. "I hope you're right, Mom. And I hope nothing happens to screw it up."

Jenna heard the front door close. She stepped back from the counter and looked into the hall. "Who was at the door?"

Her sister said, "It was Andrew, but he wants to talk to you outside."

"What about?"

"Just go. I'll finish the carrots."

Jenna washed and dried her hands, untied the apron her mother had lent her, bit her lips to make them rosy, and flipped her hair. Maybe Andrew had finally bought her a new car, and brought it over as a surprise.

She opened the door. Andrew was standing on the front walk in his overcoat, his arms behind his back, his same old car parked on the street behind him. No new car in sight.

"Hi," she said. "What are you doing?"

He brought his arms forward and revealed that he held a boom box in one hand, and a stack of hand-lettered signs in the other.

"Oh, my God." He was enacting a scene from *Love Actually*. Her favourite scene from her favourite movie. "I can't believe this is happening!" If only it weren't.

He put his finger to his lips, pressed a button on the boom box, and placed it on the ground. Jenna heard the opening notes of a choir singing "Silent Night," and Andrew held up the first sign.

THIS ISN'T A MOVIE, it said.

WE'RE NOT IN LONDON, said the second.

AND I'M NOT ANDREW LINCOLN, read the third.

Jenna had had a major crush on Andrew Lincoln for years, and had watched the whole first season of *The Walking Dead* solely because he was in it. Her Andrew didn't have half of Andrew Lincoln's looks or smoulder, but she had to give him thoughtful points for knowing that and still staging this scene.

BUT TO ME, YOU ARE PERFECT, said the next sign, and there was only one reaction possible. Jenna squealed and said, "That's a line from the movie!" and pressed her hands to her face. She hoped her brother-in-law the gadget geek was getting her performance on his phone.

The next sign said I LOVE YOU. Andrew made a vulnerable face to go with it, and Jenna said, "I love you, too." Because she had to.

WILL YOU MARRY ME? the last sign said, and Jenna cried, "Yes!" She ran over and hugged and kissed him, and her sisters and parents and brothers-in-law stood in the doorway and cheered.

She didn't know how she was going to get out of this, but get out of it she would.

An hour later, after congratulations, and toasts of Veuve Clicquot (Andrew had brought a double magnum), and dinner had been served, after Jenna had pushed the food around on her plate and the table talk had moved on to someone else's life, she excused herself. She went to the bathroom, stuck two fingers down her throat, barfed up the Christmas bread, rinsed her mouth out. She popped in some gum, scrolled through her phone contacts, and pressed send. One ring, two, three, then a pickup.

"You alone?" she asked. Cooper said he was, and Jenna whispered, "Guess what? Andrew just proposed."

———

Jenna had taken up with Cooper again at Brooke's wedding. She'd told Andrew she was going to the restroom, caught Cooper's eye, and given him the signal they'd used in high school whenever they wanted to sneak off for a quickie — she rubbed the back of her neck with her hand and tilted her head, like she had a kink. She'd used that signal in the school cafeteria at lunchtime, in the bleachers at a basketball game, at a beach party. And ten years later, at the wedding.

Cooper had held Jenna's gaze for a few seconds, smiling his familiar horny-bashful smile, then broke off his conversation and walked out of the room. Which made feel Jenna victorious, and giddy, as well as drunk — good, confident drunk. Daredevil drunk. She weaved through the wedding guests out to the hallway and spotted Cooper's broad shoulders ahead. When he ducked into a small storage room, she followed him in and locked the door. Did she shake her head slightly to make her hair swing, like in a shampoo commercial? She did, and she stuck her chest out and squeezed her tits together with her upper arms to make them rise and swell.

"This is such a good idea," he said, and kissed her mouth, her jaw line, her neck, behind her ear. Just like he used to, when he'd studded her skin with hickeys, badges of possession.

"Don't leave any marks," she said, and pulled their lower bodies close together. His dick was already hard against her abdomen. Good. She wouldn't have to hand-prep it the way she sometimes had to with Andrew, when he was "tired" after a long day at the office.

She pulled down the neckline of her dress and exposed her breasts, pushed up in a lacy low-cut bra, and was rewarded with Cooper's groan of appreciation. She unbuckled his belt, unzipped his pants, shoved them down below his butt, and pulled his springy dick out of his boxer briefs. She was ready, too, and good thing, because as exciting as it was to hear him moan and tell her he'd missed her, and to look into his eyes and see the reflection of her unspoiled fifteen-year-old self, they needed to take care of business before they were found out.

They got each other off quickly, and, when they'd straightened their clothes and passed a quick mutual inspection, Jenna left the room first. Cooper followed a few minutes later.

She went straight to the restroom, soaped her hands, fixed her makeup and lipstick, chomped through a breath mint, and sprayed herself with perfume to cover the sex smell.

Andrew was conversing with their tablemates when she slid into her seat next to him. She picked up a goblet of ice water and took a gulp. He seemed to believe her when she apologized for her absence and said she'd been waylaid (haha) by an old friend who wanted to reminisce, and he kicked up no fuss later at home either, when she pretended to have fallen asleep while he brushed his teeth.

In the six weeks or so since the wedding, she'd seen Cooper four times, always at his sad apartment in the Valley. She'd gotten him to list her number under Riley's name in his phone; in hers, she'd put his number under Kerry's first name. Kerry's real number was listed under her initials. If anyone had asked why she had two numbers for Kerry, she would have said one was a land line and the other a cell. Only no one asked. Whenever she was sick of being agreeable and upbeat, when she wanted the kind of uncomplicated attention she could get from Cooper, she'd call or message him and go over. She'd tell Andrew that she had an errand to do for Ann, or she wanted to visit her parents, or she was off to the gym.

They fucked like they were still teenagers. They tried some porny stuff — a little role playing, some dress-up, a few acrobatic positions that Andrew could never have managed. Some of those felt more stupid than hot, but she liked working out different sex muscles. As long as there was no S&M. She had no desire to submit, not after being a slave to Ann's whims at work and making Andrew feel like a Big Man Provider at home. And Cooper was not interested in being dominated, so that was that.

She and Cooper fucked, and they talked.

One day at his place, after they'd had thorough, unhurried sex for the first time since high school, Jenna said, "It kills me when I think back to how little I knew about how the world works when I was fifteen. And seventeen and twenty. I thought that fame and fortune would come my way if I worked real hard, was super-nice to everyone I met, and kept my weight down. I thought that was all it took."

Cooper lay on his side and stroked her stomach — her taut, tight stomach. "But you did become famous. And your chance to become more famous could be just around the corner."

"Do you really believe that?"

"I don't know. Maybe. When I was twenty, my goal was to make lots of money and live well, and look at me now. The bike shop isn't going to expand to a second location, let alone a third or fourth, and I'll never invent a killer phone app or a revolutionary new bike accessory."

Jenna sat up, reached for her clothes, put on her bra. "You want to live large? You can. You just have to find another way in." She twirled her black lace thong on her index finger. "Do you know how much this kind of lingerie costs? A stupidly large amount. And I sure don't pay for it."

"You're saying I should find a fifty-year-old attorney to shack up with?"

"Andrew is forty-six. And he's fit for his age."

"Sure he is."

"I'm saying that maybe you should go after the thirty-two-year-old showrunner you seemed so interested in when we talked at Brooke's wedding."

"You think I was interested in Stacey McCreedy?"

"I know you were."

"That was before you gave me the old let's-fuck signal, though."

Jenna swung her legs over the bed and started to pull on her jeans. "Look, this is fun, what we're doing together, but if you want the good life, you have to find someone who can give it to you. Stacey pulls down a salary in the mid to high six figures. And she hasn't peaked yet."

"So, you think I should become a man-whore."

Jenna looked down at Cooper, who was still lying in bed and showed no sign of wanting to get up and get on with his day. Was he chill or just lazy? "I wouldn't worry about a small thing like a job title. I'm a goddamned personal assistant right now, at my age, and with my credits, because the job is a means to an end. Stacey could be your means, is what I'm saying."

Cooper reached up and pulled her back down onto the bed. "You're such a bad girl. Sleeping around on your live-in boyfriend, scheming to get ahead at work. You could be a character on that TV show."

"And my rule-breaker side is what you like about me, admit it. That, and" — she made a circular motion with her index finger in front of her body — "all of this."

Cooper had laughed and asked her if she was sure she couldn't stay for one more round. She'd patted him on the head and left.

But, smart boy that he was, he'd asked Stacey out for a drink the next week, and gone home with her afterward, started seeing her on the regular. And he'd followed Jenna's suggestion that he drop in on Stacey after that tense meeting with Lori Painter in the juice bar. When Jenna left the kickboxing studio that night, she went out to her car and watched the meeting through the juice bar window. And when she saw Stacey's face shut down in reaction to whatever Lori had said, she texted Cooper and told him to go see Stacey and make himself indispensable.

"What's she like in bed?" Jenna had asked him, after he fucked Stacey for the first time.

"No comment."

"What's the matter? Bitch got your tongue?"

"Don't call her that."

"Awww, you like her. That's sweet."

"You're something else, you know that?"

"I'm well aware. You going to see her again?"

"Yeah. Though I'm not crazy about doing you and her simultaneously. It feels wrong if she doesn't know about it."

"Whatever you do, don't tell her. And don't fall for her either. You have to keep your eye on the prize."

"How's that going for you?"

"It's never out of my sight," she'd said.

And now? Andrew's proposal was no prize. But the guest arc on *The Benjamins* had the potential to pay off for all her effort and sacrifice and Ann-wrangling to date. She had to get it. She'd better get it. Or else she'd be as angry at everyone and everything as Ann was.

Andrew had pulled out a ring after the proposal, a two-carat diamond solitaire with a platinum band, from Tiffany, that cost (Jenna looked it up on her phone in her parents' bathroom) about as much as the entry-level Mercedes she'd been eyeing. And the car should be coming along any day, now that she and Andrew were engaged.

The ring looked fabulous on her hand. Too bad she'd have to give it back in a year or so. By then, if her current up-trend continued, she'd be a series regular on a hit show, and enough of a celebrity that the breakup with Andrew — quickly followed by a new relationship with an A-list TV actor, or a high-profile professional athlete — would net her the cover of *In Touch* or *Life & Style*. Maybe even *Us Weekly*, knock on wood.

When she got home, she called the real Kerry to tell her the news, emailed her five other closest friends, and was going up to bed — Andrew probably expected a big fat blowjob on account of the engagement, and she'd have to deliver — when her cellphone rang. Ann calling. On Christmas night.

It was only ten o'clock, not late. She took the call, in case something bad had happened. "Ann, how are you?"

"Fine, thanks. Merry Christmas."

Ann didn't sound drunk or depressed, she sounded calm. "Same to you," Jenna said. "And guess what: Andrew proposed! I'm engaged."

"Didn't I tell you he would?"

"You did."

"And you accepted. Congratulations."

"It was kind of cute how he did it — he re-enacted a scene from the movie *Love Actually*, outside my parents' house, and he gave me a beautiful diamond and platinum ring from Tiffany."

"How very nice."

Still calm. And so not negative. Had someone kidnapped Ann and replaced her with a robot, or were her prescription drugs doing the talking? "How was your day?"

"I had a peaceful and productive day, spent in reflection. I did a lot of thinking about my life, and my legacy, and I got organized. I sorted out all my files on my laptop and in my home office — you'd be proud of me."

"That's great, Ann."

"I called because I have a gift I want to give you. It's actually a Christmas bonus. I'd love if you could come by tomorrow afternoon to get it. At three o'clock."

From upstairs, Andrew called, "Bring up the bong when you come."

"Gee, thanks! And sure, I could drop by tomorrow." For a Christmas bonus, she'd go. And see if Ann had become possessed.

45

Ann's Journal

Guess what? I enjoyed my first solitary Christmas Day in eons.

I like living alone. I like doing whatever the fuck I want, whenever the fuck I want, with no one to get in my way, or irritate me, or finish the bottle of vodka in the freezer and not replace it with a new one. I like walking around talking to myself and singing random snippets of apropos songs, like "What Did I Ever See in Him?" and "Fuck You." I like to drink without anyone counting how many I've had.

As long as Rosa comes in and cleans up after me three times a week. Rim shot.

But seriously. It makes me wonder what John was good for when he lived here. Not much that I can recall. And I don't miss him.

I won't miss Stacey either, when I've gotten rid of her. I'm mad as hell that my clout seems to have gone the way of my eyesight and I couldn't get her fired, but if you want something done right, you have to do it yourself, I've heard. And I'm not afraid to get my hands dirty.

Speaking of that, I'm going to have to delete this entry after I write it, delete the whole document, in case a nosy detective questions the story I'll tell tomorrow. That I killed Stacey in self-defence. After I told her our partnership was over, and she went nuts and attacked me with my own baseball bat.

I found instructions online for how to erase and overwrite files irrevocably. It's not that difficult to do. And I can always use the bat on my laptop for good measure, go all Hulk Smash on it, and pound it to smithereens.

All in case some cop seizes my laptop and looks through it for damning evidence, like the journal entry before this one, from a few days ago. The elegant, economical six-word entry that reads, in its entirety:

STACEY CAN FUCK OFF AND DIE.

Do nosy detectives who would give a shit exist in the real world? Surely real police detectives are too lazy or corrupt to be bothered with a business dispute between heretofore law-abiding partners. Surely they'd rather apprehend terrorists and serial killers and gang lords and drug kingpins.

Surely. Don't call me Shirley, my mother used to say. And Sam, you made the pants too long. And Daisy, Daisy, give me your answer do. Say a name and she'd have a story or a song that went with it.

Now I'm rambling like an old woman. Like the old woman I've become.

I've gotta buck up, put away the maudlin. I've drunk too much Christmas cheer today, or should I say Christmas hate.

I won't drink tomorrow. There'll be no morning Bloody Mary to wake me up, no noontime bottle of wine from the cellar to savour. I've got to stay sharp and lay my trap, outwit that devil's spawn Stacey once and for all. And hit myself with the bat. That'll be a literal pain to do. Then I'll have to put on a performance for the ages and persuade that dimwit Jenna that I killed Stacey in self-defence, so she can back me up to the police.

Outwit, dimwit, fuckwit.

Goodbye, journal. It's been real.

46

At two o'clock sharp on December 26, Stacey rang the doorbell at Ann's front door. "I'm coming," she heard Ann call from inside, and the sound of her voice might have made Stacey jump if she weren't in her Zen ninja state — ready to do battle and in complete control of her senses, actions, and reactions.

In her hands was a box that contained one of Ann's favourite desserts, a triple berry cream shortcake from Sweet Lady Jane. It was a special occasion cake, but if this meeting wasn't a special occasion, what was? And having a cake to cut was how she would get access to a sharp knife.

Ann opened the door, breathless and unsmiling. She was wearing a long-sleeved baggy top over baggy pants, and had slippers on her feet — what old people wore at home, Stacey supposed. In contrast to Stacey's boots, leggings, T-shirt, and leather jacket.

Ann said, "You're punctual. As usual."

Stacey held up the box. "I brought your favourite cake. To sweeten our negotiations."

Ann made no motion to take the box from her. "I'm set up in the den, come on back."

Stacey took off her boots and walked barefoot behind Ann through to the kitchen, which was clean and tidy, not a dish or glass to be seen. She took off her jacket and placed it on a chair back, set her purse and the cake box on the counter, and said, "Have you got a knife and some plates? I'll cut us some cake." Her pulse was beating at a constant club-banger rate, and the little hairs on her arms were standing straight up, but her voice came out normally pitched and steady. The Zen ninja–state thing was working.

"No thanks, I'm not hungry."

Impossible. Ann was never not hungry. She had not once turned down a dessert in all the years Stacey had known her.

"I am," Stacey said brightly, if not credibly. "You don't mind if I have a piece, do you?"

"Go ahead, help yourself."

Stacey removed a knife — a solid eight-inch mid-weight Santoku — from the wooden knife block on the counter, and used its sharp blade to cut the string on the box with two quick movements.

When Ann turned her back to open a cupboard door and pull out a cake plate, Stacey dropped the knife into her purse, quickly withdrew another from the block, and sank it into the cake. She sliced through the layers, cut a thin but not too thin wedge, and eased it onto the plate Ann had placed within reach. "You sure I can't tempt you with a slice?"

Ann took a spoon and a paper napkin out of a drawer and dropped them on the counter. "Maybe later."

"That's a spoon. Do you have a fork?" How bad was Ann's vision?

Ann opened the cutlery drawer, felt around in it, and produced a fork.

"Thank you." Stacey picked up her plate, fork, napkin, and purse. "Shall we?"

"I'm not going to offer you coffee."

"That's fine. I've had enough coffee for one day." And more wouldn't be good for her reflexes.

Ann led the way into the den at the back of the house — one of the few rooms on the main floor that was not outfitted with floor-to-ceiling windows. She sat down behind a big teak desk in a padded office chair and motioned to Stacey to sit across from her in a matching chair.

Stacey placed her purse next to her on the chair seat. She took a bite of the cake, pronounced it delicious, and swallowed it without choking on the mouthful of sugar and butterfat she'd taken in. "How are we going to do this?" She put the stupid cake plate down on the desk. "Do you want to lead off the discussion?"

"All right," Ann said. "I'll start."

But she didn't say anything. She just sat and stared at Stacey — or in Stacey's direction — for what seemed like a minute, but may have only been five seconds.

Stacey's right hand closed around the knife handle in her purse. She lifted it out, keeping it below the desktop, and she tensed her leg and abdominal muscles, ready to spring. No fancy stunts were required — she wouldn't have to vault over the desk or run around it. She'd hear what Ann had to say, hear what insulting pittance she'd offer Stacey to walk away from the show, from their production company, from everything she'd worked for her entire adult life — then she'd pounce. She'd whip out the knife, lean forward, pin Ann's arms down with one hand, and hold the knife blade up to Ann's neck with the other. Just like that, she'd be in the dominant position, able to force Ann upstairs and into the bathtub, where she'd make her swallow a bunch of her own pills and watch Stacey slit her wrists with her own kitchen knife. And die.

Why wasn't Ann speaking? Should Stacey spring up now? She should. In five, four —

Ann said, "You know, it's funny."

Funny? There was nothing funny about this scene.

Ann said, "I had a whole speech prepared, in which I delineated my position, and explained why I'm doing what I'm doing, and how we came to be sitting here, about to walk down the path of no return." She pushed her sleeves up to her elbows, and revealed a large, ugly, bleeding bruise on her left forearm.

Stacey gripped the knife handle tighter. "What happened to your arm?"

"Isn't that something?" She leaned forward. There was madness in her eyes. "It hurts like hell. I think I might have cracked a bone when I did it. Or should I say — when *you* did it?"

Stacey started to sweat, in an un-Zenlike way. "What are you talking about?"

"Nothing. Because there's no point in talking. Talk is overrated."

What was Ann saying? What was she doing? *Act now*, Stacey's ninja voice commanded, and she jumped up, knife in hand, and yelled a *hyah!* battle cry just as Ann lifted her hand and fired a handgun at her.

A blast of sound assaulted Stacey's eardrums, a burst of sparks exploded in front of her eyes, and a slash of pain burned through her left arm — pain so searing that she cried out and collapsed onto the desk. She grabbed the bloody mess that was her left bicep with her right hand, and recoiled when her fingers slid over shredded skin to touch something raw and wet and yielding underneath.

She opened her mouth to yell at Ann to stop, but all that came out was a whimper.

"Did I miss, goddamn it?" Ann stepped back from the desk, the handgun still raised and pointed in Stacey's direction.

The crazy bitch was going to shoot her again. Stacey gathered up her strength and hurtled herself onto the floor milliseconds before the second shot hit a framed print on the wall behind the chair she'd been sitting in. She cried out when shards of glass fell and cut her where she lay tangled up in the chair legs, her back pressed against the desk apron. She pulled her arms and legs in close to her body, tried to make herself into a ball.

"Ann!" From outside the room, a woman's voice wailed, awesomely loud, and awesomely anguished. "Ann! Don't do it!" The voice was coming closer.

Stacey heard a click that might have been the sound of the gun being cocked. What was Ann waiting for? Stacey fixated on a pink, viscous blob of something the size of a ping pong ball sitting on the floor a foot away from her face. What was that? A piece of squashed cake? *A chunk of her flesh?*

Jenna yelled, "Hold on, I'm coming!" and ran into the room.

47

What with the proposal, and Christmas dinner, and the stoned sex at home afterward, and sleeping in the next day, and workouts and showers, and phone calls to Andrew's sister and parents to announce the engagement, Jenna didn't think too much about going over to Ann's at three o'clock on the twenty-sixth. Not until one-thirty, when Andrew asked her what she wanted to do for the rest of the day and she told him she had to go pick up a gift Ann wanted to give her.

"That's a little much, to ask you to come over during the holidays," Andrew said.

"I won't stay long. Though I think part of the reason she asked me is that she's lonely and wants company. When she called last night, she told me she'd spent Christmas Day organizing her files. How sad is that?"

"Yeah, well, if the gift is one of her valuable personal possessions, don't accept it."

"What do you mean?"

"Those are the warning signs of impending suicide — when people put their affairs in order and give away objects of value."

"Yeah, but —"

"Didn't you say she's been depressed lately?"

"Holy shit." Jenna grabbed her keys, ran outside, and jumped into her car to drive over to Ann's house early. It would be just like Ann to invite her over at three o'clock so that Jenna could discover her body after she'd overdosed on pills or hung herself. What a rad Christmas bonus that would be.

The drive from Loz Feliz to Ann's place in the Hills should have taken twenty minutes, but the traffic was bad, the streets clogged with holiday shoppers or tourists, who knew what, and Ann's phone was turned off no matter how many times Jenna called. It was 2:12 when she rolled up to Ann's address and through the open gate, and if she thought she was anxious when she pulled up to the house at last, that was nothing compared to how she felt when she heard a gunshot. From inside the house. When Ann had said she didn't have a gun.

"Ann!" she yelled. She opened the unlocked front door and stepped over a pair of riding boots in the foyer. A second shot sounded from the back of the house. Christ, she was too late to stop Ann from making a huge mess of herself. "Ann! Don't do it!" she screamed, and ran through the kitchen, past a tall white cake on the counter. "Hold on, I'm coming!"

She ran into the den and saw an overturned chair, shattered glass on the carpet, a framed picture on the wall with a bullet hole in it, a heap of blood-stained clothing on the floor, and Ann — leaning against a built-in bookcase. She was breathing heavily, apparently unhurt, and she held a smoking gun in her hand. An actual gun with actual smoke coming out of it.

"Are you all right?" Jenna said, and Ann yelled, "Stacey tried to kill me, she attacked me with that baseball bat" — she pointed to an aluminum bat in a corner — "and I had to shoot her to defend myself. I had to!" Or she said something like that. Jenna didn't hear her that well because Stacey yelled too: "Don't listen to her, Jenna, she's insane! She shot me twice. I didn't even touch her! Stop her, before she fires again. Please!"

Jenna looked from Stacey — who was inside the blood-stained clothing on the floor, her face cut, her arm wounded, her eyes red — to Ann, who stared blindly ahead, the gun clutched to her chest.

"Look at me, Jenna," Ann said. "Look at me! Everything Stacey says is a lie. I'm the only person you can trust. She's the bad guy here. You know that."

Jenna didn't hesitate; the crazed expression on Ann's face looked exactly like Meryl Streep's in *The Manchurian Candidate*. She tightened her core muscles and pitched her voice low. "Why don't you give me the gun, Ann? Let's put it away and talk this over."

48

Stacey hurt everywhere, and she was covered in blood, and her teeth were chattering, but she couldn't give in and pass out, not yet. Jenna's miraculous appearance might have stayed Ann's hand for a minute or two, but she didn't seem to realize how deranged Ann was, how capable of killing them both.

Stacey gritted her teeth and pulled herself up to a kneeling position on the floor, then, shakily, to standing. No, leaning. On the desk.

Jenna was trying to talk Ann into giving up the gun, playing the scene like she was the hostage-negotiator hero on a cop show. "We can work this out," she said. "I know we can. You're too smart to go around shooting people. Give me the gun and I'll put it away somewhere safe." All she lacked was a bulletproof vest marked POLICE or FBI.

"Don't come any closer," Ann said. She squinted at Stacey, raised the gun, and pointed it at her.

Stacey ducked. "Take it away from her, Jenna. Take it!"

At last, Jenna snapped into self-defence mode and executed the drill taught at the martial arts studio: she hit Ann's gun-holding wrist with her right forearm, grabbed the snout of the gun with her left hand, flipped it, and aimed it back at Ann. "Done!" she said. She turned to Stacey — what'd she want, applause? — and made the mistake of taking her eyes off her opponent.

"Get back!" Stacey said, but Ann had already lunged forward and reached for the gun. Jenna and Ann grappled with it, their hands clasped together. They grunted and twisted until the gun fired right into Ann's torso.

Stacey flinched, as if she'd been hit.

Ann's body jerked backward and hit the bookcase. Her head lolled, her eyes went blank, and she fell sideways, with a crash, to the floor, like a punching bag dropped from a height. Like a big, heavy-duty punching bag. Like she was dead.

Jenna stood over Ann, the gun still in her hand, panting, for maybe five seconds. Then she dropped the gun on the floor, turned to face Stacey, her face shocked, her eyes enormous, and cried, "Omigod, omigod, omigod! What happened?!"

Two alternate scenarios unfurled on fast-forward in Stacey's mind. In one, the police, summoned by neighbours, who'd heard the gunfire, ran into the room minutes later and found Jenna bent over Ann's body, her fingerprints on the murder weapon. Cut to Jenna being led out of the house in handcuffs and taken to the police station, where she was charged with involuntary manslaughter. Cut again, to a court scene, where Stacey testified on Jenna's behalf, the kill shot was deemed an act of self-defence, and the charges were dropped, but too late: Jenna's career was finished. Her boyfriend kicked her out, her agent and manager dropped her.

Four months later, a scary-skinny, lank-haired, and strung-out Jenna comes to Stacey — whose dark motives are never discovered, who by then reigns over *The Benjamins* as the sole showrunner, and has moved into a palatial house/love nest with gentle, steadfast Cooper. Jenna, who has nothing, begs Stacey, who has everything, for a job, any job; she'll answer phones if she has to, get coffee, make photocopies.

And in the second scenario?

Stacey said, "Is she dead?"

Jenna sob-talked: "I didn't mean to shoot her. She grabbed the gun and squeezed my trigger finger. I was trying to stop her from shooting you! From killing us both!"

The smell of freshly excreted shit reached Stacey's nostrils, mingled with the scents of blood and smoke that already hung in the air. Someone — Ann — had shit her pants.

"Is she for sure dead?" Stacey pressed her thighs against the desk to steady herself. "Check. See if she has a pulse."

Jenna stopped making sobbing noises, but didn't move. "I can't."

"Yes, you can. Bend over and feel her jugular vein. I'd do it, but I have to hold on to my arm."

Jenna looked at Stacey's right hand where it gripped her bloody left arm, and looked away.

"You can do it, Jenna."

She took a deep breath and leaned over Ann's body. "There's so much blood."

"Place two fingers under her chin."

After a minute, Jenna said, "There's no pulse."

"Good. I mean, okay. Now we know." And what a relief to hear that the wicked witch was not only dead, but by someone else's hand.

Jenna turned her back on Ann and pointed at Stacey's forehead. "You're bleeding."

That would explain why everything Stacey saw was tinged with red. "It's not serious, is it? The top of my head's not sliced off? My brain matter's not exposed?"

"What? No." Jenna leaned in for a closer look. "I think it's just a big cut. Right below your hairline."

"A flesh wound. But I need a tourniquet for my arm. Can you find me something?"

Jenna unwrapped the scarf from around her neck, stepped over to Stacey's side of the desk, and wrapped and tied it around her upper arm.

"Tighter," Stacey said, though the pressure on the wound made her feel nauseated. "Thank you." She swallowed some bile and took a step away from the desk. Put one foot in front of the other, that's what she had to do. "Now let's call 911 and get some cops and paramedics over here so we can tell them that Ann went crazy and fired at me, you tried to take the gun away from her, and she took it back and shot herself."

Stacey looked through the blood dotted on her eyelashes at Jenna, tried to will her into understanding, and hoped she wouldn't regret saving Jenna from the doomed future that lay ahead if the truth were told. Though how could Stacey not try to prevent further tragedy, when Jenna had not only saved her life, but saved her from taking Ann's? "Did you hear me? Ann took back the gun and committed suicide, right in front of us."

"She shot herself?" Jenna said. She seemed a little calmer.

"It's horrible and tragic and upsetting, and it's what happened."

Jenna stood silent for a moment, her face unreadable, then said, "Yes. It was horrible." And she started to cry, soundlessly this time. Tears spilled down her cheeks.

Stacey said, "Where's your phone? Find it and call 911. And act distraught: you require help urgently. One woman has been shot dead, and another's injured."

"My phone's in my bag. By the door. I'll go get it." Jenna ran out of the room, and seconds later, Stacey heard her make the 911 call from down the hall.

Now was her chance. Her purse was on the rug, lying on its side. She picked it up with her good hand. Where was the knife she'd threatened Ann with? There — on the floor, five feet away, pushed halfway under a chair. She took two shaky steps over, bent down, picked up the knife, and dropped it into her purse. In the time that remained before the police arrived, she could get herself into the kitchen and place the knife on the counter beside the cake. She could and she would, and then she'd lie down, just for a minute, and close her eyes and rest, and be ready to face the police when they came. She'd be ready to back up Jenna's story, and to become her partner-in-crime forever.

49

One minute Jenna had ripped the gun from Ann's grip — way to go, Jenna! — and the next a shot had been fired, and Ann was dead, crumpled on the floor, her limbs twisted, her eyes open. Blood was seeping out of her body and onto her clothes and the rug and the floor, and the smell of a monster shit filled the air.

Holy fucking shit. Ann was dead, and Jenna had somehow pulled the trigger that fired the bullet that killed her. But not on purpose — Ann had squeezed her hand, and made her fire. This was all Ann's fault. Christ, Jenna had come over to stop Ann from killing herself, hadn't she?

Fuck fuck fuck. What if she took the fall for this? What if Stacey told the police Jenna had pulled the trigger and Jenna was convicted of murder and had to go to prison for years and years? Her life would be over. She'd get fat, and wear orange coveralls, and have to do disgusting manual labour like cleaning toilets, and her hair would be cut off, and she'd get beaten up and worse by big butch lesbians, and why oh why couldn't she go back in time and have a do-over? No, that was stupid, she couldn't. She had to deal with the now. And her best option was to act confused, like she didn't know what she'd done.

Jenna let the gun fall from her hand onto the floor. "Omigod, omigod, omigod! What happened?!" Had she overdone it with the panicky inflection? No, she'd got it just right, with a gradual build.

Stacey said, "Is she dead?"

Sweet Jesus, what if Ann weren't dead? Would that be better or worse? Jenna didn't even know. "I didn't mean to shoot her. She grabbed the gun and squeezed my trigger finger. I was trying to stop her from shooting you! From killing us both!"

Stacey stayed calm and told Jenna to feel for a pulse on Ann's neck, which of course she knew how to do. She'd seen people do it on TV a thousand times. She avoided looking at Ann's face as she touched the loose folds of skin on her neck and pressed against the place where the jugular vein ought to be. Nothing. She checked her own pulse to make sure she had the right spot, to remember what a live person's heartbeat felt like, and rechecked Ann's. "There's no pulse," she said, and Stacey said okay, now we know.

Stacey had a big gash on her forehead — it was a mess of tangled hair and blood — and streams of blood tracked down her face from it, through her eyebrows, down her eyelids. "You're bleeding," Jenna said.

Stacey made a joke — a joke! with Ann lying there, all dead and stinky and dead — about her brain being exposed, and said it was just a flesh wound, but asked for something to use as a tourniquet for her left arm, which looked bad, worse than the cut on her head. Jenna didn't want to get too close to it but she thought she saw a flash of exposed bone inside the torn, oozing flesh.

When she'd taken off her scarf — not one of her better ones, luckily — and tied it around the bloody wound, Stacey told her to call 911 and tell them to send responders right away, because Ann had shot Stacey, then herself.

But Ann hadn't shot herself.

Stacey said, "Did you hear me? Ann took back the gun and committed suicide, right in front of us."

Jenna said, "She shot herself?" The thing was, Ann sort of had fired the shot, with all the grabbing for the gun. And she might even have intended to kill herself after she killed Stacey. She probably had. Definitely had. It wasn't like she had much reason to live anymore, with the blindness, and her marriage breakup, and her career over. And hadn't Andrew speculated that Ann was suicidal just that afternoon?

Stacey said, "It's horrible and tragic and upsetting, and it's what happened."

It was like the sun had come out from behind some storm clouds and shone a golden light on the path out of this nightmare, and Stacey was the person who'd made the sun shine. Smart, quick-thinking, shot up, bleeding Stacey.

"Yes," Jenna said. "It was horrible," and she started to cry, from relief, from thankfulness, and because that's what people were expected to do when someone had died in front of them.

After Jenna made the 911 call, she called Andrew. She told him what had happened — fed him Stacey's lines — and added some of her own. He shouldn't worry. She was upset and shaken, but physically unharmed. Could he come over to Ann's house, and meet her there? Because the police were on their way and she could use his support right now, she really could.

She ended the call, erased all the text messages in her phone's inbox and outbox, and, just in case, removed Cooper's number from her contact list. She went back to Stacey, who lay on a leather couch in the sunlit living room that was still decorated with Kerry's evergreen boughs and glass jars full of white Christmas ornaments. Stacey's good arm was flung over her eyes, and her face was grey underneath the streaks of blood that marked her skin like zombie makeup.

"How are you holding up?" Jenna said. "An ambulance is coming. Can I get you something? Water? Bandages?"

"I'll be okay till the paramedics get here. And thank you. For coming here today, and for stopping Ann from shooting me a second time."

"You're welcome."

Stacey raised her head a few inches and dropped it back down. "Why did you come, anyway?"

"Ann asked me to. She said she had a gift to give me."

"Some gift."

"I came early because I thought she might kill herself. But I guess the person she wanted to kill was you." Jenna heard sirens outside. "By the way, you didn't happen to see an envelope sitting around with my name on it when you came in, did you? In case she really did want to give me something?"

"No, I didn't."

The sirens came closer. When they stopped outside, Stacey groaned, reached for Jenna's hand, and pulled herself up to a sitting position. "You ready for this?" she said. "You know what to say?"

Jenna nodded. She heard car doors slam in the driveway, the static of a police radio, male voices speaking, the sound of booted feet on the tiled front steps. She let go of Stacey, and ran to the open front door to greet the cops, firemen, and EMTs.

It was showtime.

MARCH
FIFTEEN MONTHS LATER

50

tacey has been up for hours when Cooper wakes at 8:00 a.m. From her office on the new house's second floor, where she ignores the ocean view and focuses on the computer screen in front of her on a Saturday morning, she startles at the sound of his wakeup groan from the bedroom down the hall.

She almost forgot, again, that he lives with her, but he does. She raises her arms, stretches them across her body. First, the right, and more carefully, the left. She feels slight vibrations through the floor when Cooper gets out of bed and crosses the bedroom to the bathroom. His hey to Buddy, his devoted companion, is muffled. Stacey waits for the sound of water running through the plumbing system for the shower. There it is.

They've been in this house eight months now, but she's still surprised to find herself in a live-in relationship with a good-natured guy who drives a truck. Or with anyone. She would never have predicted, over a year ago, when she decided to do away with Ann, that she'd be here now, one half of a cozy couple, living the dream in a house, with a dog.

She doesn't think Cooper is The One necessarily — she's skeptical that there is such a thing as a One for her — but she still finds his mellowness appealing, his solidity reassuring.

She saves the scene she's working on, closes the document and her laptop, and gets up from the desk. She has wondered, more than once, if Cooper is her karmic reward for not having crossed the murder line. Though on bright, blue-sky mornings like this one, she's inclined to think she wouldn't have gone through with killing Ann if she'd had the chance.

Other times she fears she would have.

She's in the kitchen, filling her water bottle, when Cooper comes down in a T-shirt and jeans. His feet are bare, his hair is wet, he smells like her expensive shampoo. "Morning, babe," he says, and she doesn't mind that he calls her that. She likes it.

He kisses the top of her head, opens the fridge, takes out some orange juice. "I've got a bike tour this morning, then I'll be at the shop till six. How's your day look?"

"I'm going for a run and I've got more writing to do, then I have the Paley event this afternoon."

"Oh, yeah." He turns on the coffee machine, picks out a pod, slots it in. "Will that be a good time, or a chore?"

"It'll be a performance. A marketing and publicity exercise." Stacey's phone buzzes. She checks it, reads a text. "It's Jenna, confirming our walk tomorrow morning."

His back is turned. "You two are still in touch?"

"Less so lately, but yeah. She and I will always have that we-were-there-the-day-the-shit-went-down connection."

Stacey hasn't told Cooper that Ann didn't exactly shoot herself the day she died. She hasn't told anyone, or felt tempted to, since the story she agreed on with Jenna was never seriously challenged.

Various police officers interviewed them, and the coroner's office made some inquiries, but in the end, Ann's death was declared an act of suicide, without a note. Ann's electronic devices and papers were seized, and checked for a personal diary, or for relevant emails, texts, or messages, for anything that might corroborate or contradict Stacey and Jenna's account of what happened, but nothing was found. Ann's bizarre scheme with the baseball bat, and the gun, and the invitation to Jenna to drop over an hour after Stacey was due to arrive — the details and reasoning behind it went with her to the grave.

Cooper adds milk to his coffee. "How's Jenna's show doing?"

"It's on the bubble for renewal. But she's gotten decent reviews. And she was in *Us Weekly* last week, in a paparazzi pic that showed her out with one of the hot young Brits from *Game of Thrones*."

"What's that?"

Cooper watches *The Benjamins,* but he doesn't read the trades or follow any other serial dramas on TV. Stacey doesn't mind that about him either. "It's an HBO show, a medieval fantasy type thing."

"Sounds like Jenna's where she always wanted to be."

Stacey picks up her keys and tucks them into her running belt. "I doubt that. Actors are never satisfied with their level of fame." Neither are showrunners. "Shall we order in sushi tonight?"

Cooper shows his dimple. "Sushi, some college basketball on TV, and you? I'll look forward to that lineup all day."

He's so easy to please.

Stacey laces up her running shoes at the front door, goes outside, jogs down the driveway to the road. She should buy Cooper something special for his birthday coming up. Maybe some custom-made clothes for when he accompanies her to industry events? No — the Tom Ford suits she bought him last fall are still in good shape, he's only worn them a few times. She could spring for a luxe adventure holiday — if that's not an oxymoron — for the two of them. They could go after post-production is done on this season of *The Benjamins*. When she'll have one, maybe two weeks off, if she's lucky. Where to, though? Not another safari. Maybe they could hike someplace exotic — Peru? Patagonia? She starts to run. She'll ask Topher to call her travel agent tomorrow, ask him to look into some upscale hiking destinations. And Australia. She hasn't forgotten that Cooper said he's always wanted to surf in Australia. Maybe they can squeeze that in, too.

Later that afternoon, Stacey waits in the wings of the theatre, at the back of the single-file line the *Benjamins* cast has formed under the direction of the Paley Center stage manager. Danny Danziger, the founder of a popular TV blog site, stands at the podium onstage and gushes through an introduction of the panel. He thanks the Paley Center for the moderator gig (the gig Stacey arranged) and blathers on in his fawning, fanboy manner about the show, and so he should. Stacey granted him one of the first industry-specific interviews she gave after Ann's death — she knew he'd go easy on her — and has driven online traffic to his advertisers by feeding him quasi-spoilers, sneak-peek clips, and inside-information tid-bits for his site almost every week since.

The actors are quiet while they wait to be brought onstage. Most are in full makeup and hair, and wear their own, carefully-styled-to-make-an-impression clothes — except for Carly, whose face is scrubbed clean, hair is messy, and body is hidden inside a bulky sweater, ripped jeans, and high-top sneakers. Could she make it clearer that she can't wait to be written off the show so she can go tool around with her music, then shoot an indie movie, in which she'll appear topless and shoot heroin, in the futile hope that thereafter she'll get taken seriously? Poor deluded kid. But if that's what she wants — Stacey pulls out her phone, makes a note to wrap up Carly's character arc sooner than later, puts the phone away.

Stacey's fitted, knee-length dress and pointy-toe pumps make her look sleek, tall, executive. And way more polished than the other, older women showrunners who've done time on this stage, with their shapeless tunics and comfort shoes.

Topher stands next to her and offers to hold her bag when she goes on. He's ever loyal, and has become more respectful since Stacey took over sole command of the show and made him an associate producer, not only in name. He has more responsibilities now, and makes more money. He asks her if she'd like a water bottle. She says no, thanks.

"And now," Danny Danziger says, "please welcome to the Paley Center stage the cast of *The Benjamins*! First up, Ryan Lindson!"

At the front of the line, Ryan pumps his forearms three times to get his vascularity up, walks onstage, waves to the audience, drinks in their applause, and finds his way down to the furthest seat along the apron. The others follow his lead when they're announced. They face the crowd, heads held high, and smile and wave, like they love their jobs, their roles, their fans, their bosses. "Best cast and crew I've ever worked with," one or more of them will say when Danny asks what it's like to work on the show. Another will thank the writers for the meaty storylines, and a third will say that the actors are such good friends, they spend all their free time together.

Keep it positive and light, the network publicist told them in the green room. Let the fans in — be casual, and confiding. Share funny on-set anecdotes, but keep them short. And emphasize the love! When Stacey heard that, an image came to mind of Ann making a gagging motion. If she were there, she'd have yelled something like, "Feed them the best horseshit you've got!" and cackled like the sometimes entertaining, always volatile lunatic that she was.

Instead, Peter led the cast in singing a chorus of "All You Need Is Love," like they were a bunch of old hippies.

"And last but not least," Danny says, "show creator, showrunner, and true survivor Stacey McCreedy!"

Stacey rolls her eyes at the word "survivor" — mock yourself first, then no one else can: that's another trick Ann taught her. She throws her shoulders back, steps onstage, makes a sweeping gesture with her good arm to indicate that she owes her moment in the spotlight to all the stellar talent she has the honour to work with (who's gagging now?), and takes her seat.

51

Jenna watches the Paley panel on her tablet in a trailer on the *Knife Skills* set, while Marla, the show's hairdresser, does the daily hour-long styling job on her extensions. Long, flowing hair is essential for the role Jenna plays, an ex–CIA agent turned sous chef. Though all that hair has to be tied back whenever she does a cooking scene.

Jenna ups the volume to better hear the audio in her earphones over the noise of the blow dryer. The *Benjamins* cast members look golden when they walk onstage — it's crazy how being on a hit show can improve a person's appearance. Except for Carly. Look at her, dressed-down and not made up, like she's too cool to do publicity. Like she thinks she'll be famous for more than a year or two. Wait till she finds out her best days are behind her.

All the principals are out now, and seated. Where's Stacey? There she is, last on, and Danny Danziger introduces her as a survivor — what's that about? For sure, Stacey would have given him a list of talking points beforehand, with Ann's death listed in the forbidden topics column.

Stacey is stylish in charcoal grey and black, and talk about Hollywood hair — hers looks amazing, wavy and bouncy and long, and it almost covers up the stiff way Stacey holds her left arm, two reconstructive surgeries later.

Marla touches Jenna's shoulder and points out that a production assistant is standing behind her chair. Jenna removes an earphone, makes eye contact with him, and smiles, in case he's related to somebody important. He hands her new sides for the next scene, and she thanks him, though she hates last-minute rewrites. She prefers to learn lines alone, at home, in front of the mirror.

The pages are for a scene in which her character and the show's male lead — her character's will-they-or-won't-they love interest — prep food together for a catered event. The rewrites were done to make the conversation more flirty and crank up the romantic tension, though the caterer is played by a very good-looking, very gay actor with whom Jenna has zero chemistry, so good luck with that. And the one true love/soulmate concept is so over now anyway. Even on *The Bachelor* and *The Bachelorette*, no one stays together afterward except the Christians, and even they don't. No one over eighteen believes in that kind of fairy-tale romance.

Though since she ended it with Andrew, Jenna has thought about Cooper — her true sexmate? — more often than she should have.

She picks up her phone, finds Cooper's alias in her list, and hovers over it, thinks about sending him a dirty text. She has only seen him once since he moved in with Stacey. She dropped by his shop one sunny afternoon, leaned over the counter, and asked if he'd like to play hooky for a few hours, take her for a drive up the coast in his truck. He smiled and said it sounded like fun, but he couldn't leave the shop. Though Riley was in the backroom and there were no customers in sight.

He knew what she was suggesting, and he was mighty tempted, she could tell. Her pussy has some kind of magic hold on him. Or her tits do.

A close-up on the tablet, still in her lap, of Stacey, in sincere mode, catches Jenna's eye. When she listens in again, Danny Danziger says, "Can I just say how inspiring it is to see you here today, healthy and whole, and to see the show doing so well under your leadership, after all the difficulties you've had to overcome?"

Ooh. Juicy. Jenna two-finger zooms in on Stacey's face, and waits for her to show a sign that the question has rattled her, but no, she's nailed an expression that reads as modest and grateful with a tinge of painful remembrance. Well played. The camera goes wide to show the cast members clapping their appreciation for their brave leader — Peter leads them in a standing ovation — until Stacey lifts a hand to stop their clapping and bids them all to please sit.

"Thanks for those kind words, Danny," she says. "And thanks to my awe-inspiring and talented cast for their support, and to our dedicated fans. With a special shout-out to those who watch live and keep the ratings up!"

She's so smooth. Working in a plug to watch the show live? Jenna would never have thought of that.

Stacey touches her bad arm — is the gesture conscious? it must be — and says, "These days, I'm all about moving forward, looking ahead, and doing my best to produce engaging entertainment for a large audience."

This gets another round of applause. Jenna is about ready to puke at all the staged affection on display when Danny leans in, eager to make his follow-up comment, because, duh, this dialogue was scripted in advance.

He says, "Speaking of moving forward, what can you tell me about the future of *The Benjamins*? I'm sure I speak for everyone here when I say we want the show to go on for several more seasons, but have you gotten the official word yet on renewal for a third?"

Stacey says, "As a matter of fact, I have. I heard just today."

Yeah, right, she did.

Stacey looks down the line of chairs at the actors. "The cast doesn't even know this yet, but I'm pleased to announce that not only have we been picked up for a full season for next fall, but a pilot has been ordered to production for a spinoff about Arielle going to boarding school."

More cheers and applause. Blech. Jenna stops the stream and asks Marla, who is twisting a lock of fake hair around the big-barrel curling iron, how much longer till she's done.

"About twenty minutes," Marla says.

Jenna begins to compose in her head the script she'll use tomorrow when she meets Stacey for their once-a-quarter hike in Fryman Canyon. She'll start by saying how fit Stacey looks. Should she ask to see how the skin graft on Stacey's arm has healed? No, that might be a little weird. But she'll show concern. She'll say she can't believe it was only last year that everything happened, and what a narrow escape they had, and it still gives her chills when she thinks about it, but she's so glad that she ran into the house when she did. So glad.

What she won't say is that Stacey should be grateful Jenna killed Ann dead, grateful forever.

Next, Jenna will mention that she live-streamed the Paley event, and was impressed with how well-spoken and self-assured Stacey was — she was born to lead. And hey, it sounds like Stacey's new life strategy is paying off, yay! The last time they walked,

Stacey told Jenna that her brush with death had made her think she should become Ann's opposite in how she treated people. Stacey's new mission was going to be to share credit, help others succeed, and create a network of loyal friends and followers to go out into the brave new media world and make top-notch entertainment with. Which sounded like pretty standard bullshit to Jenna, but to Stacey, she was all "that's brilliant," and "an excellent work/life plan," and "you go, girl!"

Tomorrow, in the canyon, Jenna will find the right moment to drop in excited congratulations about the boarding-school pilot. Then she'll step back and wait for Stacey to offer her the role in it that Stacey told her about, the role of the sympathetic and idealistic young teacher who takes Arielle under her wing, but who harbours a dark secret of her own.

Jenna's current objective is simple: she wants to be cast as a potential series regular on a network pilot. Which she'd do in second position, obviously, behind her commitment to *Knife Skills*. It won't be the last favour she asks for, but to book a pilot that may never be greenlit is no biggie, right? Not after she committed murder to save Stacey's life and career.

And to revive her own.

Acknowledgements

I wish to thank my indefatigable agent Bev Slopen for her stellar agenting on my behalf. To be clear, Bev is a lovely, gracious person, and unlike the Ann character in the novel in every respect other than indefatigability. Because, of course, all the characters in the book are fictitious; no one is based on a real person, alive or dead.

Who am I kidding — Ann is me. When she's funny, that is. If you found her funny. And when she makes *Singing in the Rain* jokes — that's me all over.

Come to think of it, the Stacey character is also based on me. At a great distance, I might be mistaken for Stacey — only without the feigned perkiness, obsessive work ethic, youth, thinness, athleticism, and gorgeous hair. Okay, I'm nothing like her, except for that time in grade one when I was made It in hide and seek, and couldn't find anyone, and cried.

I give thanks to everyone who embraced, worked on, and promoted the book at Dundurn, especially Carrie Gleason, Kathryn Lane, Laura Boyle, Jenny McWha, and Jaclyn Hodsdon. Thanks to Jess Shulman for her thoughtful and insightful edit, for tactfully correcting my mistakes, and for laughing at some of my jokes. And thanks always to my core supporters: Louise, Simon, Michael, and Ehoud.

Also by Kim Moritsugu

The Oakdale Dinner Club

After Mary Ann's husband cheats on her, the suburban mom decides to have her own affair. She starts up a neighbourhood dinner club as a cover and invites three men she has earmarked as potential lovers. Along for the ride is her best friend, Alice, who has recently returned with her young daughter to Oakdale, the cozy bedroom community where the two women grew up and briefly shared a telepathic past.

Over good food and wine, new friendships develop, new dreams simmer, Mary Ann pursues her affair candidates, and Alice opens her heart and mind to ways out of her single-working-mother social rut. The stars align on the night the core dinner club members consume an aphrodisiac, go to a local dive bar, hit the dance floor, and rock their worlds.

Appetizing fare for readers who like their fiction sharp and witty with a strong dash of spice, *The Oakdale Dinner Club* is a suburban comedy of manners that proves it's never too late to start over.

BOOK CREDITS

Acquiring Editor: Carrie Gleason
Project Editor: Jenny McWha
Editor: Jess Shulman
Proofreader: Catharine Chen

Cover Designer: Laura Boyle
Interior Designer: Lorena Gonzalez Guillen
E-Book Designer: Carmen Giraudy

Publicist: Michelle Melski

DUNDURN

Publisher: Kirk Howard
Acquisitions: Scott Fraser
Managing Editor: Kathryn Lane
Director of Design and Production: Jennifer Gallinger
Marketing Manager: Kate Condon-Moriarty
Sales Manager: Synora Van Drine

Editorial: Allison Hirst, Dominic Farrell, Jenny McWha, Rachel Spence, Elena Radic
Design and Production: Laura Boyle, Carmen Giraudy, Lorena Gonzalez Guillen
Marketing and Publicity: Andre Bovée-Begun, Michelle Melski, Kendra Martin

dundurn.com   dundurnpress
@dundurnpress   dundurnpress
dundurnpress   info@dundurn.com

FIND US ON NETGALLEY & GOODREADS TOO!

DUNDURN